She heard a loud [...] n a scream.

"Oh, my God!" Joh[...] at the stage in horror. The ghosts were scrambling back down out of the frames—except for David, whose frame was empty at last.

Jumping to her feet and scarcely noticing the resulting twinge in her ankle, Joan saw the costumed body lying on the stage and the dagger sticking out of its back.

"Curtain, curtain!" someone yelled, and it closed with a rush. Now everyone was talking at once, in the orchestra and in the audience. Trapped in the pit, Joan felt helpless.

Fred, where are you?

Then she saw him running down the aisle. Ignoring the stairs, he vaulted onto the stage behind her and disappeared behind the curtain.

★

"Frommer writes of small-town Hoosierland with unsentimental affection and an observant eye for evocative detail."

—The Washington Post Book World

Sara Hoskinson Frommer

MURDER & SULLIVAN

WORLDWIDE.

TORONTO • NEW YORK • LONDON
AMSTERDAM • PARIS • SYDNEY • HAMBURG
STOCKHOLM • ATHENS • TOKYO • MILAN
MADRID • WARSAW • BUDAPEST • AUCKLAND

For Gabe

MURDER & SULLIVAN

A Worldwide Mystery/September 1998

First published by St. Martin's Press, Incorporated.

ISBN 0-373-26285-X

Special thanks to

Ross Allen, Charles Brown, Bybee Stone Company,
Joe Courtney, Mary Fenner, Mary Harrison, Joe Hensley,
Sue Kroupa, Helen May, Dr. Anthony Pizzo,
Barbara Burnett Smith, Bob Weir, Mary Ann Whitley,
and the Bloomington Writers Group;
and to Stuart Krichevsky, my agent;
George Witte, my editor; and above all,
W. S. Gilbert.

ONE

There is beauty in the bellow of the blast,
  There is grandeur in the growling of the gale.

—KATISHA, *The Mikado*

JOAN SPENCER was on foot when the siren went off.

In the morning, eyeing thunderclouds, she had considered driving to work, but risked carrying an umbrella instead. She walked between home and her job as director of the Oliver, Indiana, Senior Citizens' Center even on days as hot as this one, both for her body's sake and for the peaceful time it gave her at the beginning and end of the day.

Henry Putnam, short, bent, and white-headed, waved from his rose garden next door. Waving back, Joan inhaled his early June roses. She understood why people driving down their street crawled past Henry's corner.

It was hard to believe that Henry had lived in his new house only three years, just over a year longer than she'd lived in her old one. Of course, he'd spent about seventy years in Oliver, where Joan was only beginning to feel at home. She knew she would never be considered an old-timer, not even if she spent the rest of her life here.

"How are you, Henry?" she called, as she always did.

"Can't complain," he called back, as usual. A widower, Henry lived alone, except for his constant companion, a mud-colored hound of uncertain ancestry. The first fall and winter, she hadn't known him except to see him on the street with the dog. Last summer, though, he had begun appearing at her back door in his overalls to bring her wonderfully fragrant roses—Crimson Glory, her old favorite; Scentifolia, which Henry called an antique rose; hybrid teas such as Mr. Lincoln and Perfume Delight; and unnamed hybrids he was developing himself. He would never come into the house, but he and Andrew, Joan's eighteen-year-old son, sat out on the back steps swapping stories. And when winter returned, Andrew walked Henry's dog on days too icy to risk old bones.

Joan greeted other neighbors in the blocks between her house and the wooded park that ran through the little town. She'd learned how to direct newcomers around the park at the beginning of the Oliver College year, but she herself took pleasure in cutting through it on foot and thanked the early citizens of Oliver who had preserved this amazing forty-acre stand of southern Indiana trees with the creek that delighted children. Once she reached the far side of the park, she was only four blocks from the courthouse square—Oliver's "downtown"—and the Senior Citizens' Center.

Work was peaceful, as it turned out; only a few old regulars showed up. Of those who came, some ignored the weather and others couldn't stay away from the window.

"Gonna be a toad strangler and a gully washer," old Annie Jordan predicted, knitting furiously while she monitored the sky.

"We'll be all right, Annie," Joan said, but she could have kicked herself for not driving today.

Only Margaret Duffy and Alvin Hannauer came for the two o'clock meeting of the board of directors, which Alvin chaired. A retired anthropology professor, Alvin had worked with Joan's father during a long-ago sabbatical spent in Oliver. Margaret, Joan's sixth-grade teacher that year, had told her about the vacant director's job when she'd come back to stay and rejoiced with her when she got it. Joan appreciated them both for their good humor and calm.

"I'm just as glad to go home early," Margaret said. "The others had more common sense than we did, coming out today."

"Want me to schedule a rain date?" Joan asked.

"No," Alvin said. "We didn't have anything on the agenda that can't wait for next month. Come on, Margaret. I'll drive you."

By the time the center closed at five, the threatening clouds had produced only intermittent drizzle and occasional sprinkles. Joan checked the windows, locked up, and started for home. A soft rain began, pleasantly cool on her face at first, but then heavy enough to make her put up her umbrella.

Marching along in leather strap sandals designed for a gentler pace, she watched the sky turn dark, and then an eerie greenish-yellow. It was still hours before real dusk, but the birds began twittering. At the edge of the park, sudden wind whipped her cotton skirt around her legs, tore at her long hair, and jerked the umbrella from her hands. She chased it into the park but lost it in the trees.

The rain stopped as abruptly as it had started, and the wind died.

That's better, Joan thought, but she picked up her pace anyway. She had just crossed the sycamore-edged creek that meandered through the middle of the park when the siren rose from nothing to blast her ears. She'd heard it before, on a sunny Friday noon back in March—after explanations on the radio and in the paper, so that no one would worry when it was tested. Hoosiers took their tornadoes seriously, she knew. Back in sixth grade, Margaret Duffy had taught them what to do if they were ever caught outdoors in one.

They wouldn't test the siren on a day like this, she thought. This is a warning! Knowing she wasn't quite halfway home, she started running.

When she saw the funnel dip down out of the darkest cloud, a part of her recognized real danger; the rest of her didn't want to miss a thing. It was moving toward her, and she looked around for the closest shelter. The nearest house stood at the top of a hill on the edge of the park, an impossible distance, she was sure—even if the top of a hill were safe in a tornado. A ditch, that's what she needed. Or the creek bed.

The wind rose again, this time with a vengeance. Sticks and little branches swirled around her, mixed with sand from the playground and scary, twisted things. Frozen, afraid to go forward or turn back, Joan spotted the child—a little girl of three or four with Alice-in-Wonderland hair, bare feet, pink shorts, and a pink tank top. She was leaning into the wind, her hair streaming out behind her. Joan could see her mouth crying "Mama! Mama!" but the siren drowned her out.

No point in calling to her. And no time. Joan ran to her, scooped her up, and carried her to the creek.

"It's all right!" she screamed. "We're going to be all right!" The wind tore the words from her mouth—she couldn't tell whether the child could hear her, much less believe her, but the little arms had a stranglehold around her neck.

Don't panic. Don't scare her even more.

"Here we go! Hang on!" With the little girl clinging frantically to her, she dropped to the ground and slid backward down the muddy bank into the creek, all the while watching the funnel cloud reach the ground and advance. A line of beech and shagbark hickories toppled toward the sycamores. Then it was too dark to see anything, and the siren was wiped out by an even louder sound.

It really *is* like a freight train, Joan thought in amazement. Just the way they always said.

At what felt like the last possible moment, she threw herself down over the little body in the creek bed.

TWO

> But duty, duty must be done;
> The rule applies to every one,
> And painful though that duty be,
> To shirk the task were fiddle-de-dee!

> —SIR DESPARD AND RICHARD, *Ruddigore*

EVEN BEFORE the first siren, the Oliver Police Department began moving all staff and citizens to the weight room in the basement of the old limestone building. Officers and civilian staff members matter-of-factly started down, but Detective Lieutenant Fred Lundquist wasn't surprised to see some of the citizens doing business at the station resist the move.

"I'm a busy man," objected Paul Litten, president of the First Oliver Savings Bank, who had been reporting the theft of some jewelry from his home. "I'll come back tomorrow."

"Sorry, Paul," said Detective Sergeant Johnny Ketcham, who had been typing Litten's particulars into his computer. "We can't let you go." He pulled a paper form out of his desk drawer and picked up a pen. "But we don't have to waste your time. Let's finish this job downstairs."

Exchanging glances with his sergeant, Fred smiled. Ketcham wasn't thrown by officious, self-important types. He'd probably gone to school with this one. Like Fred, Ketcham was pushing fifty, but Ketcham was a graying Hoosier who had grown up in Oliver, not a blond Swede from northern

Illinois. Both men kept themselves in excellent physical condition, in part by taking advantage of the equipment in the basement.

At first, peace reigned down in the weight room. Ketcham and the bank president soon droned quietly in a corner. An old couple who'd come in to apply for a private parking sign in front of their house held hands. A mother kept a tight hold on her four-year-old son, who had wandered away from home and been brought in by one of the younger uniformed officers.

Having grown up in the Midwest, Fred knew tornado warnings meant business, even though the odds were good that any particular twister would pass them by. The solid station house wasn't in the danger faced by mobile homes and even relatively sturdy frame buildings. But policy was policy in public places throughout Oliver.

Over at the hospital, all the visitors and ambulatory patients would have been herded down into the basement-level cafeteria. Bedridden patients would be lined up in corridors, with doors closed between them and flying glass. And emergency room staff would be preparing for casualties.

Thank God, he thought, the kids would be home from school by now. The new Alcorn County Consolidated School building was all on one floor, and school buses were particularly vulnerable.

The police units already out on the street would be trying to spot the tornado and would be ready to respond to emergency calls—trees across the road, power lines down, injuries, doctors and nurses needing transportation. Other requests could wait.

Once Captain Warren Altschuler unlocked the basement radio console and moved the command post to safety, the people in the weight room could hear what was going on outside, and tension mounted. The little boy was tuning up to cry until a young man wearing an Oliver College T-shirt lifted him onto an exercise bike and showed him how to stand on the pedals to ride it.

Fred listened to the tornado spotters with growing concern. Finally the crackly voice of a man attempting to stay calm yelled into the radio. "It's a bad one! Passed over downtown, but touched down in the middle of the park and in the neighborhood on the other side. Looks like it hit a bunch of houses. Trees and lines down all over Prospect."

Joan's neighborhood, Fred thought. He checked his watch. She ought to be home by now—if she drove. But she likes to cut through the park on foot. And I'm stuck here. Damn!

Altschuler's voice cut into his thoughts. "Better call in the off-duty people."

"Yessir," Fred said, and began making notes as they agreed on how to assign the work that needed to be done. He and Altschuler worked well together. First, and most urgently, Oliver's small force would function as an adjunct ambulance service for all the injured who needed transport to a doctor or the hospital, but who didn't need a stretcher or the services of an EMT on the way. Outside help would arrive before long, but right now they were on their own.

From siren to siren felt like an eternity.

When the all-clear finally sounded, the switchboard looked like an old man's birthday cake. Fred took the stairs to his office two at a time and began handling nonstop calls that ranged from real emergencies to anything but.

"No, ma'am," he said as politely as he could to one caller. "I can't assign an officer to bring you a pack of cigarettes."

"But I'm all out," the husky voice wailed. He cut her off.

"No, sir," he said, feeling like a broken record. "We can't deliver a bottle of whiskey to you. Try the liquor store."

"I did. They won't come." This voice was already slurred. "I'm going to report you to the police!"

How can these people clog up the 911 line? Fred asked

himself for the nth time, leaned back in his old wooden swivel chair, and reached for the next call.

"Lieutenant, it's old Mrs. Snarr," said the dispatcher in his ear. "I tried to calm her down, but she insists on talking to you."

"Put her on." Bud Snarr owned the local funeral home. His mother spent too much time alone and comforted herself by calling the police at least once a day to talk at length about every worry that crossed her mind. But that didn't mean she didn't have a real one this time. "Lieutenant Lundquist," he said into the telephone.

"Oh, Lieutenant, I'm so glad it's you," she fluttered. "Those young people mean well, but they don't really understand, not the way you do."

Yes, dear, he wanted to say—she was a sweet old lady. But not today. "Mrs. Snarr, do you have an emergency?" he asked firmly.

"I certainly do! You know that new roof I had Virgil Shoals put on my house last spring?" She waited for him to answer.

"Yes, ma'am."

"Well, you'll never believe this, but it blew right off today! A little wind, and it's gone! I want you to arrest him. I paid plenty for that roof."

"Mrs. Snarr, that was no little wind—that was a tornado. Didn't you hear the sirens?" He jotted down her address from memory. A neighborhood the tornado spotters hadn't mentioned yet.

"I certainly did! Isn't there a law against that kind of noise in town?"

"No, ma'am. Not when it's warning people to take shelter. I'm sorry, but we can't arrest Mr. Shoals. If you like, you can come in tomorrow and file a complaint."

"Well, I never! My roof is gone, and that's all you can say?"

"No, ma'am. I'd advise you to call your insurance company. They'll probably pay to have a new roof put on."

"They will? Are you sure?"

"If you have tornado insurance, yes, ma'am."

"Well, thank you, Lieutenant. I knew you'd understand."

THE FIRST TIME he sent an officer to Joan's neighborhood to check downed power wires, he asked the man to check in on her for him.

"Sure, Lieutenant. And you won't mind if I swing by to check on my wife?"

"Go on—you'd do it anyway. Thanks."

But the man didn't find her. In a few minutes he radioed back. "There was a young fellow looking over the damage to her house, but he said he hadn't seen her. Sorry, Lieutenant."

"Her son?" Fred had grown fond of Andrew.

"I didn't ask—just about the lady."

At least the house was still there. Fred thanked him and sent him to a mobile home that had sustained substantial damage. He promised himself that he'd call Joan right after the next crank call he handled.

They stopped as if by magic.

THREE

*But the darkness has passed, and it's daylight at
last, and the night has been long—ditto ditto
my song— and thank goodness they're both
of them over!*

—LORD CHANCELLOR, *Iolanthe*

HOURS went by that must have been only minutes, and then
it was still.

The child was silent beneath her. For a moment Joan was
afraid she'd gone deaf. Then her foot bumped a pebble and
she heard it splash. She sat up on her knees and looked. The
little girl lay on her back with her eyes squeezed shut. Alive,
then. Joan patted herself all over. Nothing broken. Just a few
scratches and a goose egg on the back of her head.

Thank you, she thought.

"It's all right now," she said. "It's all gone." She stroked
the muddy face. Two blue eyes opened.

"I want my mama." The lips puckered, and the chin began
to quiver. "I want my mama!"

"We'll find your mama," Joan reassured her, and hoped it
was true. "Is she in the park?" The little girl shook her head
emphatically. It was going to be a guessing game.

"Is she at home?" A big nod. Well, all right. "What's your
name?"

"Laura." At last, an answer.

"Okay, Laura, let's go home and see her." Now if you just know where home is, Joan thought. If you still even have a home. "Up you go."

She hoisted the child out of the creek and clambered after her. Suddenly Laura began running toward the house on the hill. Of course. No wonder she was alone, if she lived that close. Blink twice and a little girl that age would be at the playground before you could say "Stay in the yard."

Joan stumbled after her, past trees that looked as if someone had twisted them out of the ground and then stripped off the bark. Already stiff, she couldn't keep up, and she quickly lost sight of the little figure. The only people in sight were a man, a woman, and a teenage boy and girl wandering around near the house at the top of the hill shouting something she couldn't hear. Shingles had blown off their roof, and the yard was littered with twisted debris, but the main house itself was standing. The wood frame of an addition under construction had splintered. Joan wondered how her own little house had fared—and Andrew. Doggedly climbing the hill, she tried not to think about what might have happened to Andrew.

Suddenly the woman screamed and pointed in her direction. Joan swiveled, but saw no new funnel cloud behind her—the tornado was truly over. Turning back toward the family, she saw Laura running to the woman, who dropped to her knees in the mess.

"Mama!"

"Laura! Oh, Laura! Thank God!" Hugging her, Laura's mother was laughing and crying at the same time. The others crowded around them. Joan watched, relieved. Laura's mother, as blonde as her little girl, looked to be several years younger than Joan, probably in her late thirties, and a little more comfortably rounded, though her legs were slender in their tight jeans. Laura's father was about the same age and of medium height, with a full head of dark hair and a good suntan. He, too, wore jeans and a T-shirt. The boy, several inches taller, resembled his dad, and the older girl, her mother.

Coming close now, Joan said, "Hello."

"Oh my God!" Laura's mother said, and Laura hid behind her.

"It's all right, Laurie." Her father smiled warmly and picked her up. "She won't hurt you." The older girl and boy were staring frankly.

Joan looked down at her muddy arms and legs and tugged at the front of her skirt, still wadded up and saturated with clay from her slide down the bank of the creek. The hem relaxed, almost to her knees. She kept tugging.

"Do I look that bad?" she couldn't help asking.

"I'm sorry," Laura's mother said, and gulped. "You startled me—I wasn't expecting to see anyone come up out of there alive. I can't imagine how Laura survived."

"She was with me."

"With you! Where?"

"In the creek. It was the lowest place."

"How can we ever thank you!" Laura's father said. "We thought—" His face crumpled and he couldn't go on.

"One minute she was right here," her mother said. "And then—"

"I know," Joan said. "I'm glad I saw her." She felt suddenly wobbly. "Is there—is there someplace I could sit down for a minute?" Silly question, she thought. Their lawn chairs are probably in the next county by now.

"You poor thing! Are you hurt?" Laura's mother ran to support her. Normally independent, Joan didn't resist. Just leaning felt good.

"I don't think so. A little muddy." She stood on her own again, relieved to find that she could.

"David, can you drive her home? She doesn't look so good."

"You bet," Laura's father answered. Passing Laura to the

girl who might have been her twin except for the ten years or so between them, he attacked the worst of the mess on the driveway. The boy helped.

"Please don't bother," Joan said. "I just have a few blocks to walk." If only my legs would stop shaking.

"It's no bother," David said. "Get us a towel, won't you, Ellen?"

Checking first that Joan could stand alone, Laura's mother ducked into the house and emerged with a huge beach towel, which she wrapped around her while David backed a neat white pickup truck out of the double garage.

"I'm all right, really," Joan said, and realized she was shivering in the cool air that had replaced the sweltering heat before the storm. "But thanks." She huddled inside the towel.

"It's the least we can do," David said. He held the door open, and Joan glimpsed the truck's pristine interior.

"I'd better take off my shoes." She peeled off the first sandal. The contrast between the astonishingly clean skin beneath it and the rest of her foot gave her some idea of how her face must look.

Even so, when David helped her into the cab of the truck, the mirror on the sun visor shocked her. Every inch of exposed skin was covered with a layer of fine mud. Her eyelashes were coated. Her long brown hair, blown in all directions, stood out with its own stiff support. When she closed her lips, her mouth disappeared entirely.

Andrew will laugh, she thought. Andrew—the fear washed over her again. She hung on. Come on, David, let's go.

David tucked her in and fastened her seat belt gently, as if she were Laura. He backed out of the driveway and drove slowly past the devastation, past downed trees and around huge branches and sputtering power lines, past bricks and boards and rubble where she had seen her neighbors' houses in the morning, where families were now wandering in shock.

"Look at that," he said, shaking his head. "Those poor

folks are going to have to build from the ground up. If they can afford to rebuild at all."

At least they're alive, Joan thought. Does Andrew even know where to go in a tornado? How could I bring him to Indiana and not tell him that?

After a block with little damage, they came to her own block. On the corner, Henry Putnam's new house stood with the crown of a silver maple sprawled across its roof and its secrets exposed to the world. Looking through Henry's smashed picture window, Joan held her breath for him. Then she saw him come around the corner of the house. Good. He's all right.

"Thank God," David said. "At least Uncle Henry's okay."

"He's a dear old man," Joan said. So Henry was David's uncle. Some days she thought everyone in Oliver was related to everyone else.

And there was her house, still standing, but looking vulnerable. The wooden wraparound porch was gone, and the front door hung five feet off the ground.

"Ours is next door to Henry's," she told David. "The one with the door up there." He pulled over carefully. Joan scanned her windows for Andrew's curly head.

"Watch out for those live wires, now," David said, and walked gingerly around the truck. He opened the passenger door and offered a tanned hand to help her down.

"Uh-huh." She scarcely heard him. Then her front door flew open and Andrew leaped to the ground, ran to the curb, and hugged her, mud and all. Joan dropped her sandals and towel to hug him back.

"Mom! You're alive!"

"Andrew! I was so worried!"

"I went down to the furnace room. But what happened to you?"

"I hid in the creek." She looked down at her skirt. "Got a little dirty."

He roared, and she grinned. Belatedly, she turned to thank David, but he was already deep in conversation with Henry. She heard David say "board it up" before they disappeared around the back of Henry's house.

"Who's the guy who brought you home?" Andrew asked

"David somebody. Henry's nephew. He lives down the street, by the park. I spent the tornado in the creek with his little girl."

"Figures. You look like the creature from the mud lagoon."

"It'll wash off. How about the house?" She took a step toward it, but Andrew stopped her.

"The yard's full of glass. You'll cut your feet." He knelt to strap on her sandals. For the second time, she realized how wobbly she was and didn't argue.

They made a quick tour of the yard. Except for broken windows and the corpse of her silver maple tree out back, which had missed their power and telephone wires by mere inches, the only serious damage appeared to be the missing porch and steps.

"I'll have to find a carpenter," Joan said.

"We can use the back door for a while. And I found some plastic in the furnace room to tack up for temporary windows."

"You do that, Andrew. I'm heading for the shower."

Ten minutes of steamy shower and three shampoos restored her. With the mud gone, more scratches and bruises appeared on her arms and legs, but she felt lucky to have escaped with nothing worse. She felt a twinge in her right ankle, but was sure it wasn't serious.

Why is it we always feel lucky to have only minor injuries? she wondered. Luck would be no tornado at all.

The telephone rang while she was still dripping. Rats.

"Andrew?" she called. But she could hear him hammering downstairs. She left a trail of drops across the bedroom floor and answered the phone in the altogether.

It was Fred Lundquist. Both Andrew and her daughter, Rebecca, who'd met Fred when she'd come to Oliver for the quilt show a year ago, called him "Mom's cop."

"You all right? I hear your neighborhood was hit hard."

"We're fine. Lost our front porch, but we're safe."

"Good. I may be able to come by later, but the department's jumping."

"I can imagine. It was sweet of you to check." Worth answering the phone right out of the shower to know you cared that much, she thought, and smiled to herself as she hung up. Andrew safe, strangers helping, and Fred caring—she wasn't nearly as alone in the world as she had felt down in the creek.

The phone rang again. This time it was Alex Campbell, the woman who conducted the Oliver Civic Symphony. A different matter altogether.

"Joan, I have a job for you."

No "How are you?" from Alex, but then there never had been—certainly not since Joan had taken over as manager, a part-time job that had swelled to take all the free time she was willing to give it, though her low monthly pay hadn't budged. But she didn't owe Alex anything now. Preparations for the symphony's fall season were well in hand.

"A what?" Joan stretched an arm for the terrycloth robe draped over the end of her bed.

"I've just agreed to conduct a Gilbert and Sullivan orchestra this summer. You won't need more than two or three firsts and seconds, a couple of violas and cellos, a bass—"

"Wait a minute, Alex." Joan shrugged the robe on, a shoulder at a time, passing the receiver from hand to hand. "What do you mean, I won't need them? I didn't agree to anything."

"You're the manager." Alex combined authority with wounded innocence.

"Sure, of the symphony. Not of any other orchestra you happen to agree to whip up."

"I can't do it without you, Joan."

"Then you should have asked me first." Listen to me standing up to her, she thought. Compared to a tornado, Alex is just a big wind.

"Joan—" Suddenly nothing. Then a dial tone. Good, Joan thought, and hung up. With luck, you won't be able to call me back tonight.

She wiped up the wet trail back to the bathroom before pulling on jeans and a T-shirt and starting to unsnarl her hair. It was still tangled when someone began pounding on her back door.

FOUR

My pain and my distress
I find it not easy to express.

—SIR JOSEPH, *H.M.S. Pinafore*

JOAN FLEW down the steps with the comb in her hand, ignoring a sudden sharp jab in her right ankle. "Coming!"

Throwing the back door open, she barely recognized the grim face of the man who had just driven her home. It's Laura's father, she thought. Henry's nephew. David. But why is *he* so dirty all of a sudden?

"Your phone working?" he demanded, skipping the niceties.

"Come in," Joan said, and handed him the receiver of the kitchen wall phone.

"Call 911."

I knew it, she thought, and dialed the old phone. Someone *did* get hurt next door. At least Henry's okay. Andrew emerged from the basement while David paced her kitchen, tethered by her long phone cord. Fred wasn't kidding, Joan thought. It never takes this long to get through to 911.

"This is David Putnam," he said finally. "My uncle, Henry Putnam, is trapped and hurt in his house at the northeast corner of Chestnut and Prospect. I can't get him out, and he looks bad. There's a beam on his back. No, he can't. He's seventy.

Just a minute." He turned to Joan. "What's Uncle Henry's address?"

"I don't know. This is 716." Not Henry, she thought. It can't be. I just saw him. He was fine.

"One house west of 716 East Prospect. It's the northeast corner. No, I can't tell you the phone number there—the phone's dead anyway. Yes, I'm calling from 716. Dammit, cut the Mickey Mouse! He needs help now! Good." He hung up and started for the back door. "They're on the way."

"What happened?" Joan asked.

"Uncle Henry insisted on going back in the house to look for his dog. The floor collapsed, he fell through, and a beam landed on his back. It shouldn't have happened." His face was grim.

"I'm so sorry. You'd better take him some blankets. He may be in shock." She wondered whether David wasn't feeling shock too. "Andrew, can you run up and get them?"

Andrew took the stairs two at a time and returned with a load that included Joan's sneakers. Bending to lace them while Andrew and David went ahead with the blankets, she winced at a sharper pain from her ankle.

Why now? she wondered. I was all right in the park. Could I have jolted it on the way downstairs? But I felt it when I got out of the shower. Maybe I hurt it in the park after all, and the adrenaline is just now wearing off.

She tried a step or two, and it bore her weight, but the pain increased.

They're going to have to take care of Henry without my help, she decided, and limped to the refrigerator to fill an ice bag. Propping her right foot on the sofa, she listened for the ambulance. The siren wailed closer and then died abruptly. Through the plastic on her front window she saw lights flashing next door and heard the men calling to one another. Then there was nothing but the lights and sporadic, unintelligible bursts from the radio in the ambulance.

It was taking much too long. The urge to go over was almost overwhelming, but common sense kept her where she was. Finally the voices returned, and then the siren began again.

Andrew came back alone.

"How is he?" Joan asked.

"Conscious. But I don't think he can move his legs. No one said much. David took off after the ambulance."

She shook her head. It wasn't fair.

"What happened to you, Mom? I thought you'd be over there."

"I don't know. There's something wrong with my ankle. It can't be too bad—I walked out of the park on it."

"Don't count on it. Remember the quarterback who played ten minutes with a fractured leg?"

"No," she said honestly. "Andrew, it's not broken! All I need is a little more ice." Spending a hot, muggy southern Indiana summer trussed up in a cast was more than she could bear to think about. Henry's summer is probably going to be much worse, she told herself, but as usual, competitive suffering failed to comfort her.

"What were you doing in that creek, anyway?" Andrew asked after a trip to the kitchen for more ice.

"Darned if I know. Kneeling over Laura and trying to keep my head down."

"You probably just hyperextended it. You can use my old crutches if you want to. I'll lower them for you. If it gets any worse, I'd better take you to see a doctor."

She smiled at his mothering, but she needed him.

"Thanks, Andrew."

Two hours later, Joan was sitting on the examining table of Dr. Robert Cutts, who had been recommended to her when she first moved to Oliver almost two years ago. She'd seen him only once before, for a routine physical. She hadn't yet been treated to the wonderful bedside manner she'd heard old ladies at the center rave about.

Liz MacDonald, Dr. Cutts's buxom, no-nonsense nurse, refused to guess what he would say. She sat down at a little desk and wrote something on Joan's chart.

"Take your shoe off, please. He'll be with you in a few minutes. He barely took time for supper—we're kind of an auxiliary emergency room tonight, with all the minor injuries from the tornado. How did you do this?"

"I don't know. My son thinks I hyperextended it when I got caught in the creek."

Liz looked up.

"In the creek? What were you doing in the creek?"

"I was halfway through the park when the tornado hit. I ended up hiding in the creek with a little girl named Laura Putnam."

Liz stared at Joan's chart—there wasn't enough on it for her even to pretend to read it. The silence grew.

"David Putnam's daughter?" she asked finally. In a town the size of Oliver, Joan knew better than to ask how she knew. Liz and David were about the same age—odds were good they'd known each other since childhood. But what was the long pause about?

"Yes. David drove me home."

"Lucky you," Liz said, and snapped the chart closed. Color rose in her cheeks. Oho, Joan thought, remembering how thoroughly married David and Ellen Putnam had seemed. Liz stood up, picked up the chart, and slid it into a pocket on the outside of the examining room door.

"The doctor will be with you soon," she said, and shut the door behind her.

Dr. Cutts entered the room humming. Joan admired his big eyebrows and the whiskers in his ears. She wouldn't have called him handsome exactly, but she could understand why the old ladies liked his pixie smile and wavy white hair. He exuded cleanliness—just right for a doctor. After manipulating her ankle, he asked a few questions and ordered an X ray, "just to be on the safe side." Liz set it up right there in the office, and in no time Joan had the verdict. No fracture, but a hyperextension, just as Andrew had thought.

"I'll wrap it for now, and you can keep it wrapped for a while," Dr. Cutts told her, rolling an Ace bandage around her foot and ankle. "Don't ice it after today. And when the swelling goes down, leave the bandage off." The elastic rose up her leg, bringing instant comfort. "Liz will give you something for pain."

"Do I have to stay off it?"

"Nope. The more you walk, the better." He smiled up at her. "That's how I keep my girlish figure." Dr. Cutts was indeed trim, and Joan suspected that he meant it.

"That's it?"

"That's it. You're going to be fine. Come back if the pain intensifies after tomorrow or doesn't subside in three or four weeks." Three to four weeks—there went her summer.

"How about swimming?"

"With my blessing. It's great exercise and good for the ankle." He pinned the top of the bandage, gave her foot a pat, and washed his hands before heading out the door to the next patient.

Joan squeezed her bandaged foot into her unlaced sneaker and hobbled out to collect whatever painkillers Liz was dispensing. She wasn't looking forward to the next few weeks.

FIVE

Judge: For now I am a Judge!
All: And a good Judge too!

—Trial by Jury

THE NEXT DAY was Saturday, and it was a relief to stay at home. Joan was relaxing with her foot propped up on the sofa when David and Ellen Putnam arrived at her back door, bearing spectacular peonies that she thought must have come from a distance—nothing living in their yard could have survived the storm. She put her foot down, but kept her seat while Andrew let them in.

Outside, a chain saw began its racket. Someone was taking care of the tree that had fallen on Henry's house.

"We had to thank you properly," Ellen told Joan, handing her the flowers. "Even though there's no way we can thank you enough. Laura's running around as if nothing had happened. It's amazing."

"They're beautiful," Joan said, looking at the peonies. Ants were marching around the buds—her mother used to say they opened them. "But you would have done the same for me." And having seen David in action, she was sure it was true.

"That doesn't make us any less grateful," David said.

"Won't you sit down? And Andrew, could you find some water for these?" Andrew carried the peonies off to the kitchen. When he brought them back in her pewter pitcher and set them on the mantelpiece, she introduced him to the Putnams.

"We've met." David smiled at him from the big chair.

"Of course," Joan said, remembering. "How is your uncle?"

David's face darkened.

"It looks as if he's going to live, but there's some paralysis. They can't say yet whether the damage is permanent. It never should have happened."

"You mustn't blame yourself."

"I don't." His tight lips didn't invite further discussion. "But I'm going to spend some time today boarding up that house, so no one else will get hurt there."

Joan and Andrew exchanged glances. Their porch!

"Are you a carpenter?" Andrew asked him.

Ellen laughed. "He'd like to be. Any day now I expect him to quit the bench and set up shop."

"The bench?" Joan was puzzled.

"He's a circuit court judge." Ellen beamed at David.

"A judge—I've never known a judge. And here I was going to ask whether we could hire you to rebuild our front porch. The insurance adjuster hasn't been by yet, but I don't expect much, and the deductible is going to take all I can spare. I'm afraid it'll have to be no-frills. I don't suppose you could recommend anyone…"

"Not as good as I am!" David grinned. "But you might try Zach Yoder. He's done a lot of the work for Virgil Shoals—the builder on our new addition."

"And now he's going to have to redo a lot of it," Ellen said.

Joan shook her head sympathetically.

"Yoder—isn't that an Amish name?" Andrew asked. "We read about the Amish in Indiana history a couple of years ago." Transplanted to Indiana as a high school senior, Andrew had just finished his freshman year at Oliver College.

"That's right," David said. "But Zach left the Amish community when he was about your age. Married an English girl. They have a nice little family."

"English?" Joan asked, wondering how an Amishman would have met someone from England.

"Non-Amish," Ellen explained. "They speak a version of German, so they call us English."

"Zach's a good worker," David said. "And he understands wood. He'll do you a good job, at a reasonable price."

"Is he in the phone book?" Would he be that modern, Joan wondered, even if he had left the Amish community?

"Oh, sure. But Virgil's got him helping me next door today." That explained the hammering she was hearing in between bursts of the chain saw. "Come on over and I'll introduce you."

Hobble over is more like it, Joan thought. But Dr. Cutts said to walk. I ought to be able to make it that far.

It was a generous offer—carpenters had to be at a premium after the tornado. It would be good to have Andrew's plastic windows replaced with something sturdier, even if temporary, but she couldn't ask them to put off their own repairs. She stood up—and winced.

"Why, you're hurt!" Ellen exclaimed, looking at the elastic bandage on her ankle. "What happened?"

"It's not even a sprain." Joan waved it off.

"It happened while you were protecting Laura, didn't it?" David demanded, and she couldn't say no.

"Our addition can wait," Ellen urged. "We're still a long way from moving into it. I'll tell Virgil we owe you, and he'll let Zach come over to help you as soon as he finishes helping David board up Uncle Henry's place. There's lots more to do, but there's no hurry."

"That's right," David said. "Uncle Henry won't be home for a long time, at best. He'll be in a rehab center for weeks after he leaves the hospital."

"What about the dog?" Andrew asked.

"David brought him home to us the other day," Ellen said. "Scott and Amy like him, but Laura's ecstatic."

"Let me know when I can visit Henry," Joan said. "He's a good neighbor."

"We will," David promised. "And you'll use Zach."

They left in a flurry of mutual goodwill that was still warming her cockles when the telephone rang for the first time since Alex had been cut off the day before. As always, there was no preliminary greeting.

"You're right, I should have asked you." Alex capitulating? Unheard of. "I really need you."

It was almost an apology. Joan felt herself softening.

"Actually, I enjoy Gilbert and Sullivan. What's the operetta?"

"*Ruddigore.* They've been working with a piano for over a month now, and they're sounding good. When they begged me for an orchestra, I couldn't resist. I grew up on that stuff."

"Me too. And I always did like *Ruddigore.* It's not *Pinafore or Mikado,* but it's good, spooky fun. I could play, if you're short a viola. I won't manage the orchestra, though."

"Do you think we'll find enough players in the summer?" Oh, no, Joan thought. *You* might, if you ask them as a favor instead of telling them they have to.

"You might," she said aloud. "How many rehearsals?"

"Only a couple. Plus a dress rehearsal and five performances, of course." Of course. What have I let myself in for?

"Where? And when?"

"Oh, over at the college," Alex said, and Joan could see her waving a pudgy hand in the air. "We're performing in their theater." Odds were good she hadn't booked an orchestra rehearsal room yet. That was the kind of detail Alex preferred to leave to underlings like Joan. Not this time, Joan thought.

"Tell me when you know more," she said firmly.

"I knew I could count on you!" Alex hung up in a burst of enthusiasm.

SIX

Each lord of Ruddigore,
Despite his best endeavour,
Shall do one crime, or more,
Once, every day, for ever!
This doom he can't defy
However he may try,
    For should he stay
    His hand, that day
In torture he shall die!

—DAME HANNAH, QUOTING WITCH'S CURSE,
Ruddigore

JOAN never did find out who had arranged the hot, stuffy room for the orchestra-only rehearsal. Not a player, she was sure. She had survived it. Tonight, though, two weeks after the tornado, she was seated near the edge of the pit in the lovely little air-conditioned Oliver College theater, with a good view of the stage. Grateful that Alex had chosen to put the violas outside the cellos, who could see only a little of the action by turning and stretching, she felt sorry for the winds, who played with their backs to the stage and never saw a thing.

Not that there was much opportunity to look, as long as things were going smoothly. Until that first rehearsal she had forgotten how exhausting it could be to play the viola part in Sullivan's operettas, often repeating the same rhythm on the

G string until she thought her bow arm would drop off—or was afraid it wouldn't, and her shoulder would have to last to the end after all.

Tonight, with the singers, she was grateful for the stage director's frequent interruptions and for dialogue segments in which she could rest and enjoy what was happening onstage while watching from the corner of her eye for Alex to raise her baton. To her surprise, she knew a number of the cast members. Liz MacDonald, Dr. Cutts's nurse, made a fine Dame Hannah, the aging contralto who accompanied Rose Maybud and the chorus of bridesmaids. Dr. Cutts himself was a most effective Sir Despard Murgatroyd, the accursed lord of Ruddigore. And Ellen Putnam was singing Mad Margaret— the best singer so far, Joan thought. Her older daughter, Amy, was in the chorus, as was Catherine Turner, Fred's old flame and the only caterer in town. Joan resolved to keep out of Catherine's way—their last encounter had been less than pleasant.

Not only was all the singing better than she would have expected—Alex had been right about that—but so far, at least, the leads even had their traditional Gilbert and Sullivan gestures and dance steps down pat. She wondered who had coached them.

Less precise, the chorus of bridesmaids ranged from schoolgirls to grandmothers. It figured, in a town as small as Oliver. The men's chorus was a little older. Sure, Joan realized. The boys' voices have to have changed.

The stage director called another halt, this time to build a fire under the laggards in the chorus.

"You bridesmaids, don't just stroll off the stage when Sir Despard moves toward you! He's no ordinary man—this is Sir Despard Murgatroyd, the evil baronet of Ruddigore! You all know he commits a dreadful crime every day. When you sing 'No! No!' you sound as if you mean it. But look at what you've been doing after that." He minced a few steps away—and turned back on them with a leer.

"Would you *stroll* away from an attacker you met in the park? I should say not. So let's see you run! Boo!" He lunged at a knot of girls, who scattered and ran from him, giggling.

John Hocking, who ordinarily sat third in the Oliver Civic Symphony's viola section but who was sitting first for *Ruddigore,* leaned over to Joan.

"Wonder what he's like in the classroom."

"Who?"

"Duane Biggy." He waved his bow at the curly-headed stage director. "He teaches English at the college."

"No wonder he couldn't resist playing a part."

"A hammy one," John said.

Hammy was right, Joan thought. When he wasn't directing the movements of the rest of the cast, Biggy was Richard, the sailor who believes in following his heart, even when it tells him to win Rose Maybud for himself right after promising to court her for Robin Oakapple, the man he calls his dearest friend. Biggy had been throwing himself into the role to good effect, and Joan had to admit that his singing and acting more than justified casting him in it. On the stage now, he had rounded up the bridesmaids again.

"That's more like it," he said, "but without the giggling. You're not embarrassed—you're scared. Now you fellows follow suit. The girls have just put you down as clumsy clodhoppers not worthy of them, so you'd like to prove them wrong, but you're as terrified as they are. Shake a fist here or a hoe there, but look scared, and clear the stage as fast as the girls. Find your places, and let's take it from Sir Despard's line, 'I once was a nice-looking youth.' Above all, I want speed."

He got it this time, and they moved on. Alone onstage, Sir Despard mourned, "Poor children, how they loathe me—whose hands are certainly steeped in infamy, but whose heart is as the heart of a little child. But what is a poor baronet to do, when a whole picture gallery of ancestors step down from their frames and threaten him with an excruciating death if he hesitates to commit his daily crime?''

Richard followed his heart again and told Sir Despard that the older brother who should have inherited the accursed life he, Despard, has been forced to lead, is none other than Robin Oakapple, who is to marry Rose Maybud that very day. And Sir Despard rejoiced, ''Free—free at last!''

Joan grinned. Not what I usually think of when I hear those words. Then she had to tuck her viola under her chin and play again.

She enjoyed prim Rose Maybud, who tested the moral worth of her suitors with her etiquette book (''The man who bites his bread, or eats peas with a knife, I look upon as a lost creature'') and who kept switching the object of her love, first from Robin to Despard and then from Despard to Richard. At each switch the bridesmaids caroled, ''Hail the bridegroom— hail the bride!'' It was the good fun Joan remembered, if not yet spooky.

''That's it for Act One. Take ten,'' Duane Biggy said finally, shifting again from happy sailor/suitor to stage director. The members of the cast flopped where they were or ran around, depending on their age. Real-life couples began pairing off.

Down in the pit, Joan was suffering from viola player's back—sore muscles that almost made her wish her viola were a smaller, lighter violin. Serves me right for not practicing more, she thought. She shrugged her shoulders forward and back, trying to get the kinks out. The orchestra-only rehearsal had ended promptly at nine, but it was almost that late now, with the whole second act still to go. She was tempted to ask John for a back rub—she didn't think he'd take it wrong. John, a happily married man with a couple of kids of his own, had never treated her with anything but good-natured camaraderie.

She laid her viola in its case on the floor and straightened up to see him smiling at her.

"Want a back rub?" he offered cheerfully.

"John, you read my mind."

"Only your gyrations." Laying his viola on his chair, he stood up and moved behind her.

Gratefully, Joan let her head flop onto her chest and her arms rest in her lap. No point in having a back rub unless you relax, she thought. Gradually, her tight muscles loosened as his strong fingers kneaded the sore spots in her neck and shoulders and moved methodically down her back, finally beating a quick rhythm across it. She sat still a moment, feeling as if her arms could rise into the air without any effort on her part. Then she made herself offer to reciprocate.

"That was great. Want a turn?"

"No, thanks," he said. "My back is fine, but my eyes are killing me." He unscrewed the bulb on their stand light and went off in search of a brighter one.

Glad not to have to move while she felt so good, she watched the scenery being shifted without benefit of curtain. A couple of men were pushing heavy-based frames into place for the portrait gallery in Ruddigore Castle. The black steps leading down from each frame wouldn't show from the audience, at least if the lighting were right, but they'd let the ghosts of the family portraits step down for their parade in the second act. The hard part would be standing still in the frames until the time came. She said as much to John, who had returned in triumph and screwed in the new bulb.

"I think Virgil Shoals has rigged something to help them," he answered.

Where had she heard that name before? "Who's Virgil Shoals?"

"That fellow Esther Ooley's flirting with." He pointed to a wiry man with a shock of straight blond hair falling across his forehead, deep in conversation with Rose Maybud. Esther

Ooley was going to need considerable help to look like the sweet young thing Rose Maybud was supposed to be. She was wearing taut black stirrup pants and ballet slippers—the only thing about her that looked young. "He's a building contractor."

Of course. David Putnam's. The one Zach usually worked for.

"And Esther?" she asked.

"Has that bridal shop on south Main Street." He grinned.

"Bridal Delights? The one with the sexy underwear in the window?"

"Uh-huh."

Joan watched Esther display her ample cleavage to Virgil—Rose Maybud would have been shocked. Then Esther laughed and came downstage, where Duane Biggy was comparing the heft of a couple of daggers from the prop box.

"Duane, honey, you're not planning to take the second act in order, are you?" Esther asked him.

"You have a problem with that?"

"It's just that I've got so much to do in the bridal shop—June is our very busiest month." She turned the cleavage on him. "We've been rehearsing my last scene and the finale right after my first scene, so I could leave early. I'd be soooo grateful if you'd do that for me, too."

"Sorry," Biggy said. "I can't leave the ghosts hanging up there all that time."

"Couldn't you let them climb up later?" Joan couldn't see Esther's face now, but her voice pouted.

"I could, but I won't. More of us will get out on time if we go in order. Besides, people need to recognize their cues. But I'll try to speed this up—for all our sakes." He clapped his hands and called for the ghosts to take their places. Esther stalked offstage.

The ghosts climbed into their picture frames from behind. The base of each frame was a stile, Joan realized—a sturdy contraption with steps both fore and aft that gave the men access from both directions.

Liz MacDonald leaned against the frame on the far right. She began making what Joan thought was an obvious play for the ghost in it, a dark, good-looking man she suddenly recognized as David Putnam. She tuned in.

"No, I don't think I could look deep into your eyes during your ballad," he was saying. He wasn't smiling.

"Oh, Davy," Liz said softly, looking up into his. "That's what it's all about, don't you see? We've just found each other after all these years, and we're falling in love all over again." She reached her hand up to touch his. For a moment Joan thought she might weep.

"Nope, it's too risky." David's voice was matter-of-fact. "If I don't watch the conductor, I'll come in wrong on the Hey, lackadays. Wouldn't I, Ellen?" he asked his wife, who was standing quietly behind Liz.

"Probably." She laughed. "It's a good thing they can't hear you singing it in the shower." As I can, she implied, oh, so naturally. Good girl, Joan thought. Remind her who you are, but don't kick her while she's down.

A few moments later, the next ghost, a broad-shouldered towhead, seemed to be courting Liz, but getting no further with her than she had with David. They spoke too softly for Joan to hear, but their exchanges were as clear as anything in the play. Finally Duane Biggy clapped his hands and both women left the stage.

David was still arranging himself on his invisible supports when Alex tapped for attention and Joan had to lift her bow to play the introduction to Act Two. Robin and his faithful servant Adam began the scene in the gallery by thinking of daily crimes for Robin, now the accursed Sir Ruthven Murgatroyd, to commit. The chorus of bridesmaids escorted Rose Maybud and Richard into Ruddigore Castle. After some ten

minutes of Gilbertian nonsense, they left Robin alone with the
pictures, begging his forefathers to accept his crimes.

"And the stage darkens," Duane Biggy called. "Only not
tonight." He came out from the wings. "Then the lights come
up again, and you ghosts come down. So let's do it." He
waved an arm, and Alex tapped her baton for the chorus of
family portraits.

Here, at last, was the spooky music. Joan couldn't look
away from the music to watch the ghosts marching slowly
around the stage, but she could hear them when they ordered
poor Robin to his knees and sang,

Earthworm, maggot, tadpole, weevil!
Set upon they course of evil,
Lest the King of Spectre-Land
Set on thee his grisly hand!

She had just made it past some octaves and was thinking
she'd have to figure out a more convenient fingering for them
when a strange thing happened. Baton raised for the next
downbeat, Alex looked puzzled. Finally she put her arms
down and waited.

Joan peered up at the stage. The ghosts had come to a halt
and were staring up at David's picture frame. He was still in
it, motionless.

"Psst, David," one of them said softly. No response.

What's the matter with David? Joan thought. She saw
Duane Biggy advancing on him.

"Sir Roderic!" the ghosts called. Still nothing. Biggy
whacked the frame with old Adam's cane.

"Wake up, Putnam!" he shouted. "It's your cue!"

Slowly, David descended the steps of the frame to the stage.
At last, Alex began conducting again.

On key, as if nothing at all had happened, David sang, "Beware! beware! beware!"

That was as far as he got. Biggy broke in.

"What's the matter with you?" he demanded. "You missed your cue."

"I did?" David sounded suprised. "The last I remember is 'For she is such a smart little craft—' for the umpteenth time. I must have fallen asleep."

"I knew it!" Biggy said. "It's those damn supports. Virgil? Virgil!"

Virgil Shoals materialized in Sir Roderick's frame.

"Dammit, Virgil," Biggy yelled at him. "These things are supposed to help them stand still, not put them to sleep!"

"I know," Virgil said, looking down at the assembled ghosts. "Zach, why did you change these angles? I should have known better than to trust an Amish carpenter to follow directions."

For the first time, Joan spotted Zach Yoder's blond head among the ghosts. During the past two weeks she had appreciated his good work on her porch and enjoyed his good humor, but he'd never mentioned *Ruddigore*.

Why should that be such a surprise? she thought. Neither did I.

Zach didn't answer Virgil. He stared at the floor.

"I don't care who did what," Biggy said. "You fix it before the next rehearsal."

"It's not Zach's fault," David said. "I've been working too hard. The supports are fine."

"Get some sleep, then!" Biggy snapped. "But don't get it here! You have a responsibility to the performance!" He marched off, leaving David silent.

Poor David, Joan thought. And poor Zach.

They made it to the end without further mishaps. The viola part to David's "When the Night Wind Howls" was easy— the clarinets and flutes did the fancy work—and she enjoyed hearing David do it justice. Dr. Cutts as Despard, no longer the bad baronet of Ruddigore, danced a staid little dance with

Ellen Putnam as no-longer-mad Margaret, and with Robin they finally sang Joan's favorite patter song, ending with "This particularly rapid, unintelligible patter isn't generally heard, and if it is it doesn't matter!"

Liz MacDonald's Dame Hannah, the elderly maiden Robin had attempted to abduct for his crime of the day, challenged him to a duel with the daggers Joan had seen Duane Biggy testing. Sir Roderic, who turned out to have been engaged to Hannah when he was still alive, intervened, and sang a sad little love song with her. Robin, in a flight of Gilbertian legality, persuaded Sir Roderic that since for a baronet of Ruddigore to refuse to commit a daily crime is tantamount to suicide—itself a crime—Roderic ought never to have died at all and was "practically alive." Quickly, all the lovers were reunited and sang the rousing finale.

Joan lowered her instrument with relief.

"Made it," she said to John.

"All right, everybody onstage," Duane Biggy called. "Let's get your steps right for the curtain calls."

Alex tapped her baton.

"We're going to play for them—take it from the Allegro con spirito in the Finale to Act One. I cut you off at the first place marked 'End of Act One' when the act ends, but for the curtain calls, you'll need to play all the way to the *second* 'End of Act One.' Got it?"

Wearily, Joan flipped the pages back. Better mark that with a paper clip for the performance, she thought, or I'll never find it. She rummaged in her purse for one and clipped it on the page.

"Good," John said. Scarcely needing to glance at the easy notes, Joan watched the curtain calls—first the choruses, then the ghosts, and then the principals. Ellen Putnam and Dr. Cutts kept their faces straight, as befitted the newly staid demeanor of Margaret and Sir Despard, but Liz MacDonald glowed up at David, who seemed to be concentrating on his footwork.

How can she stand to play Dame Hannah to his Sir Roderic? Joan wondered. It's obvious how he feels about his wife.

Before releasing them, Biggy called for attention.

"Up to now, I've been lenient, and you've all been able to watch each other. You've had your fun. From now on, I want nobody in the wings who isn't waiting for a cue. The rest of you will wait all the way downstairs. Chorus, this means you!" Giggles. "And orchestra, leave your cases in the dressing rooms. Please take the time to find them now, so we can start promptly at seven tomorrow. We'll lower the pit then, so you can enter that way, but just for tonight you'll have to climb up here and go down from backstage."

One more thing to remember. Joan picked up her case, leaving the music with John, and climbed the steps to the stage. At stage right, she found David and Ellen Putnam talking with Zach Yoder.

"I'd never call a man a liar," Zach said. "But so help me, he didn't say a word about any special angles. He just said to make armrests. I'm awful sorry."

"Think nothing of it, Zach," David said. "I should have known better than to take this on. I've been pushing too hard since the storm, and all I've done is our roof. Maybe I should quit while there's still time. Pete could sing Sir Roderic. He knows it."

"Oh, no, David!" Ellen said. "You love it—you know you do. You'll just have to figure out a way to get some rest."

"Maybe," he said. "But I think I'll bring my tools over and do a little work on the supports."

SEVEN

There is beauty in extreme old age—
    Do you fancy you are elderly enough?

—KO-KO, *The Mikado*

TOO TIRED even to chat after the rehearsal, Joan couldn't imagine how she'd feel by the performance on Friday. She limped into the house at half past eleven, muttered something to Andrew, and flopped into bed.

Zach Yoder's hammering and power saw generally woke her at eight. He was making good progress on the porch. With luck, he said, they'd be able to use the front door again in a few more days. On Thursday, though, she woke at the crack of dawn to the sound of a backhoe over at Henry's. Andrew grumbled his way into her room at seven.

"Sheesh, Mom, isn't there a law against blasting people out of bed this early?"

"It's the coolest part of the day." She looked out the window. "Besides, that's a judge out there. He knows the law."

"Probably thinks he is the law." Andrew yawned again and headed downstairs to brew coffee. He had a point.

By the time Joan finished her shower and heard Zach arrive, the backhoe had stopped. I'll bet he has to be in court today, she thought. Lucky David—the courthouse is bound to be air-conditioned.

What passed for air conditioning at the Oliver Senior Citizens' Center was woefully inadequate, but she knew it was better than many of the regulars had at home. With movies, once the low-cost answer to a hot day, now out of range of many old folks' budgets, Joan worried about people who lacked so much as an electric fan. Finding them and cooling them was an ongoing project of the center.

She ran a comb through her hair and pulled it back into a thick French braid. On a day this muggy, it wouldn't dry for hours. Good. The damp weight felt cool on the back of her head and neck.

Still in her bathrobe, she poured two mugs of coffee and carried them outside, where she offered one to Zach. He drew a sharp pencil line on a floorboard before accepting it. He'd measure it again before cutting it, she knew by now. Zach had turned out to be a careful, methodical carpenter. Where did Virgil Shoals come off, anyway, insulting him?

"How're you coming?"

"Pretty good. I have to take off awhile today, though, to take back that backhoe for David."

"That was quick."

"He didn't do anything—just looked. Said it was worse than he thought."

"I see." She didn't, really, but she didn't expect to understand whatever explanation might be forthcoming if she asked. It was probably a good thing Henry wouldn't need his house in the near future. She'd have to ask David whether he thought his uncle was ready for visitors yet. In the pressure of rehearsals, she hadn't even tried to see him.

When she went back into the house, Andrew looked startled.

"You're here!"

"It's early, remember?"

"I just told Fred Lundquist you'd left. He said to tell you he'd pick you up at the center at five-thirty."

"Omigosh, that's right. I told Fred I'd go to dinner with him tonight. You'll have to scrounge for yourself."

Upstairs, she sighed over her sparse clothes closet. Oliver's restaurant scene was anything but upscale. Still, as often as Fred had seen her looking grubby, it might be nice to dress up a little for a change. Right, she thought. And die of the heat at work? He probably won't even notice.

In the end, she chose her favorite—a soft, blue cotton, mini-pleated dress with short sleeves, cool enough for work and loose enough to be comfortable at tonight's dress rehearsal, which was bound to go even longer than last night, if everything went wrong that could. From every dress rehearsal she'd ever played, that was a good bet. She tucked a bottle of aspirin in her purse for her back and shoulders. Her sore ankle would benefit, too. She left off the Ace bandage, though—it wouldn't do a thing for the blue dress. Dr. Cutts had said her ankle would be okay to walk on without it. She hoped she wouldn't be sorry.

The morning programs—an exercise class led by a vivacious Oliver College student and a lecture by the new librarian on "Great Summer Reads Available at the Oliver Public Library"—let Joan retreat to her tiny office to make plans and cope with the endless stream of mail. Much of it was from businesses with little sense of what the center was all about, or how lean its budget had to be. In the afternoon, a group of old ladies at the craft table making octopus doorstops out of plastic peanut butter jars, sand, and yarn fussed over her dress. They'd give Fred the once-over, too, she knew, if they were still around when he arrived. Even though she'd ducked their questions about her plans for the evening, she could tell they saw through her. It was beginning to look as if they'd hang around to watch. At last Annie Jordan, usually the worst tease of all, winked at Joan and diverted everyone else's attention with a game of "Ain't it awful?"

"Did you hear the government isn't going to help at all

with the tornado damage?'' she asked in an innocent voice. "Seems it doesn't qualify as a disaster."

"That's awful!" A woman with knobby fingers tugged at a braided tentacle. "My grandson's mobile home was demolished, and he lost every stick of furniture. Some of it not even paid for. He's living with his folks, but they don't have the space—he's got a wife and four kids."

The others picked up the tune without missing a beat.

"There's still families camped out in the National Guard Armory. They've been counting on government loans to get back on their feet."

"The ones I really feel sorry for are the ones in the hospital. Did you hear about Henry?"

"Henry who?"

"Henry Putnam—you know, the one who gets all the good parts in the Senior Players." Oops, Joan thought. I'd better have a word with the director if Henry has a corner on the best roles. "His spanking new house caved in on him when he went to look for his dog. Turns out the dog wasn't even in there, but it looks like Henry might be paralyzed for life. He's still in the hospital."

"Not for long," Annie said. "They're gonna bump him out. Insurance says he has to go."

Joan was shocked. "Annie, Henry can't go home! There's no one to take care of him, and anyway, his house isn't fixed."

"They'll send him to a nursing home, I expect. I don't know who'll bother with the dog. Ain't it awful, the way they do old folks?" Annie's eyes sparkled, and she sat back, waiting for the flood that would follow. It obliged.

"Nobody cares, that's why," said one.

"I hear Social Security is about broke," said another. "We paid into it all our lives, and they're using it up on everything else."

"They make you practically spend down to your last cent

for Medicaid—and now they're cutting that. What's a person supposed to do when nursing homes charge so much?"

"And have you seen the gobbledygook the hospital calls a bill?"

"There was things on my John's last bill I know nobody ever done to him, but I never could get anyone to listen. If you ask me, some of them doctors was lining their own pockets." Heads nodded grimly.

Joan still remembered the awful cost of Ken's death, even though her young husband had lived only a few hours after his sudden collapse. Thank goodness his ministerial insurance had covered most of it. But these old women, mostly widowed, needed to know more than they did.

"Would you like me to ask someone to come talk to us about Medicare and Medicaid?" she asked. A lawyer, maybe, or a social worker, she thought.

"Ask why they charge four dollars an aspirin in that hospital."

"I'll see what I can do." Maybe the hospital administrator would come. Or she could ask Dr. Cutts—if he didn't know, he ought to.

By the time Fred arrived, they had all left but Annie. The last to go, she pointed a knitting needle at Joan and Fred on her way out the door.

"Don't do anything I wouldn't do," she called.

"You take all the fun out of it," Joan said, and waved.

"They give you a rough time?" Fred said, smiling down at her. They both remembered the gauntlet he had run the first time he'd called on her at the center. His eyes crinkled and reflected the blue of his shirt. Those eyes got her every time, but his body was no slouch, either. Fred was almost fifty, but only his thinning blond hair and the depth of the lines in his face suggested it.

"Not bad. Annie got them going on the medical system, and that took the heat off. Besides, I don't really mind."

"Where would you like to go?"

"Any place that doesn't take too long. I forgot to tell you, Fred, I have a rehearsal at seven." She looked at her watch. Pushing six already.

"On Thursday?"

"I'm playing *Ruddigore*. Tonight's the dress, and tomorrow is our first performance. I'll have a couple of comp tickets for you." That means he could bring a date. He wouldn't, would he?

"Sure, I could use one. Since you're buying."

She smiled up at him. "You're a cheap date, Lundquist."

"So, how about a pizza?"

"Great." Not that there was a lot of choice in this small college town—and there wasn't time to drive to Nashville or Bloomington and back before the rehearsal. They left her viola in the relative cool of her office, rather than worrying about the effects of heat and humidity on its wood and strings.

Over deep-dish pepperoni and surprisingly fresh salad she and Fred compared his tornado in the station house to hers in the creek bed.

"I don't know what we'd have done if it hadn't been so dry for the past month."

He nodded. "It could have been worse. Compared to Martinsville, Oliver got off lucky."

Henry Putnam didn't, she thought. And they moved on to more cheerful topics.

Strolling down Main Street afterwards to pick up her viola—hardly limping at all—she thought, here I am, hand in hand with a handsome fellow after going out for pizza. I feel like a college kid.

A horn from a car full of cruising teenagers made her jump, and a kid yelled, "Hey, Grandpa!" The others laughed. Joan looked for the doddering old man, but saw no one. Then the boy yelled again, "Hey, Grandma!" And suddenly it hit her.

They mean us! They think we're ancient—and I guess to them we are.

Fred, whose ears had turned red, said, "I'll show them Grandpa! Come here, woman!" He grabbed her around the waist, bent her backwards, and bussed her solidly. It was like being kissed by Clark Gable, only with sweet breath.

"Fred!" she cried and he did it again, but gently this time, omitting the calisthenics and caressing the sensitive corners of her mouth. She put one hand up to his temple, wrapped the other around his neck, and kissed him back.

The kids whooped and the horns blared, but she no longer noticed.

EIGHT

*I don't believe you know what jealousy is! I don't believe
you know how it eats into a man's heart—and disorders
his digestion—and turns his interior into boiling lead.
Oh, you are a heartless jade to trifle with the delicate
organization of the human interior!*

—WILFRED, *The Yeomen of the Guard*

THE PIT was still in the basement when Joan approached it
from the auditorium, her mind on Fred, not on Duane Biggy's
new rules. She leaned over the railing and called down to John
Hocking.

"How do I get down there?"

He stood in the pit and pointed his bow to show her. "Go
out up there where it says Stage Door. Take the stairs on your
left. You can leave your case in the women's dressing room."

"Thanks." Duane probably said all that the other night, but
darned if I remember. I did well to show up tonight.

She descended the steep stairs cautiously, feeling her ankle
again, found the dressing room, and cleared a spot for her case
among piles of costumes and street clothes. Good pickings for
a thief, she thought, and shook her head at unguarded purses
while rubbing rosin on her bow. Grateful not to have to go
onstage in costume, she hung her bag firmly on her shoulder
before heading for the open door to the back of the pit. She

squeezed between the woodwinds and past the cellos to her seat near the front edge, next to John.

No sooner was she seated than someone yelled, "Keep your hands in!" The door closed and the pit vibrated and moved upwards. It felt more like a minor earthquake than an elevator, and Joan wasn't surprised to see the irrepressible John ignore the warning and touch the wall sliding ever so slowly past them. She had yearned to do the same thing years ago, when her parents had taken her and her little brother to Chicago and they'd gone down into the old coal mine in the Museum of Science and Industry. That elevator had been just as creaky and slow as this one, but the walls had sped past to give the illusion of rapid descent into the bowels of the earth. Here there was no such illusion.

At last they stopped, slightly below the level of the orchestra seats in the audience. Tonight, for dress rehearsal, the curtains were closed as they would be tomorrow before the performance. For a moment Joan felt jittery about the few tricky bits in the music. Then Alex raised her baton for the first upbeat. Too late now, Joan thought, and dug in.

Tonight's disasters were minor. No one tripped, no one forgot lines, and the orchestra and singers hit most of the same notes at the same time. The bridesmaids shrieked and ran most convincingly from Sir Despard Murgatroyd—Duane Biggy's coaching had worked well in that scene. He stopped the rehearsal only once, to banish a few overeager choristers from the wings to the lower regions of the theater.

"I told you last night!" he bellowed. "No one—and that means *you*—is allowed in the wings unless you're going onstage in that scene. Out in the audience they'll hear every little whisper." He came downstage. "That means you down there in the orchestra, too, even though you can't leave. I can hear what you're saying all the way up here. Unless you're blowing a horn, keep your mouths *shut!*" He turned his back on them.

"Yes, your majesty," John muttered. Biggy whirled on the pit.

"I heard that! Who said that?" His eyes raced from one player to another, and Joan felt like an innocent schoolchild accused of something unthinkable. Cold perspiration trickled down her neck and under her arms. She wiped her chin rest and carefully avoided looking at John, who sat beside her like a stone. For a long minute Biggy stared down at them, while the singers behind him rolled their eyes.

"All right, Duane," Alex said calmly. "We get your point. Let's get on with it—we don't want to be here all night." Joan blessed Alex for demonstrating more common sense with him than she sometimes did with the symphony.

At last Biggy shrugged. Looking daggers back at them, he slowly left the stage, and they finished the first act.

By the time the pit was lowered for a break and she escaped from its tight quarters, Joan found the couples already pairing off downstairs. She felt for Liz MacDonald, whose crush on David was even more painfully obvious tonight than it had been the night before, and just as matter-of-factly ignored. Tonight, though, the towhead ghost Liz was rebuffing again would not take no for an answer, and the dynamics had gone from piano to mezzo forte.

"Liz, let the man be!"

"You just butt out, Chris Eads. What I do is no longer any of your business."

"It's my business if you make a fool of yourself. He don't even want you, and I do!"

"It's too late now. We're divorced."

"And whose fault is that!" He stared tight-lipped at David.

"You know whose fault it was."

"Let me make it up to you, Liz. I'll be a better husband this time."

"Run along, Chris. You had your chance." Liz turned her back on him. Chris clenched his fist, but put it in his pocket.

Joan turned away. The whole exchange was too painful.

The orchestra members hadn't wasted words on Biggy's explosion. Joan figured they were inured to it by Alex's frequent outbursts—almost all were members of the Oliver Civic Symphony. But she wasn't surprised to find choristers complaining while they sweated in the hot dressing room. Standing with a gaggle of girls in line for the all-too-scarce toilets, she heard a high young voice float out of a bilious green stall.

"I don't know who he thinks he is! And the other night he was, like, so *rude* to Amy's father! What did your dad say, Amy?"

"Not much." In line ahead of Joan, red was rising in the already made-up cheeks of a blonde bridesmaid Joan recognized belatedly as Amy Putnam, Laura's big sister, but Amy sounded calmer than she looked.

"Well, *my* dad would be *furious!*" said the closeted voice. "He'd probably stomp out and never come back."

The stall door opened, and Amy swapped places with a girl about her age who set to repairing her eyeliner without bothering to wash her hands.

"Dad's pretty cool," came Amy's voice from inside the stall. "Compared to the characters he gets in court, Biggy's nothing."

"I guess not." The other girl made a face at herself and then giggled. "Biggy's not as big as he thinks, is he?"

"Not as big as my dad," Amy said, and flushed the toilet. Joan entered the next cubicle before Amy emerged. You're lucky in your father, Amy, she thought. But then, so were my two—I only wish they could have had him longer.

Andrew had loved Ken, but Rebecca had idolized him and clung to his memory. For years after his death she had turned a stony face toward any man who so much as looked at her mother, but she had warmed up to Fred. Or was that wishful thinking?

When she went back for her viola, Amy was gone, but the

lower hall was still crowded. She was stuck in a traffic jam of singers keeping out of Biggy's way and ghosts hurrying to get up onto the stage and into their frames. She pushed carefully, not wanting to risk viola or bow, and tried saying "Excuse me," but no one seemed to notice. Certainly no one yielded.

Great. All I don't need is to be late for the pit to rise. I hope they'll at least wait for me—I can just imagine what Duane Biggy would do if I tried to climb down from the stage after the pit was up. How did I get myself into this, anyway?

Virgil Shoals and David Putnam pushed through the crowd toward her as they headed for the stairs behind her. David wore Sir Roderic's black frock coat, with a gray waistcoat and trousers. His collar was turned down over a loosely knotted tie. Very becoming.

"Don't get me wrong," David was saying. "I understand what you're up against."

"I didn't do the work," Virgil began.

"But the other guy's shoddy execution makes you look as bad as if you had," David finished for him. "You can't let him get away with it. That kind of thing will ruin your reputation."

Joan was shocked. The man who sent Zach Yoder to her knocking him behind his back? What had happened to David's protestations of last night?

"Excuse me!" she said loudly. Over several heads, David spotted her.

"Make way for the orchestra!" he sang out good-naturedly. "Let this woman through—she's about to miss her pit." The crowd parted magically, and Joan saw a clear path to the door. Still indignant, she thanked the people who let her by, but couldn't bring herself to acknowledge David's making them move.

"Boy," she said to John, as the pit rattled upwards again. "You think you know someone."

He cocked his head at her.

"Trouble?"

"I'm just disappointed in someone."

"Sorry to hear it. You sure were glowing when you came in tonight."

Had it been that obvious? She started to answer—what? What if Fred, too, turned out not to be what she thought? The elevator stopped, saving her from the need to reply, and Biggy's silence reigned until Alex got the signal to begin. Then the music—even the filler notes the violas spent so much of their time playing—commanded her concentration and put thoughts of men in a back corner of her mind while she counted rests and repeats.

NINE

Alas, poor ghost!

—ROBIN, *Ruddigore*

THE ADVANTAGE to playing viola, Joan thought, beyond the deep, lovely tone of the instrument itself, was that most of the time she could manage the notes. The advantage to playing in an orchestra was that she never had to manage them alone. Comfortable with the knowledge that she would never achieve perfection, she seldom suffered from preperformance jitters.

On opening night, though, she wasn't surprised to see plenty of jitters in the cramped dressing room. Most of the teenagers in the chorus couldn't stop chattering as they squeezed into what looked like miserably hot costumes and slathered on greasepaint under the supervision of Esther Ooley. Joan had dressed at home in her coolest black cotton skirt and scoop-necked shirt. Long black was the uniform for every orchestra she'd ever played in, and she chose comfort over formality every time.

A few of the older chorus members and most of the women principals, who didn't have individual dressing rooms, kept to themselves and scarcely responded to greetings. Catherine Turner was one of them. Even though Fred had broken up with her almost two years ago, Joan was relieved not to have to decide whether to speak to her.

In the pit, wind players were practicing solos or just blowing warm air into their instruments, and string players were running over passages with tricky fingerings and string crossings. Some were truly warming up; others were skittering panicky bows across strings instead of pulling tone out of their instruments.

Inhale that, and you'll be sorry, Joan told herself. With more than half an hour to curtain, she gave herself permission to climb the stairs and wander backstage, as much to avoid the tension as to escape the heat and stretch her legs.

Things looked different back here. The frames for the ghostly portraits in Act Two were clustered together behind the backdrop for Act One. She couldn't tell how they had been modified since David's disaster—was it only two nights ago? They were the only sturdy things in sight. Up close, the stone walls for the castle in Act II and Rose Maybud's cottage in Act I revealed themselves as insubstantial fakes. The trees were flimsy cutouts, and even the fishing nets of the seaside village had been painted onto the scenery. Knowing that real walls and nets would have been impractical and added nothing to the operetta, she nevertheless felt vaguely cheated.

A faint buzz was rising from the early comers. She resisted the temptation to peek around the curtain to look for Fred, who was due to attend opening night if no emergencies kept him away. He wasn't likely to waste time sitting there early, though.

"I'll get there eventually," he'd promised, and she was sure he would. Solid, reliable, that was Fred. But not what you'd call predictable. She grinned, remembering.

She meandered back to the dressing room, tuned her instrument to her tuning fork's 440 A in relative quiet, and slipped into the pit in plenty of time. She felt in her handbag for the set of well-broken-in strings she always carried in case of emergency. They mattered here more than usual, as there was no way to escape from the pit to change a broken string, or time for a new one to stay in tune.

The concertmaster stood and pointed to the oboe to sound the A, first for the woodwinds, then for the brasses, and finally for the strings. Joan checked her tuning softly and waited in the hush that followed. Then Alex entered the pit, the lights dimmed, and they rode up to applause that sounded as if more than a few out-of-towners had driven to little Oliver for some summer fun. Alex bowed to the audience, turned, and began the overture, this time for real. It went well. Then the curtain rose.

With an audience things were different, and not just because there was no chance to start over again if something went wrong. The first laughter rolling out of the darkness (at Rose Maybud's gifts: "a set of false teeth for pretty little Ruth Row-bottom, and a pound of snuff for the poor orphan girl on the hill") perked up the members of the cast, who were soon performing their best by far since the orchestra had begun rehearsing with them. So, for that matter, was the orchestra.

From time to time, when something went particularly well, Joan and John grinned at each other. At the end of the first act, even Alex applauded the orchestra before leaving the pit. Not inclined to move, Joan relaxed in her chair and looked up at the faces peering down at them over the railing. And there was Fred. He jerked his head toward the stairs. Well, all right. She loosened her bow and laid it on the stand, but tucked her viola under her arm, unlike John and several violinists, who had left their instruments trustingly on their chairs.

If I did that, I'd sit on it, sure as anything.

Fred met her at the top of the stairs. She thought he looked tired.

"It's going well," he said.

"We're not too loud?"

"No, the balance is fine."

"That's good. I'm really impressed by some of the singers. I'd hate it if we drowned them out."

He nodded. "The program says Judge Putnam is in the cast. I didn't recognize him."

"David's a ghost in the second act."

"David, is it?" Deadpan. "You theater types get chummy awful fast."

Joan wouldn't bite. "It was the Putnam's little girl I spent the tornado with." Looking out at the audience, she spotted Laura's blonde head, second row center. It didn't reach the top of her seat. "Fred, they let her come. Look—she's down front with her big brother. Still awake, too."

He smothered a yawn. "Sorry. Long day."

"See you afterward?"

"Sure." He smiled. "You'd better scoot."

She ran back down and made it through the doors after everyone had already been seated. She threaded her way through winds and cellos to her seat just in time for the pit to rumble stageward, only to wait interminably before Alex got the signal to begin conducting and the curtain finally went up on Act Two.

"Hurry up and wait," John murmured. "Just like the army."

The second act began smoothly enough. But ten minutes later, while the orchestra played an interlude and the stage darkened briefly before the ghosts' scene, a peculiar look on Alex's face told Joan that something must be wrong onstage. Funny, though—the audience wasn't responding or laughing, as you would expect them to at a major goof. It must not be that obvious.

She marked time while the ghostly portraits came down out of their frames for their slow march. Then she played in unison with their eerie chorus:

Baronet of Ruddigore,
    Last of our accursed line,
    Down upon the oaken floor—
    Down upon those knees of thine.

John, who could see the stage out of the corner of his eye, even while playing, whispered during a rest, "He's done it again." He could mean only one thing—David had fallen asleep.

Now what? Joan wondered, while shifting positions to negotiate moving octave sixteenths with as few string crossings as possible. Duane Biggy can't go over and yell at him in the middle of a performance.

The answer turned out to be simple. A voice Joan didn't recognize sang David's "Beware! beware! beware!" It had to be one of the ghosts already onstage.

That ought to wake him, she thought. And the audience won't know that he should have sung it—well, most of them won't.

But David didn't climb down from his frame. Instead, his understudy stepped seamlessly into the role of Sir Roderic. The voice sang,

I am the spectre of the late
Sir Roderic Murgatroyd,"
Who comes to warn thee that thy fate
Thou canst not avoid.

"Alas, poor ghost!" answered Robin.

Right, Joan thought. But it's going to be all right, as long as David doesn't suddenly wake up and start singing "Beware!"

He didn't. The understudy made it through "When the night wind howls" as if he'd been rehearsing with them all along. His voice was stronger and better trained than David's. Joan wondered why he hadn't been given the part in the first place. Political pressure?

When the long dialogue began and she was free to watch, she could see how Alex and John had known that David was out like a light even before he should have sung—his head was on his chest.

By now the word had spread throughout the orchestra, with those who could see whispering into the ears of the ones who couldn't. Her hands folded, Alex was shaking her head.

When Robin refused to carry off a lady, as his ghostly ancestors commanded, and began to cry out in pain, Joan thought surely David would wake up, but he didn't move. Could it be that he was awake now, but had decided not to disrupt the operetta? Then Robin yielded, and the ghosts sang,

We want your pardon, ere we go,
For having agonized you so.

Finally, singing softly, they returned to their frames.

Painted emblems of a race,
All accurst in days of yore,
Each to his accustomed place
Steps unwillingly once more!

The tremolo swelled to Alex's cutoff. Knowing that the following dialogue would be brief, Joan reached forward promptly to turn the page to the next number. But instead of old Adam's line, she heard a loud thud and shocked gasps. Then a scream.

"Oh, my God!" John whispered. Alex was staring at the stage in horror. The ghosts were scrambling back down out of the frames—except for David, whose frame was empty at last.

Jumping to her feet and scarcely noticing the resulting twinge in her ankle, Joan saw the costumed body lying on the stage and the dagger sticking out of its back.

Behind her a child's voice cried, "Get up, Daddy!"

Laura. Dear God.

"Curtain! Curtain!" someone yelled, and it closed with a rush. Now everyone was talking at once, in the orchestra and in the audience. Trapped in the pit, Joan felt helpless.

Fred, where are you?

Then she saw him running down the aisle. Ignoring the stairs, he vaulted onto the stage behind her and disappeared behind the curtain.

TEN

Pallid ghosts,
Arise in hosts,
And lend me all your aid!

—MR. WELLS, *The Sorcerer*

THE BODY WAS SURROUNDED by costumed ghosts, a weeping woman wearing sedate Victorian black, and a man in jeans. Fred pushed his way through, repeating "Police" and "Back off!" in a louder voice than he would have chosen had the noise level been lower. A white-haired man in black kneeling beside the body looked up, his stage makeup grotesque at close range.

"He's dead." The man spoke calmly.

"Don't touch him," Fred said. It was too much to expect, but at least the weapon was still in place. He bent to feel the carotid, just in case.

"I had to establish that there was no pulse." The man stood up. "I didn't let anyone else touch him."

"Who are you?" Fred straightened.

"Dr. Cutts."

Fred had heard of Cutts, a G.P. of the old school. "Lieutenant Lundquist, Oliver Police. Thank you, Doctor."

"Lieutenant, thank God!" cried a man in a sailor suit. Fred recognized Richard, the Jolly Jack Tar of the operetta. "This is terrible!"

"This is murder," Fred said quietly. The noise level had dropped, at least behind the curtain. "Who's in charge here?"

"I am," said the sailor. "I'm the director. Duane Biggy."

"Mr. Biggy. Is there a phone to call 911?"

"We did call. Isn't that why you're here?"

"No. I happened to be in the audience."

"Oh, my God! The audience!" Biggy lost his directorial cool. "What do we do about them?"

"They all saw it. Tell them a doctor and the police are here, and ask them to be patient and stay in their seats for a few minutes." Those who haven't already left by now, Fred thought.

Biggy took a deep breath and stepped outside the curtain. The buzz in the auditorium died down as he made his announcement, adding on his own hook that all tickets would be honored for a future performance. The orchestra struck up the overture again, and Biggy returned.

"Who is he?" Fred asked. From the back, and in costume, the body could be any dark-haired white man of medium build.

"David Putnam," Biggy answered, and he looked toward the woman in black.

"Judge Putnam?" God help us all.

"I'm his wife." The woman in black choked back a sob.

His widow, Fred thought. "I'm sorry for your loss, ma'am."

"The children!" she said, and her sobs stopped. Fred waited. "The children are out there—our little girl and our son. They must have seen it!"

"And you?"

"I didn't see anything. I was waiting backstage to come on after the next song. Our older daughter is still downstairs. Lieutenant, I need to find my children!"

"Yes." Fred turned to Biggy. "Is there someplace private

for Mrs. Putnam and her children to wait? I'll want to talk to them."

"There's an upstairs dressing room," the director said.

"My nurse is in the cast," Dr. Cutts murmured. "Could we ask her to stay with Ellen and the children?"

"Of course," Fred said. "Where are the others?" Why haven't they all come running?

The doctor rolled his eyes toward Biggy.

"I insisted that they all stay downstairs until just before their next scene," Biggy said. "That's why only Ellen and Bob, here, saw it from the wings."

"Bob?"

"Bob Cutts." Dr. Bob Cutts, Ellen Putnam.

"So right now no one should be backstage?"

"Only the crew." Biggy pointed to the man wearing jeans.

"Good. I don't want anyone going back there until we can check it out." No siren yet—where were they? "And as far as the rest of the cast knows, the performance is continuing?"

Biggy nodded. "By now they must be wondering why they haven't been called."

"Suppose you tell them Mr. Putnam's been injured and ask them to wait down there. Remind them that Dr. Cutts is here and ask the nurse to come with you—you know who she is?" Biggy nodded. "And the Putnam child."

"Amy," Ellen Putnam said. "Her name is Amy. Duane, don't tell her he's—" She couldn't say it.

"Mrs. Putnam, you go with him," Fred said. "We'll bring your other children to you." And you can all watch each other until I have some backup, he told them silently.

"Don't let them see," she said. Too late, he thought. Then he remembered what the little girl had called out. Maybe she didn't realize yet what had happened.

"We won't," he promised, wondering again when "we" would arrive. When she left the stage in the direction of the stairs, he heard a little voice.

"Mama? Mama!" Turning, Fred saw Mrs. Putnam united with her son and small daughter. Behind them, two uniformed officers entered by the stage door. Good.

He filled them in quickly and left one to preserve the crime scene onstage while the other went to radio for help and report his presence. Now, finally, he could look at what had been behind David Putnam while he was so vulnerable in that picture frame.

Pausing a moment to let his eyes adapt to the dim light backstage, he recognized the scenery from the first act. A few folding chairs were scattered around. To his right, or stage left, were a clothes rack with a couple of costumes hanging on it and a box of theatrical props. Was that where the dagger had come from? The back wall was plain brick—fire brick, he hoped, looking at the flammable sets and curtains. He crossed behind the stage. Against the wall near the corridor that led to the stairs he saw pulleys for the curtains. Overhead were lights, more pulleys, and other things he didn't have names for.

He came back to the picture frames. Putnam's frame was stage left, the one farthest from the stairs. Was there any other entrance? He'd have to ask, but it looked as if whoever stabbed him had to cross behind all the other frames to reach him. What had the other ghosts noticed behind them? Probably not much, once they were facing forward. His own loafers made little sound on the wooden floor.

He looked at the steps without expecting to see anything—no blood had leaked around the dagger onto Putnam's dark coat. There couldn't have been much of a struggle with all those people watching and listening, or he'd have heard. He himself didn't remember seeing any movement during the first minutes of the second act, before the ghostly portraits came to life. Nor had he noticed the one who stayed in his frame—until he fell. He'd have to ask the other actors, who would have known what to expect.

"Fred?" A familiar voice came from the stairs. Peering into the gloom, he saw a middle-aged man in a sport coat and wire rims, and smiled.

"Over here, Johnny." Good with crowds, slow to panic, Sergeant Ketcham had a calming influence in situations like this one—if there was such a thing as a situation quite like this one.

"They said that you were back here." Ketcham crossed behind the frames to where Fred stood. "And that the victim's Judge Putnam."

"Of all people, and we've got the cast and a whole audience full of witnesses, though we probably won't get much from that bunch. I was in the middle of them, and I didn't notice a thing." He shook his head.

Ketcham nodded. "We're calling in off-duty guys to help. And you caught this one."

Fred nodded. He already felt relieved, just knowing that he'd be working with Ketcham. Quickly, he told the sergeant what little he knew.

"So," Ketcham said, "unless someone from outside sneaked in, it looks like one of the people on the stage now."

"An outsider would stick out back here, with Biggy even keeping the cast away."

"Do we know for sure that no one slipped up here long enough to do in the judge and then disappeared back down there?"

"Could be." Fred pictured the scene out front. "Or it could even be an orchestra member, if it happened before the pit went up. They're pretty well trapped in there, once it rises. We need to establish when Putnam was last seen alive."

They looked at each other and headed for the stage, where the photographer and evidence techs were already at work. Dr. Henshaw, the coroner, hadn't arrived yet; the body still lay as it had fallen, facedown, crumpled, legs curled. The black handle protruded between the shoulders of the frock coat at an angle that suggested an assailant shorter than the victim—unless, Fred thought suddenly, he'd been standing on a lower step. In that case, it meant a tall man—or a woman who would stand out in a crowd. He put Putnam at about five ten.

Without discussion, Ketcham took over calming the agitated cast and crew, assuring them that with their help, the police would do their best to find the killer, and that they would be detained for as short a time as possible. He stepped outside the curtain, where Fred heard him telling the audience and orchestra that Putnam had indeed been murdered. They were free to leave, he said, but he asked for voluntary statements from anyone who had noticed anything unusual before Putnam fell to the stage, or who had talked to him between acts, or who had any other information that might help the police. Officers would be waiting at the exits to take their statements.

Fred sent Officer Jill Root, a young woman with a good dose of common sense, to stay with Mrs. Putnam.

"Keep your ears open. We'll be there before long," he promised. Ketcham returned, and the two of them took the cast members and the others backstage, out of sight of the body, but in view of what had to be the murder scene itself.

"We need your help," Fred told them. "Were you all backstage before the second act began?" Mistake. Everybody started talking at once. He spread his palms out toward them. "Whoa. One at a time. Mr. Biggy, can you answer that?"

"Yes, this group was here. After Robin and old Adam— that's Steve here, and Ed over there—" He waved, and Fred recognized the tall young redhead and the short servant with big ears from the operetta. "After they opened the act, I brought up Esther Ooley, our Rose Maybud, and the chorus."

"They were downstairs until the end of the first scene?" So it wasn't a mob scene at first, either.

"That's right. So were Ellen and Bob." Mrs. Putnam and the doctor. "Their little dance comes after the song Steve and

Bob sing when the ghosts go back to their frames—but we didn't get that far.''

Reaching into his breast pocket for his ever-present note-book, Fred's fingers touched the program he had folded and stashed there. Good. Between the cast list and the synopsis, he could keep track of who was who and where, at least the ones who had been onstage.

''And when did you last see Putnam alive?''

''He passed me on the stairs. I didn't talk to him after that. I checked that all the ghosts had climbed into their frames and then went downstairs.''

''Did anyone actually see Judge Putnam climb into his?''

''I did,'' said a blond ghost whose muscles were visible through a double-breasted cutaway and canary-yellow waist-coat.

''Your name?''

''Chris Eads. My frame's next to his. We talked some.'' His voice was pleasant enough, but it betrayed him as Hoosier rather than the English lord he was portraying.

''Did you see anyone come past your frame?''

''Just him.''

''What did you notice after he was in his?''

''Nothing. You don't see much, once you're in that thing.''

''Anybody else?'' No response. He looked at the stage crew, who stood apart from the actors. ''You guys see any-thing at all behind Putnam? A person who shouldn't have been there? Anyone doing anything out of the ordinary?'' They all shook their heads. He turned back to Eads. ''When did he quit talking?''

''He didn't say much. Nothing after I climbed up. He never did. Not that I could have heard him. You don't hear each other in those things, either.''

''Is that true?'' Fred asked the others. There were general murmurs of assent.

''It made the ensemble singing difficult,'' said a tall, dark, good-looking, middle-aged man in a blue satin costume that made him vaguely resemble Gainsborough's Blue Boy. "We really had to watch the conductor to stay together before we climbed down out of the picture frames to the stage."

"So even if he made some kind of noise, you might not have heard him?" Fred asked.

"Might not," Eads said. "For a while there it was pretty noisy."

"Or he could have been alive until right before he fell?" By then only the crew, the doctor, and the wife would have been backstage—and Biggy.

"He was long gone by then," said Blue Boy. "I had to sing his solo."

"You kept going *after* you knew he was dead?" Fred thought that was carrying "the show must go on" too far.

"We thought he was asleep," said a bewigged ghost wearing a long brown velvet coat over white satin. Asleep? In a performance? Fred raised an eyebrow.

"Like the other night," said a balding ghost with a mustache and trim beard, wearing doublet and hose, a ruff around his neck, and a sword at his side. "He fell asleep in rehearsal."

"It's true. That's why I had Pete ready to take over with no warning," Biggy put in. "I heard his voice when it should have been David's, and I was sure David had done it again."

"You're Pete?" Fred turned to the ghost in blue, who nodded.

"Pete Wylie."

"When did you notice, Mr. Wylie?"

"I had my eye on him when we started marching around. He was supposed to stay up there when the rest of us came down, but his chin was on his chest. It was still there when his cue came, so I took over. Once I started singing, I just hoped he wouldn't wake up all of a sudden."

"Yeah, well, you got your wish," Fred said, and was sorry

he had. He tried to remember what had happened before the ghosts had started marching around, but it was hopeless.

"Did anybody notice him before that?" Ketcham asked.

"The frames are too deep," said a blond man of twenty-five or thirty, about five ten, wearing a loose robe tied with a sash. "Like blinders on a horse. I wish now we hadn't built them that way."

"You are…?"

"Zach Yoder. I helped with the sets."

"I didn't notice him either," said young Robin. Fred pulled the program out and checked it. His name was Steve Dolan, and he looked young enough to be carded at a bar. "I was talking to the portraits, but I didn't actually see them—I was concentrating on that speech about calling welcome Death to free you from your cloying guiltiness. That's a real bear."

"Before that, I was onstage with Esther—Rose Maybud—and the chorus," Biggy said. "But I didn't see him; we had to watch the conductor. And nobody else mentioned him when we went off."

"And before *that*, it was Steve and me," said the man Fred had recognized as old Adam. Edward Kleinholtz, according to the program. His lines and wrinkles had been painted onto a baby face—impossible to guess his age. "We opened the second act. We were running over our lines together while they were climbing into their frames."

"What about the weapon?" Ketcham asked. "Is it part of the play?"

They all looked at Biggy this time. He gulped.

"It looks like the little one Liz threatens Steve with at first."

"At first?"

"First she threatens me with the little one," Steve said. "When I say, 'And this is what it is to embark upon a career of unlicensed pleasure!' she throws it at me and challenges me to take her on—only she's got a big one."

"They should both be in the prop box," Biggy said. "Liz was still downstairs."

They followed him over to it. In clear view was a very large, very sharp-looking dagger.

"I'm sure the one in his back is the little one we used," said Steve. "I thought so right away, so I looked at it up close."

"I'm surprised you fought with such sharp weapons."

"It's not really dangerous. We didn't ever actually fight." He stopped abruptly. "I mean…"

"All right," Fred said. "That's it for now, unless you think of something we should know." He paused. To a man, they looked at the floor, at the walls, anywhere but at the two detectives.

"We can leave?" asked the man in dark jeans, cut from the same mold as Chris Eads and the man in the robe. Fred wondered how he'd ever tell them apart, once the ghosts changed into street clothes. He'd have to start from scratch if they told him anything useful.

"For now. Just stay where we can find you. We'll have more questions later." He turned to the director. "Mr. Biggy, do you know how to reach all of them?" Biggy nodded. "Then I think we'd better talk to the rest of the cast."

Downstairs, the men and women had bunched together in the women's dressing room. Rose Maybud's eye makeup was a smeary mess, and she seemed to have aged a good fifteen years since he'd seen her onstage.

When Biggy introduced Fred and Ketcham, she threw her still-luscious body at Biggy and clung to his neck.

"Who would want to kill David? He was the sweetest, kindest man I knew!" she cried, as if her heart was broken. Maybe it was, for all Fred knew about Putnam's personal life. He heard gasps. Biggy looked startled, as any man in his shoes might.

"We don't know—yet," Fred said. "What can you tell us?"

"Me?" She disentangled herself. "Not a thing. I was down here, waiting for my cue."

"Ever since your last scene?" She had left the stage with Biggy and the chorus just before the music that brought the portraits to life.

"That's right. Duane insists on it." She batted her eyes at Biggy.

"Then how do you know he's dead?" She looked blank. He asked the others, "Did someone tell you?" Heads shook.

"They said he was hurt," a man said. "Is it true? Is he dead? Murdered?"

"Yes." He turned to Rose Maybud. Esther something. "How did you know?"

"Why—I don't know. When I saw you, I just knew."

"You'd already been crying." Her hands rose to her face. He saw her consider another lie. Then her whole body sagged. When she spoke, her voice was flat.

"A little while after Duane and Ellen came to get Liz and Amy—when Duane told us David was hurt—I said I was going to walk down the hall, but I went halfway up the stairs. I heard."

"Did anyone see you leave?"

"I don't know." She turned to the others, her hands out in mute appeal. No one answered. They seemed to shrink away from her.

"What did you hear?"

"I don't know—I can't think. It's so awful!" Her mascara ran again.

"Try," he said, and waited. She swiped at her destroyed face.

"Someone said something about blinders. Isn't that silly? That's all I can remember."

Fred and Ketcham exchanged a look. It was enough. She was telling the truth, at least about that.

The cast added nothing to what they'd already heard. Several of them had seen David Putnam alive before the second act, but no one admitted to having noticed anything between then and when he fell from his frame. And no one, not even Catherine Turner, who Fred knew could usually find a reason to think ill of almost anybody, suggested a motive.

ELEVEN

Hark, the hour of ten is sounding!
Hearts with anxious fears are bounding.

—CHORUS, *Trial by Jury*

DOWN IN THE PIT, the orchestra was still trapped. Joan had no idea who ordinarily set the elevator in motion. They had all heard Sergeant Ketcham's request for statements, but there was no way to make one—the wall separating them from the audience was too high to climb over. A few people began to panic; others practiced solo passages, concertos, or finger exercises; more philosophical types settled back to wait it out. At least they no longer had to observe Biggy's silence.

"Wonder how long it will take them to remember us," John said.

"They know we're not going anywhere," Joan said, but she, too, suspected that no one was thinking much about the orchestra.

"It's taking forever," wailed a young second violinist. She stood on tiptoes, stretching, as if that would help her see behind the curtain. "What are they doing up there?"

Trying to figure out who did it, Joan thought. At least they know we're innocent. Or do they?

"John, when did you first think David was asleep?" she asked softly.

"I dunno. When I saw his head down on his chest "

"Sure, but when was that?" He shrugged. Joan tried Alex, the one person who had been watching the stage all the way through. Just now she looked half-asleep. "Alex, when did you spot something wrong with David?"

"When the lights came up and the other ghosts stepped down," Alex answered so promptly that she must have been thinking about it herself. "Before that, they were all so still, and behind a scrim."

"A what?"

"You know, a see-through curtain. Whether you can see through it depends on the lighting. The light on the portraits was dim—you could see them, but not very well. Besides, I wasn't paying any attention to them until they had to sing. The scrim goes up during the blackout right before they come alive. Good thing. They don't have enough volume to carry through it."

"And then?"

"And then I saw David's head down. I knew one of the others was primed to sing if he fell asleep again, but I didn't know where he'd be standing, so I couldn't cue him. It was a little hairy there for a moment or two." Not to mention later, Joan thought.

"Did anyone see David's face during the first part of the act?" she asked them all. Nobody answered. "Think—was his head on his chest before the ghosts walked? Or how about during that long dialogue between Robin and old Adam, at the beginning of the act?" Still nothing.

No wonder. Much of the time they'd been busy with the music, but during the dialogue, Joan, too, had watched the actors who were doing something, not the pictures on the wall. It's only human nature, she thought. You don't notice boring things.

"Who cares?" the concertmaster asked. "Leave it to the police. It's their job."

"You're right," Joan said. "But it's too bad we won't be

able to tell them for a fact that David was alive after we were all safely locked in this pit.''

They got it.

"Why should they suspect *us?*" the string bass player objected.

"I didn't even know him!" cried a flutist.

"I did," said the second violinist who'd been in such a hurry. "I used to sit with his little girl. Do you think they'll hold that against me?" She looked ready to cry. "He was such a nice man. He always drove me home, and he never once made a pass."

"Maybe we did see him alive, after all," said the bassist. "We could all agree on a story." Alex glared at him, and he wilted. "Just a thought."

"I was the last one to enter the pit," Joan said firmly. "And I was talking to a policeman just a few seconds before that. Once they find out I didn't do it, the rest of you will be in the clear." It didn't really follow, but the panicky ones cheered up and went back to grousing. She shook her head.

"One minute they're afraid the police will come, the next minute they're mad because they're not here yet," she said to John.

"Ain't it the truth?" He grinned at her, and she caught herself laughing back. This is all wrong, she thought suddenly. How can I be laughing down here when David Putnam is lying up there dead? The laugh, far from stopping, threatened to turn into an uncontrollable giggle.

It's okay, she told herself. Laugh if that's what you need to do. She felt her diaphragm relax, and the giggle stopped before it got a good start.

Why did that get to me? It's not as if I'd never been around sudden death before.

Maybe because you were ready to kill him yourself? asked a little voice in her head.

I wasn't.

Yes, you were. You were angry at him for throwing Zach to the wind.

I wouldn't have killed him.

No. But someone did. And you know he wasn't *always* the world's nicest man. Better tell Fred.

What difference does it make? Zach didn't hear that conversation.

Maybe he did.

She shuddered, not wanting to think of gentle Zach Yoder—or any man she was trusting around her house—as a murderer. Then the image of Liz MacDonald leaning on David's frame floated into her mind. Liz, who wanted David, and Chris Eads, who wanted Liz. How many of the rest of these people might have had a motive for killing David?

Without warning, the floor lurched. John quickly unplugged the extension cord that supplied all the stand lights on their side of the pit. Others did it for the other side and the back. Joan clung to her viola in the gloom of the pit while the wall above them lengthened. Someone had decided to take them down.

In her heart of hearts she let herself hope that Fred would meet them at the bottom, but when the double doors opened, a tall, slender black man in a light-blue summer suit stood waiting with Duane Biggy. His dark skin glowed in the light from the hallway.

"I'm Detective Chuck Terry," he said quietly. "I hope we won't have to keep you here long."

"It's already long!" the bassist grumbled.

"I know," Terry said. "Some of us are going to have a late night. Right now I need to ask you a couple of questions."

"Come on, people," Biggy said. "Do your civic duty." Out of the corner of her eye, Joan saw John heave an exaggerated sigh. She hoped Biggy wouldn't try to take over the police investigation. Terry didn't acknowledge the interruption. His eyes scanned the orchestra.

"Let me tell you what we know already." That got their attention. "David Putnam was alive before the second act began. He climbed into his picture frame and spoke to the man next to him. At some point between then and when he fell to the stage, he was stabbed in the back."

"When was he killed?" the bassist asked.

"Good question. What can you tell us about that?" Terry returned. The bassist subsided.

"We've talked about it," Alex said. "I was watching the stage, of course. Most of the time, the players weren't, even those who could see it. But none of us paid any attention to the portraits until they moved. That's when I saw David's chin on his chest."

"I saw it, too," John said. "At the same time." He hadn't been so sure before, Joan thought.

"I thought he had fallen asleep again," Alex said. "You heard about that?"

The detective nodded. "We heard. Anyone else remember how he looked before that?"

They all shook their heads.

Alex spoke for them. "We wish we could. We want to prove to you that the orchestra couldn't have been involved. I was the last person in the pit, except for Joan, here," and she laid her hand on Joan's shoulder. "And I saw her coming before I went in. Before that, she says she was talking with a police officer, and I was alone in the corridor for a good five minutes. Whatever you think about me and her, you have to let the rest of these people go."

"That's true," Biggy told him. "I went downstairs and sent the pit up as soon as we got the ghosts settled in their frames. No one passed me going down those stairs."

"Who was that officer, ma'am?" Terry asked Joan, looking into her eyes.

"Fred Lundquist. We were standing at the top of the steps

until the last minute, and I lost track of time. I had to run down.''

''Thank you. I'm sure the lieutenant will confirm what you say.''

Joan hadn't realized she was holding her breath. Terry unfolded a program and looked back and forth from the orchestra to the back cover, on which the members' names were listed.

''Anybody missing—out sick, maybe?'' He kept looking.

''They're all here,'' Alex said.

Apparently satisfied, Terry tucked the folded program into his notebook. He looked again at their faces.

''Any of you know who would have a reason to want Judge Putnam dead?''

''No one would want to hurt Mr. Putnam! He's a good man!'' The little second broke into tears. She wept on the ample breast of her stand partner, a regular in the symphony's second violin section. Terry consulted his program again.

''Are you Emily?'' he asked. She nodded, snuffling. ''How did you know him?''

''I babysit Laura.'' Snuffle. Emily's stand partner offered her a real cloth handkerchief. She blew hard, and met his steady gaze.

''His child?''

''Yes.''

''How would you describe his family?''

''They're a regular family. Except they had their little girl when the other kids were so old. They spoil her rotten.''

''You think the older kids resent that?''

''They're as bad as Mr. and Mrs. Putnam. Laura gets away with murder—oh!'' She clapped her hand over her own mouth. ''I didn't mean that. She's just a little kid, you know?''

''Sure. Anybody else?'' No one volunteered. Joan thought, I can't say what I've been thinking in front of all these people.

''All right. If something occurs to you later, call the police department. Or me personally, Detective Terry. Thank you.''

He looked at them one more time and strode off down the hall.

One by one, the players stood and began picking up the belongings they had brought into the pit. Joan, who had left her case in the dressing room as ordered, tucked her viola under her arm. Biggy blocked the doorway.

"We all greatly regret this terrible event," he said. "But the police have assured us that by tomorrow night there will be no problem in using the stage again. Understudies will sing both Sir Roderick and Mad Margaret, of course. Your call is at the usual time."

Something in Joan squirmed, but it made sense. This was not a group of old friends, but people who had come together for a specific purpose. David's family and friends would mourn him.

And do I count myself as one of them?

Unable to answer her own question and intent only on going home, she was limping up the stairs with her head down when she bumped into Fred at the top. She managed to hang onto her viola case, but the music flew out of her hand. They both knelt to pick it up.

"I'm sorry," he said into her ear. "You all right?"

"Oh, Fred, it's awful."

"That, too. Doesn't look as if I can see you home, after all." But he settled his big frame on the top step. Joan sat down beside him, glad to have a moment alone with him.

"I know. Do you have to interview everybody?"

"Not alone. Ketcham's here, and Terry."

"I just met him."

"That's right, you would have. I haven't talked to him since then." His eyebrows invited her to respond.

"You will. You're my alibi. He didn't learn much from us, except that I think Alex and Duane Biggy pretty well cleared the orchestra."

"Good."

"Fred, there's something I think I should have told him."

"Go on."

"I feel silly." He waited. "Liz MacDonald had a crush on David. I gathered that when I first met her, and it was obvious during rehearsal breaks. She'd hang around and talk to him while he was getting into his frame."

"How did he respond?"

"Hardly at all. But Chris Eads—the man in the frame next to his—wasn't happy about it. I heard them fighting."

"Eads and Putnam?"

"No, Chris and Liz. They're divorced, but Chris wants her back, and he talks as if it's all David's fault."

"Thanks. We'll look into it."

"And Fred, there's something else, only I don't quite know how to say it." She stopped, and he put his arm around her shoulder.

"Just say it."

"It's probably not important, but it left a bad taste in my mouth. After David fell asleep in rehearsal, Virgil Shoals— he's in charge of building the sets—chewed Zach Yoder out for doing something wrong that made David fall asleep while he was leaning on Zach's supports. David stood up for Zach and said it was all his own fault. But last night, downstairs, he took it all back."

"What did he say?"

"That Virgil shouldn't let shoddy execution make him look bad. He said, 'You can't let him get away with it. It will ruin your reputation.'"

"That's it?"

"It doesn't sound like much. But a man who says one thing to your face and another behind your back like that probably has lots of enemies." Or ought to.

"Hmmm." He looked thoughtful. "Anything else?"

"Not now."

"You keep your eyes and ears open." He stood up, dusted off the seat of his trousers, and offered her a hand. "I've got to go talk with the family."

TWELVE

All must sip the cup of sorrow—
I to-day and thou to-morrow.

—MADRIGAL, *The Mikado*

BEFORE FACING the Putnams, Fred went back to the stage. The body still lay where it had fallen—the coroner was on his way. Someone had turned off most of the lights. The stage was noticeably cooler without them.

He took Ketcham with him to the dressing room where the Putnam family was waiting. The heat rose with them; the air conditioning wasn't strong enough to cool the upstairs. Officer Root opened the door.

"They've been very quiet," she murmured to Fred as she left the room.

Surrounded by her children, Ellen Putnam appeared calm. She was perspiring—no wonder, sitting in an overstuffed chair in her gloomy black costume. Her older daughter, a small-boned blonde dressed as a bridesmaid, was weeping openly. Both of them had cleaned off the greasepaint. Fred was relieved to see faces that looked normal, if grieving.

Red blotches around the eyes betrayed the son, who turned a stony face to the detectives. He was shorter than his father, and well muscled. Fred was sure that the lump in his pocket was a clenched fist. The little girl was curled up in her mother's lap, teardrops still shining on her closed lashes.

The buxom woman near the window was the nurse. She played Dame Hannah in the operetta and looked the part. She, too, was perspiring, and appeared to have been crying. She hadn't managed to remove all of her makeup.

"I'm Lieutenant Lundquist, and this is Sergeant Ketcham," Fred told them. No one offered a hand or a chair.

"This is our son, Scott, and our daughter Amy." Ellen Putnam bent over the little one. "I think Laura's finally asleep."

"We'll try not to disturb her," Fred said. He wished he didn't have to work around the children. The boy paced and looked ready to attack somebody or something. But there was no avoiding this. At least he hadn't had to notify them.

"You were in the audience?" he asked Scott, knowing the answer to that one.

The boy nodded, and stopped pacing.

"So was I," Fred said. "And I have to admit that I didn't notice your father until he fell." Scott winced. "I was hoping you were watching him sooner." Scott opened his eyes wide at that, but didn't answer. Fred continued, "Some people have told us that he looked asleep. Did you notice?"

"Yeah." It came out as a croak. Scott cleared his throat and avoided Fred's eyes. "His head was kind of hanging down on his chest. He told us the other night about dozing off in that picture frame. I thought he'd done it again."

"Uh-huh. And when was that?"

"When?"

"When was his head on his chest?"

"It just was."

"When the other ghosts walked?"

"Yeah. And before that."

"How much before?" A break, at last?

"I don't know. I guess I wasn't watching him at first. There was stuff going on, you know?"

"I know."

"And then I looked at the pictures, and I knew it was Dad's

big scene and he was about to miss his cue again." His face crumpled. "I was mad at him. Do you hear? I was mad at him!" The fist came out of his pocket and banged the wall once, hard.

Laura stirred and murmured something. Her mother stroked her hair. Scott jerked his fist back and held it with his other hand. Fred hoped he could reach the boy before he fell apart.

"It's a terrible thing not to be able to say you didn't mean it."

"But I did mean it! Don't you see? If he was going to—" he glanced at his mother "—to louse up in public like that, I didn't want to be his son. Not tonight. Not in front of my friends." He stared at the floor.

"Son," Fred risked the word, "we've all had those feelings. Right now we need to find who took away your chance to talk to your dad about them." He waited. "You can help."

Scott looked up. "How?"

"First, by thinking as hard as you can about what else was happening on the stage when you first saw your dad look as if he was sleeping."

Scott stood still.

"I don't know. But right before, my sister left the stage. That's when I finally remembered to look for him."

"Thank you." Fred turned to the girl. "Amy, is it?" She nodded. "What did you notice when you were onstage?"

She gulped and took her mother's hand.

"We were supposed to watch the conductor."

"Of course."

"Mostly I did. I mean, I knew Daddy was right there watching me, and I wanted to do a good job."

"Uh-huh." This one didn't need a push.

"But Mr. Biggy has a long song before we start singing."

"Uh-huh."

"So I kind of peeked." He kept his face still. "Daddy was way down at the other end, but I could see him, and it was

just like Scott said. I felt awful. I thought he wasn't bothering." Big tears ran down her cheeks. "Do you think he was
already…?"

"We're not sure yet. But it looks like it." He offered them
the only comfort he could. "We haven't heard from the coroner yet, but it looks as if he died very fast, without suffering."

"Thank God!" said Ellen Putnam.

"And you, Ms.….?"

"MacDonald," the nurse said.

"Can you add anything that might help us?"

"No. I was still downstairs. My big scene came later."

Fred's eyes met Ketcham's and asked for a breather. He
wished for cooler air.

"There's a question we have to ask you all," Ketcham said,
and paused to let them want to hear it. "Can you think of
anyone who might have wanted to harm Mr. Putnam? Or possibly wanted him out of the way?"

Amy gasped, but Ellen answered.

"I've been thinking about that—I couldn't help it. You
know my husband was a circuit court judge." Both men nodded, as if murdered judges were routine. "I've worried for a
long time that someone he angered in court would come after
him."

"Had someone threatened him?" Ketcham asked.

"I don't know. He always pooh-poohed me when I talked
like that. He never told me about his cases."

"So you wouldn't know if anyone involved in the operetta
ever appeared in his court?"

Now it was her turn to gasp.

"No." She looked suddenly frightened.

"That's a matter of public record," Fred said. "We can
find out."

"Oh." She relaxed a little.

"Mrs. Putnam, there are some questions you might prefer

to answer in private," Ketcham said. Scott bristled, but he needn't have worried.

"I have no secrets from my children." Composed again, she put the emphasis on "children." Taking his cue from her, Ketcham dismissed the nurse with thanks for her help.

"Who will gain from your husband's death?" he asked when they were alone with the family.

"We left everything to each other."

"Did he have insurance?"

"Yes, of course. And we bought a lot of new term insurance when Laura was born." She shook her head sadly and stroked Laura's hair again. "David was afraid he wouldn't live to see her grow up, but he was thinking of a heart attack. They run in his family."

"You're the beneficiary?"

"Yes."

Ketcham looked at Fred.

"How would you describe your marriage?" Fred asked, and for the first time, her eyes filled with tears.

"It's the best thing that ever happened to me," she said. "Nobody's perfect, but I couldn't ask for a better husband."

"There was never another woman?"

She smiled, and the sun shone in the dingy little room.

"There were lots of other women. Women threw themselves at David. But it didn't get them anywhere."

"In the cast..." He let it trail off.

"In the cast there was Esther Ooley," she said. "Esther hardly counts, though. She throws herself at everyone. But Liz MacDonald—" She frowned. "Of all people, I don't know why you sent Liz up here with us." Fred groaned inwardly. "Liz was David's first kiss in high school—he told me so years ago. I don't think she ever got over it. She's been hanging around him lately as if I didn't exist."

"I'm sorry," he said. "Dr. Cutts suggested that his nurse might be helpful. I didn't know anything about her. And until you told me just now, I didn't realize that she was the woman I had heard about. I understand that Mr. Putnam and another man had some words about her.'' That wasn't what Joan had said, but he wanted to hear her response.

"Not exactly. Liz and Chris Eads were fighting about David. That's nothing new. I remember once last year we were out square dancing. So was Liz. Chris came in drunk, saw David swinging Liz, and yelled at her and—oh.'' Warm as she was, she turned pale. Her eyes got big.

"And?''

"He threatened David—threatened to kill him.''

"Did you and your husband take him seriously?''

"No. As I said, he'd been drinking. And it's not as if they were still married.'' As if that would stop a jealous man, Fred thought.

"Anybody else come to mind?''

"No.'' Her voice shook. "It doesn't matter now, does it? He's gone.'' Amy hugged her, and even Scott awkwardly put his hand on her shoulder. Her eyes glistened.

She was right. Fred felt useless.

"Is there any way we can help you? An officer to take you home?''

"Thank you,'' she said. "My son will drive tonight. And I do understand what you have to do, Lieutenant. We'll answer any questions you have. Anytime.''

"Did you believe her?'' Ketcham asked Fred on their way back downstairs.

"Yeah. Joan Spencer witnessed Chris Eads and Liz MacDonald fighting over Putnam.''

"Great,'' Ketcham said. "Eads was next to Putnam. All we have for when Putnam was last heard alive is his word, and now that's not worth a plugged nickel.''

"The kids put the time of death sooner than any other witness,'' Fred said.

"That points to Eads.''

"Maybe. But they didn't see anything wrong before the chorus entered. That mob had to pass behind all the ghosts—they went onstage from the far side. Good cover for a quick stabbing."

"If it happened then, it couldn't be Eads," Ketcham said. "You might not notice the position of the head on a painting, but if one of them disappeared—if he left his frame to kill Putnam—someone in the audience would have spotted it, and we'd hear about it for sure."

"Maybe Putnam was dead before Eads climbed into his frame." Fred said. "And maybe Eads wasn't the only person here with a grudge against him. Check it out."

THIRTEEN

In this college
Useful knowledge
*   Everywhere one finds,*
And already,
Growing steady,
*   We've enlarged our minds.*

—HILARION, CYRIL, FLORIAN, *Princess Ida*

JOAN caught a ride home with John Hocking and found Andrew asleep. Wishing for his company, she resisted the brief temptation to drag him out of bed and tell him the whole story. In bed, she tossed and turned briefly, but a healthy body and the fatigue she'd built up all week took over. She was asleep long before her clock radio turned off the Charlie Parker retrospective on the college station's Friday night jazz program.

In the morning, it was Andrew who resisted the temptation to wake her. "I thought you'd never get up," he said when she yawned into the kitchen around ten in her robe and slippers. "David Putnam's all over the front page. I brewed a pot of coffee."

"Thanks." She dropped a couple of slices of whole-wheat bread into the toaster, poured herself a cup of coffee, and looked at the paper. It was true. The murder had happened near enough to the paper's deadline that the sketchy story gave only the bare facts, but the obituary must have been ready and waiting for whenever and however Judge Putnam died. She scanned it, inhaling the smell of the coffee while she waited for the toast.

David had spent most of his thirty-eight years in Alcorn County. A graduate of Oliver High School, Oliver College, and the Indiana University School of Law, he had practiced law in Oliver and served as school-board president and county commissioner before becoming a circuit court judge. At the time of his death he was on the Oliver Hospital board of directors and a trustee of both the First Baptist Church and Oliver College. Included among his many honors was his selection as Alcorn County Father of the Year in 1989—that was before Laura, Joan thought. He was survived by his wife, Ellen (Day) Putnam, his son, Scott David Putnam, and his daughters, Amy Louise and Laura Ellen Putnam, all of Oliver. There would be no visitation. The funeral would be three o'clock Monday afternoon at the church. Memorial contributions to the church or to Oliver College were suggested.

The accompanying photograph was a formal portrait of David in his black robe, looking pleasantly serious in front of a wall of books. A separate, black-bordered box announced that the Alcorn County courthouse would close Monday at two in memoriam.

She skipped the quotations from Mayor Deckard and other prominent Oliver politicians and laid the paper on the table in time to catch the toast before it hit the floor. Their toaster had a mind of its own.

"Pass the butter, Andrew." He did, and pushed the jam jar across the table. She buttered the toast while it was still hot. The jam could wait.

"Tell me all about it, Mom." He propped his chin on his hands and his elbows on the table, across from her.

"The paper got it right. In the middle of the second act, David dropped dead onstage, with a dagger in his back."

"And they don't know who did it? Why not? Who was near him?"

"It's not that simple. He had to stand still in a picture frame for a long time before that. He looked asleep, and he'd fallen asleep in rehearsal a couple of nights before, so we all thought he'd done it again until he fell. It was like this." Between bites, she drew the picture frames on the kitchen table with her finger and explained how David had been vulnerable to anyone behind him, but that such a person would have been invisible to the audience. Andrew leaned forward, watching closely.

"Where did the dagger come from?"

"I don't know, but they used a couple in a scene near the end."

"Sounds like an inside job." He picked up the program she had tossed aside when she finally arrived home Friday night. "I was looking at this while you were sleeping. I know some of these guys."

"Mmmm?" She couldn't help being interested.

"Pete Wylie, one of the ghosts, teaches choir at the high school. The choir always sounds good. The girls will do anything for him because he's good-looking, but married, see, so he's no threat to them. The guys like his sense of humor. It says here he rehearsed the chorus for *Ruddigore*."

"They were pretty good. I wondered who'd been working with them."

"It figures. And you know Steve Dolan, the guy who played Robin."

"I don't think so."

"He lives around the corner in that old green house on Chestnut. He's a year ahead of me in school. I met him last year, but I see more of him now that I'm in college and we have more in common—we're both broke and we both live at home. He's supposed to come over here today, as a matter of fact."

"Maybe I'll recognize him when I see him."

"You've got a couple of professors, too. I had Biggy this year for English lit. He made it tolerable. He's tough, but fair. And a campus character. Lives alone with this big Irish setter—you see him out walking that dog at all hours. The girls flirt with him, but they kind of wonder if he's gay, 'cause he's still single."

"Is he?"

"How would I know?" Andrew shrugged. "Then there's Ucello."

"Who?" She yawned.

"Tony Ucello, like the instrument. Another ghost. Teaches psych. Steve and I are human subjects in his research."

"I didn't know you were interested in psychology."

"I'm not—he pays six bucks an hour. Steve told me about it."

"Good for Steve." She yawned again, and poured another cup of caffeine. "When did you say he was coming over?"

"Pretty soon, unless he's as slow today as you are. What do you know about the rest of the cast?"

"Not much. Well, Dr. Cutts and his nurse are in it. She seemed to have a thing for David."

"Putnam? He's married. Was, I mean."

"I know, and his wife was right there in the cast. So was the ex-husband of the nurse, and he wasn't happy about it."

"The plot thickens." Andrew snitched a piece of her toast and slathered jam on it.

"I told Fred about them." She frowned. "I kind of wish I hadn't."

"Why not?" He chewed around the words.

"I don't know. I guess I can't see that man stabbing David in the back. He'd be more likely to sock him in the face, or shoot him, if it came to that."

"You don't think he'd use a knife?" He licked his fingers.

"Maybe. But not in the back. If he went after David, I think he'd want him to know it, and to know who did it."

"And why?"

"Exactly. But I told Fred anyway."

"Good for you." He stood up. "I'd better get busy."

She washed her plate and cup, glad to find Andrew's supper and breakfast dishes in the drainer, instead of waiting for her in the sink. A faint hammering told her that Zach Yoder had arrived to work on the porch. He was running late this morning, but then so was she. She was surprised to hear him at all. Zach had said up front that he saved Saturdays for his family.

Maybe he figures he's so close to being done he might as well finish, she thought hopefully. Being able to use the front door again would be a relief. All her morning routines felt wrong since the tornado, and she had set off for work more than once without an umbrella or some other essential item she'd laid automatically on the little table by the front door. Feeling cheerful, she went upstairs to dress.

But it wasn't Zach. Looking out her bedroom window, she saw a man working over at Henry Putnam's house. That explained why the hammering had been so faint. David had boarded up the broken windows right after the tornado. Maybe he'd finally hired someone to do the repairs so that Henry could come home after all. She went over to see.

To her surprise, she recognized Virgil Shoals.

Why am I surprised? He's David's builder.

"Good morning," she said. "I'm glad to see you're doing something to this poor house."

"It looks worse than it is."

"David had a backhoe over here one day. I thought he gave up on it."

"He gave up too soon." He looked a little huffy. "The damage will be easy to repair."

"Oh, really?" Zach had made it sound ominous. She was

glad she hadn't quoted him to his boss. But Virgil was still frowning.

"Don't I know you from somewhere?"

"Not really. I'm in the orchestra for *Ruddigore*. I live next door—Zach Yoder's rebuilding my front porch." And if you don't like that, tough.

He eyed the porch, but kept his opinions to himself. She decided she'd better do the same and went back home.

Andrew hailed her from the kitchen. He was waving some pages in the air.

"Look what Steve brought!"

"Hi, Steve." Joan smiled at him. She couldn't look at this young man without seeing him as Robin Oakapple.

"Hi, Mrs. Spencer." He hopped to his feet. Gracious. She waved him back down.

"So tell me, what is it?"

"It's Professor Ucello's first journal article about the research we're in," Andrew said. "It came out yesterday. Steve just copied it at the library."

"That's pretty quick turnaround," Joan said.

"Oh, Andrew's data won't be in this article," Steve said. "He just started spring semester. This one reports on what we did a year ago. Dr. Ucello had to hurry to get it published—he's applying for another NSF grant."

"That's how he can pay us," Andrew said. "We made three hundred eighty-four bucks last semester."

"Between you?"

"Each. If he gets his grant renewal, we'll end up with around twelve hundred apiece. All we have to do is reach out and touch these targets while we're looking through lenses that change how we see things. It's a lot easier than working in the lab." Andrew had been a lab assistant to Professor Werner of Biology since volunteering in high school. That, plus a hefty tuition scholarship and living rent-free at home, made it possible for him to attend Oliver College. If he'd mentioned being a human subject, Joan had missed it, or confused it with his lab job. "You have to keep your mind on what you're doing, though," Andrew continued. "If you drift off, you'll distort the results."

Steve pored over a graph on the second page of the article.

"That's odd," he said.

"What's odd?" Andrew and Joan asked in unison.

"My graph is wrong."

"What do you mean, your graph?" Joan said.

"This one, with SD on it—it shows my data. And it's wrong."

"How?" Andrew said.

"It fits his mathematical model all right, but I had one data point way up here, not down where the line is."

"What about the error bars?" Andrew asked. Joan wondered what error bars were, not to mention how Andrew would know. College must be doing him some good.

"They don't account for that big a difference. That point was way off. Maybe that's why he left it out."

"You can't dump anomalous data that don't fit your model." Andrew sounded shocked.

"Yeah, well. It looks like he did—or changed it."

"That's even worse!"

"Maybe he had a good reason."

Andrew shook his head.

"He'd better hope NSF doesn't find out about it. You violate scientific ethics, and you're out on your ear—or worse."

"Well, they won't find out from me," Steve said. "I need the money."

FOURTEEN

A policeman's lot is not a happy one.

—SERGEANT, *The Pirates of Penzance*

FRED left the Saturday paper unread on the floor of his spartan apartment. He showered the sleep out of his eyes, shaved, and pulled the pins out of a new shirt. Tying his four-in-hand precisely, he brushed the shoulders of his good summer suit and gave his already shining shoes an extra swipe. It was his routine before appearing in court. Not that court would be in session today, but there was no telling what bigwigs he'd deal with. Not that they'd notice how he looked.

He stopped for a sack of doughnuts at Dan's Donuts, an Oliver fixture often patronized by the police force. They'd go fast at the station. He wasn't the only cop who skipped breakfast.

"Well, now, Fred." Dan reached for the doughnuts with a slick tissue. "You reckon it was his wife killed the judge?"

"Two more chocolate." Fred wasn't surprised at the question. Mounted on a shelf behind the counter, Dan's police scanner searched for something to make his life more exciting. A man about Putnam's age, Dan might have known him for years. And he was a born gossip. "What do you know about it, Dan?"

"Nothin'." Dan tucked the tissue on top of the last doughnut and folded the top of the sack down over it. "But I figure maybe she didn't take to him playin' around."

"Who says?"

"You hear things. I wouldn't want to name names."

"But you're going to." Fred didn't expect to have to lean on him much. Dan generally took great pleasure in telling him everything he knew, or thought he knew, about any case. "Come on, Dan, this is murder. And you knew him, didn't you?"

"Hell, yes. Me and David played ball together." Fred stared at him until he looked away and fiddled with the doughnuts under the glass counter. "It was Chris Eads—you know Chris?" Fred remembered Eads, the muscular ghost who claimed to be the last person Putnam had spoken to.

"What did he say?"

"He said David had the hots for his wife." Dan looked him in the eye again.

"Liz MacDonald? His ex-wife?"

"Well, sure. But you know who gave Liz that divorce."

"No, who?" Fred gave him a twenty.

"Judge Putnam, that's who." Of course. "Chris fought it—he figures David had his own reasons." Dan handed back his change.

"Thanks, Dan." Expressionless, Fred picked up his doughnuts and left.

At the station, he set the sack on the table by the coffee maker and tore it open. Crumpling the tissue into a tight ball, he banked it off the wall into the wastepaper basket. If there was any point in keeping Dan's fingers off the doughnuts, he thought while he bit into a cruller, then why stick the paper in the bag with them? Or was it the other way around? Was the paper to keep the doughnuts from making Dan's fingers sticky? He suspected that Dan and the board of health had different views on that subject.

Ketcham and Terry arrived together and helped themselves

to doughnuts and coffee. No autopsy results yet. Dr. Henshaw had promised to do it early this morning.

"Not that we're likely to learn much," Ketcham said. "We already know the knife handle was wiped clean."

"We bagged his hands," Terry said. "But the man didn't have a chance to fight back."

"And the autopsy isn't going to narrow down the time of death any," Ketcham said.

"We've got his keys and his wallet," Terry said. "He was carrying ID, insurance and credit cards, a picture of his wife and kids, and $47.26."

"Check the keys," Fred said. "Dan the doughnut man thinks he's been carrying on with Liz MacDonald."

"He'd be crazy to have her key on him."

"Yeah, well. He had no reason to think we'd be looking in his pockets."

"I'll start with Mrs. Putnam," Terry said. "She ought to know what locks most of them fit."

"You haven't met her yet, have you? See what you think. Dan thinks she killed him over Liz."

"Mrs. Putnam sure wasn't happy about having her spend time with the family." Ketcham polished his glasses with his handkerchief. "But she volunteered that."

"She knew we'd hear something."

"Uh-huh," Terry said.

"From there, come on over to the courthouse," Fred said. "Check his office key and then help us search through the records to see whether any of the men who were backstage or in those frames before Putnam died ever appeared before him in court."

"On my way." Terry took off, and Fred handed Ketcham the list he'd made with Biggy's help.

"Run these names through the computer and see whether any of them has a criminal record. I'll call the clerk of courts for the rest."

"Go easy on her. Maude's always had a soft spot for Judge Putnam. She used to be his Cub Scout den mother."

Trust Ketcham to know. Fred wasn't surprised to hear Maude Kelly snuffling over the phone when she agreed to meet him at the courthouse in half an hour.

The computer yielded little useful information. Dr. Cutts had a couple of moving traffic violations, and Chris Eads had once been arrested for possession of a small quantity of marijuana—nothing that suggested murder. No one on the list had a juvenile record.

Fred walked with Ketcham over to the Alcorn County Courthouse, a plain brick building with white pillars and a white tower that looked like a steeple. It might have been mistaken for a church, except for the Stars and Stripes flapping over the memorial to Oliver's fallen heroes of every war since 1860 and the cannons on the perfect green lawn. Brick storefronts facing the courthouse made up the bulk of Oliver's business district, with the town hall, police station, jail, and fire department only a block from the central square.

The two men flushed a flock of pigeons roosting on the cannons. Fred sniffed the humid air, pleasant for July. The temperature was still in the low eighties, but the morning sun was already beating down on them.

"Gonna be another scorcher," Ketcham said.

"Yeah. Let's hope they don't store their records in the attic."

They did. Some of them, anyway. Maude Kelly, a plump, sweet-faced, white-haired little woman wearing shorts and sneakers on a Saturday morning, fussed while she unlocked the courthouse door for them.

"I keep telling them we need some help around here. It's no way to do, having records here, there, and everywhere. My predecessor just poked them wherever he found space, and now there's no time to clean it up. You'll find my records in much better order. Before I came, no one bothered to have them computerized. Costs too much, the commissioners said, and Mr. You Know Who didn't care—probably was afraid he couldn't learn how. After I took office, I made them join the information age. At least we can check the computer for the past year and a half.'' They waited while she brought it up and running and then typed in the names, but she found nothing. It was too much to hope for, Fred thought.

''Now what?'' he said.

''Now you get to look through the entry books. I'll show you.''

The temperature dropped and the humidity rose as Mrs. Kelly led them down a steep flight of stairs to the courthouse basement. At the bottom, she turned on fluorescent lights and paused before stepping onto the floor. Looking over her shoulder, Fred saw big black water bugs scurry like cockroaches.

''Watch out for the slugs,'' she said. ''There aren't as many, but they can't get out of your way as fast as those things do.''

Metal shelving along the walls held huge books labeled with recent dates.

''These are from the last three years,'' she said. ''The current session's records are upstairs, but they were on the computer. It's a good thing you don't need anything from before Judge Putnam came on the bench.''

''Do you keep records that far back?'' Ketcham asked.

''Have to. The state requires us to keep files for at least ten years, and David's only been a judge for eight.'' Suddenly her eyes filled up. ''I can't believe he's gone—he was the sweetest little boy.'' She pulled a handkerchief out of her shorts pocket and honked once. Then she folded it into quarters and tucked it away. ''I'm sorry. Records for the past nine years are down here. Before that, they're up in the tower. I don't know how far back the tower goes. I don't think that pack rat ever purged anything—just stashed them away. Pigeons got into the tower a few years ago when a window broke and no one bothered to fix it. Now there's pigeon droppings all over everything. You're lucky you'll find what you want down here."

She opened the door into the next room and turned on the light. Again, the bugs ran. But here they saw no neat shelves. Instead, cardboard boxes, stacked three and four high, were filled with massive books. Water stains on the bottom boxes suggested damage to the records stored inside them. She waved her arm.

"This is the mess he left me! Can you believe it?"

Behind his spectacles, Ketcham rolled his eyes at Fred, who cleared his throat.

"I, uh, don't suppose you've got them catalogued."

"Are you kidding?" She looked up at him. "No, you're not, are you?" She opened the top volume in the closest box. "Here, you see, there's an index in each book. You can check it for the names of people you're hunting—saves looking through all the cases on the docket. Course, the correct information might not be in the index. Shouldn't happen, but it does."

Ketcham picked up a book, read the date on the back, and put it down.

"Where's the book for eight years ago?"

"Could be anywhere. I told you it was a mess. People looking for something in these boxes put them back any which way."

Ketcham groaned.

"But don't let me catch you doing that on my shelves. They're in strict chronological order. Too bad you don't know what date you're looking for. Then we'd have you out of here in no time."

"Yes, ma'am," Fred said.

"I'll be upstairs if you need me." And she left them, taking with her all hope that she would help them search the chaotic records for a lead to the killer of the sweet little boy she remembered.

"Might as well start in the other room," Ketcham said.

"Might as well." Fred checked his watch when he started looking. Fifteen minutes later, they'd hardly made a dent. "I'm going to get us some help," he told Ketcham. "And Terry ought to arrive any time now. I'll ask Mrs. Kelly to take him down to you."

He didn't have to. At the top of the stairs to the first floor Fred saw Terry's tall shadow through the window. Before he could reach the courthouse door, Terry opened it. Fred crossed the scuffed oak floor to him.

"Learn anything?"

Terry nodded.

"The keys are okay." He held out the key he had just used on the courthouse door. "This is the only one that didn't fit his house or vehicles. Mrs. Putnam thought it would open his office door, too."

So there wasn't a key to a love nest. That didn't prove anything, one way or the other.

"Okay." Fred accepted the key. "I'll tell Mrs. Kelly you're here." He waved at the basement stairs. "Go down there and let Ketcham fill you in."

The key opened the door to Putnam's chambers. No indication of trouble there. He flipped through the appointment calendar on the desk. Putnam hadn't kept detailed notes. Nothing cryptic, either. It looked routine, but he'd take it along. No need to preserve the scene here.

"I've already been in and out a dozen times since he left yesterday afternoon," Mrs. Kelly said, as if she'd read his mind. "Last thing I said to him was to sing pretty. I was going to hear him tonight." Her mouth twisted briefly, and her eyes glistened, but she had herself under control. "You let me know anything I can do to help you, and I'll do it." Did she mean it?

"I don't suppose you'd be willing to help us look through those records."

"For David? You bet I would," she said. "I would have offered, but I didn't want to get in the way."

"Trust me, ma'am, you won't. We need you." Why hadn't he asked her before?

She was already heading down to the basement when he left the courthouse. The heat blasted him as soon as he stepped outside. Had the temperature risen that much in the few minutes he'd spent in the dank basement, or was it just contrast? By the time he'd walked back to the station his new shirt was stuck to his back under his suit coat.

He was only a little cooler half an hour later when his phone rang.

"Lundquist."

"Are you sitting down?" Fred recognized the voice of Dr. Henshaw.

"Tell me what you've got." Fred wasn't in the mood for games.

"Cause of death is cardiac tamponade. Blood collecting in the pericardium squeezed the heart and stopped it."

"From the stab wound."

"Yes, but not the one you think." Henshaw sounded almost gleeful.

"Not—"

"That little dagger didn't do it."

Fred leaned back and shut his eyes, blocking out everything but the voice on the other end of the line.

"Why do you say that?"

"For a couple of reasons. The simplest one is that it didn't reach the heart."

"So where'd the blood come from?"

"Exactly. And why wasn't there any in the pleural cavity? I expected to find blood in the pleural cavity. Zilch. None on the surface, either. That knife went in postmortem."

Great. Now we have to find someone who gets his jollies out of stabbing corpses.

"You found another wound?" Fred asked.

"Had to look hard." Henshaw continued to sound pleased with himself, as well he might have. "It had closed up—all the bleeding was interior."

"Where?"

"I found a small penetrating wound near the posterior midline, between the sixth and seventh ribs. Darn near invisible."

"What kind of weapon are we looking for?" Fred opened his eyes and reached for pencil and paper.

"Something long and sharp, at least ten inches long and not more than a quarter inch in diameter. Probably less."

"Diameter? It's round?"

"Maybe."

"Sounds like an ice pick."

"Yeah, that would do it."

"How hard a blow?"

"Depends on how sharp the instrument was."

"Could a woman have done it?"

"Sure. Penetrating the skin is the hard part."

Fred thought back to what witnesses had said. "He was standing there for as much as ten minutes before he fell. You think he was wounded, but alive?"

"Not that long. He died fast."

Just what I told the family, Fred thought. "How fast?"

"There was a vertical tear in his heart muscle that must have bled fast. I doubt that he lived a minute."

"How could a skinny pointed thing tear it?"

"If the killer pulled down hard on it, maybe while pulling it out."

"Does that mean we're looking for a short guy?"

"Could be. Or maybe someone backing down those steps."

Right. In other words, anyone, Fred thought gloomily.

"Anything else?"

"Nothing interesting. I'll send you the written report."

"Thanks." For shooting down the one piece of hard evidence we had.

"My pleasure."

FIFTEEN

The hour of gladness
Is dead and gone;
In silent sadness
I live alone!

— KATISHA, *The Mikado*

BY NOON, Andrew and Steve had left for the library, and the pounding next door had stopped. Joan had puttered through the morning, not wanting to wear out her bow arm with house-cleaning or working in the yard, which was still recovering from the effects of the tornado. She started a grocery list, wrote checks for the electric and telephone bills, and sorted the accumulated junk mail into trash and recyclables. Her concentration was worthless for anything that took any great thought. Her mind kept turning to David Putnam and his family.

The obituary had said no visitation, and she was glad not to call at Snarr's Funeral Home. But her heart went out to Ellen, widowed as young and as suddenly as she herself had been, and to the Putnam children. Laura was going to grow up scarcely able to remember her father.

It must be even worse, she thought suddenly, to have him struck down violently like that. Amazing. I didn't think I'd ever come to the place where I'd think that anything could be worse than losing Ken. Ellen will probably be swamped—the

Putnams must have hordes of friends. Unless they all stay away for fear of saying the wrong thing. I ought to go over there. But I scarcely know them.

As the voices in her head argued, her single-minded hands began opening kitchen cupboards. She didn't want useful food this time; she wanted comfort food, especially for the children.

An hour later, she pulled a batch of Ken's mother's richest brownies out of the oven. Leaving a few on a plate for Andrew and, if she was lucky, for herself, she packed the rest into a box Ellen wouldn't have to return. Before she left the house, she checked her appearance. Hair brushed and in place, clean jeans, sneakers, a pale yellow shirt. Nothing that would disgrace her on a Saturday.

This isn't a formal call. And I'm not the widow. Nobody's going to pay any attention to me.

Dr. Cutts had said to walk, and it was only half as far as she usually walked to work. Even so, she was hot and sore by the time she arrived at the house on the hill. The yard was bare of debris—and everything else—trees, shrubs, flowers. If there had been shade before the storm, it was going to take a long time to grow back. The roof looked whole again, but only the foundation remained of the new addition. She couldn't remember how it had looked on the day of the tornado.

Zach was working on it, she thought. That means there must have been at least the beginnings of a frame before the storm hit. With David dead, will Ellen bother to rebuild the new addition now?

There were no cars outside, but windows and the front door were open; someone must be home. When she rang the bell, the older girl came to the screen door with Henry's dog at her side. Amy, that was her name. Her red-rimmed eyes looked blankly at Joan.

"Yes?"

This is awkward. I thought they'd at least know who I am.

"I'm Joan Spencer. I came to say how very sorry I am about your father. Is your mother at home?"

"Does she know you?" Amy was on the leery side of polite. Was this visit a mistake?

"A little. She brought me flowers after I was in the tornado with Laura."

"Oh!" Amy's whole face lit up. She unhooked the screen door and opened it wide, holding the dog's collar. "Come in! I'm sorry, I didn't recognize you." A compliment, all things considered. She led Joan into a living room filled with primary colors, comfortable-looking furniture, and abundant evidence that the whole family used it. "Have a seat. I'll go get Mom." The dog followed her out of the room.

The sofa hosted a gathering of teddy bears. Joan chose a soft red chair instead, from which she had to move a couple of well-worn picture books. Robert McCloskey and Ezra Jack Keats—Laura was getting a good start.

"Here, fellows, improve your minds." Joan gave the books to the teddy bears and sat down in the chair. The smell of warm chocolate wafted up from the box on her knees, and she couldn't help inhaling. *I should have given it to Amy*, she thought.

But when Ellen entered the room, she was glad she hadn't. Laura clung to her as if she was afraid her mother would disappear if she let loose. Joan stood up.

"Joan, how good of you to come," Ellen said. She, too, was wearing jeans, and looking very much as she had on the day of the tornado, except for her eyes. She was holding it together, though.

"I just wanted to tell you how very sorry I am, and to bring a little something to the children." Joan held out the box to Laura, who hid behind her mother's legs. Ellen bent down and put an arm around her.

"It's all right, Laurie. This is the lady who took care of you in the tornado, remember?"

Laura peeked around her mother at the box.

"What's that?" Almost inaudible.

"Brownies." Joan didn't push it.

"Take them to Amy, Laura. She'll share with you." It worked. Laura let go of her mother, took the box with both hands, and ran out of the room calling, "Aymeeee!"

"She's scarcely let me out of her sight. Please, sit down." Sweeping the books and bears out of the way, Ellen took a seat on the sofa.

Joan nodded and sank back into the red chair. "My children were older when their father died, but Andrew was like that."

"People say, 'At least you have the children.' I love them to pieces. But in a way I feel more alone when they're around."

"Uh-huh."

"I can't very well let go in front of Laura."

"Have you tried it?"

"Pardon me?" Ellen's eyebrows rose.

This is risky, Joan thought. I don't know her that well.

"When my husband died, I thought I had to be strong for my children. But when I finally broke down, it was a great relief to them. Turns out they'd been confused. They were so sad, and they thought I wasn't until I just bellowed. They thought I didn't love him."

"Oh, no." Ellen's eyes filled with tears. They were silent together for a few moments.

"I didn't mean to tell you what to do. You're probably getting too much advice."

Ellen sat up straight at that.

"I'll say. Sell the house, don't sell the house, get a job, stay at home for the children. You name it, someone's said it. Don't they know I can hardly think, much less plan? And when I can think, all I think of is David, and how in the world I'm going to live without him."

"I was afraid the media people would be giving you a hard time."

"We had the Indianapolis television stations here—all of them. I finally went out and let them take my picture so they'd go away. But not the children's." She looked suddenly fierce. "They can't have my children."

"Good for you."

"And the police. They have to ask questions, I know, but right now I don't even care who did it. I'm just numb."

"Uh-huh." It was time for Joan to leave. "I know people just say it to be saying something, but if there's anything I can do to help, I mean the offer. Answer your phone, fend off busybodies like me, notify distant people, you name it."

"I'll be all right. Amy's doing a great job answering the door and the phone. She needs something useful to do. The church women are doing everything we can farm out, and they're bringing in meals and putting up relatives coming for the funeral Monday."

"Of course."

"What I really need is someone for all the things David used to do, like deal with the construction men."

"Let me send Zach back to you."

"We're not ready for Zach, and I don't know if we ever will be. David had some hang-up about rebuilding the new addition. I don't know what it was, and I don't know how to find out. Maybe he was right. Besides, I don't see how we can afford it, even with the insurance. I'm still not sure how much I'll have to live on. I hope I can afford to stay home with Laura, but I don't even know that for sure. David was a wonderful husband and father, but there are so many things he didn't tell me. Now I'm supposed to figure them all out by myself." She blinked back angry tears and punched a teddy bear in the midsection. "Why couldn't he have told me the things I need to know?"

Joan shook her head. She knew better than to point out that

David was a young man who hadn't expected to be murdered. Ellen needed to yell at him, as Joan had needed to yell at Ken for dying and leaving her to fend for herself.

"I saw Virgil this morning," she said. "Next door, at Henry's house. Did you arrange that?"

"No, David did. Virgil was the contractor on Uncle Henry's house, so he knows where all the bodies are buried. I mean…" Her voice trailed off.

"I know what you mean." It wasn't funny.

"I haven't even talked to him yet. I just don't think I can cope with Uncle Henry's house right now." She sounded exhausted. She has every right to be, Joan thought.

"From what he said this morning, they shouldn't be too bad." Joan stood up. "I'd better go, Ellen. I didn't mean to stay so long."

"Thank you for coming." Ellen saw her to the door. "I'm sorry I dumped on you. I'll be all right."

SIXTEEN

*I hate a duel with swords. It's not the blade I
mind—it's the blood.*

—ERNEST, *The Grand Duke*

THE PHONE WAS RINGING when she opened her back door.
"Joan?"

"Fred! How are you?"

"Hungry. Have you had lunch?" Her stomach growled as
if it could hear him.

"Not yet."

"I'll pick you up."

He took her to Wilma's Cafe. Wilma didn't believe in over-
air-conditioning, but it was cool enough. A ceiling fan stirred
the air above hanging baskets of green plants. Even though
the restaurant was nearly empty, they sat in a back booth. Fred
liked to have his back to the wall. Joan had teased him about
it at first—now she took it for granted. While they waited for
her BLT and his ham on rye, he poured out his frustrations to
her.

"It's not enough he's a judge. Not enough we all saw him
drop dead but nobody saw who did it. Now it turns out we
don't even have the weapon."

"What happened to it?"

"Oh, we've still got the dagger. But Dr. Henshaw says it

didn't kill him. Something longer and skinnier got there first. We haven't found it yet—the killer may have carried it off."

"Oh, Fred."

"Yup." He traced circles on the paper place mat. "We were so damn sure we had the weapon that it didn't occur to us to search anyone for it."

"And two people tried to kill him?"

"Come again?"

"I thought that's what you meant. He was standing there in that frame for a long time. Someone coming up behind him wouldn't have known he was already dead, any more than the rest of us did."

He nodded. "Could be the killer faded into the background and then someone else who wanted him dead came along and stabbed him with the dagger." He went back to his circles.

"Only I've been wondering something all along." She leaned forward.

Fred looked up.

"What's that?"

"Why choose the little dagger? Why not the long one?"

"Yeah." He abandoned the circles. "Henshaw said the little one didn't reach his heart. There wasn't any blood around it at all—that's how he knew to look for another wound. The long one was just as convenient, you know—the two daggers were kept together in the same prop box for the fight scene."

"It's as if the second attacker—if there was one—just grabbed whatever was closest, without caring whether it would reach his heart." Joan had a thought. "Maybe he knew he was already dead. Maybe there was only one attacker."

"Then why stab him again?"

"You didn't search anyone, did you?"

He shook his head.

"We didn't even start looking around for another weapon until Henshaw called today."

All those wasted hours, Joan thought. The most important

hours after a murder—she knew that much. She didn't rub it in. He felt too bad already.

"Is the stage still sealed off?"

"Yeah. We have to decide soon whether to let tonight's show go on. Once it does, any remaining evidence will be compromised."

"You haven't given up." She thought he looked haggard. The investigation was wearing him down.

"Shifted priorities is all. Searching through old records by hand just got pushed to a back burner."

"Looking for criminals in the cast?"

"No, we'd know about the criminal cases. We've been checking whether anyone who was backstage last night ever appeared in Putnam's court. We've already heard gossip about one domestic case that suggests a motive—a couple of motives, in fact."

"Chris and Liz?" For the life of her, she couldn't think of more than one motive they suggested. If Ellen had been murdered, now that might be a different story.

"That's right, you knew about those two. There may be other cases, but it's slow going, slogging through those records. Mrs. Kelly volunteered—that helps."

"I could look." It was out of her mouth before she had time to think about it. Well, why not? Someone had robbed Ellen Putnam and her children of a husband and father. Maybe she *should* help. Fred was slow to answer.

"I don't suppose there's anything against it," he said finally. "Those records are open to the public. And God knows, we could use you. Any conflict of interest?" He looked her straight in the eye, without a twinkle. Was he serious?

"With what?"

"Do you know anyone in the cast or backstage? Got a grudge against anyone yourself? Or is there anyone you'd be reluctant to tell us about if you found his name—or hers?"

"I don't think so. I wouldn't be too thrilled if the murderer turned out to be my doctor, or the man who's been working on my house, but I'd want to know."

"All right, then. I'll take you over."

Wilma brought their sandwiches, and they ate in silence for a few moments. Joan hadn't realized how hungry she was. Then she remembered what she'd wanted to tell Fred. "Andrew and Steve Dolan were showing me something odd this morning."

"Dolan. The one who plays Robin?"

"Uh-huh. But it's not about Steve. It's about Professor Ucello, one of the ghosts." She told him about the experiment for which Andrew and Steve were subjects and about the graph that seemed to be hiding inconvenient results. "If they're right, Ucello's doing something unethical at the very least. Andrew seemed to think he could get in real trouble." She knew her father, an anthropologist, would have been as shocked as Andrew.

"You see a connection to the murder?"

"I don't know. David was a trustee of the college, but that's pretty slim. There are chairmen and deans and such between a professor and the trustees. I didn't have anything specific in mind. I just thought that a man who would cheat on his own research might not stop at that."

Fred nodded, pulled out a little notebook, and scribbled something before picking up his sandwich again.

"Steve has the article," she said.

He nodded and chewed. So did she. Then she shifted gears without bothering to warn him.

"No matter who it was, how did he expect to get away with it?" She was thinking out loud now. "Even if David managed to fall asleep and stay on his feet, that didn't mean he wouldn't fall down right away this time. The killer couldn't count on having time to mislead you about the weapon. He must have had a hiding place in mind."

"If it was premeditated."

"Oh."

"Or he got lucky and found something on the spot."

"David's tools!" Of course. Why didn't I think of it sooner?

"Tools?"

"David did carpentry for fun. He said he was going to take his tools over and work on the supports. He was embarrassed by falling asleep in rehearsal. He wanted to make his supports less comfortable, to keep it from happening again. Wouldn't his carpenter's tools have something long and skinny and sharp enough?"

"Probably. Question is, where are they?" He gulped the last bite of his sandwich and washed it down with coffee. "Come on, let's find out."

Joan had been willing to search the records, but she was delighted that Fred wasn't banishing her to them just yet. He tossed a couple of bills on the table.

"Thanks, Fred," she said. He waved it away.

"I'd better check in at the station. You have time?"

"Sure." That was another thing she appreciated about this man. He never took her for granted, or treated her as if her time were less important than his own.

They walked the block from Wilma's. Joan avoided looking at the bank's time-and-temperature sign to find out how hot she was supposed to be. Good thing it didn't register humidity, too. Inside, the station house felt almost chilly.

"I'll just be a minute," Fred said, and Joan waited on the old wooden bench near the dispatcher's window. Someone had removed the ashtrays since the last time she'd waited here. It was hard to imagine the whole police station smoke-free. When Fred came trotting back down the short flight of stairs at the other end of the long hall, she forgot about asking him. His face looked grim.

"Let's go," he said. He had parked his Chevy in the shade of a sugar maple. Even so, her jeans soon stuck to the passenger seat. She leaned into the breeze when he opened the windows for the short drive to Oliver College.

"Captain Altschuler's putting the pressure on," he said.

How could he not? she thought, and watched Fred drive. His hands rested lightly on the wheel, and his acceleration into turns was as smooth and unhurried as if he were out for a Sunday drive. From the expression on his face, she would have expected clenched fists.

"I had to explain to him just now why I trusted you, when you were on the scene. For a little while there, I thought he was going to question my integrity. Fortunately, though, he'd talked to someone behind my back who had seen us together on the stairs before the second act, exactly where and when I'd told him."

"I guess he has to," she said.

"That doesn't mean I have to like it." But his face began to relax.

Inside the little theater, Fred lifted the yellow police barrier tape around the stage for her to duck under. He reminded her to keep her hands in her pockets. The auditorium and pit were dark and the stage dim, but backstage, the strong light made the costumes hanging on the racks look as cheap and unconvincing as the sets. Joan recognized Detective Terry, who had interviewed the orchestra, and Sergeant Ketcham, whom she had met a couple of years earlier, when the orchestra had its troubles, and again at the quilt show.

"Any luck?" Fred asked, but the answer was obvious from their faces.

"Nope," Ketcham said.

"You find a toolbox?"

They looked at each other.

"How did you know?" Terry said. "It was under Putnam's frame." Fred nodded at Joan.

"We went over it with a fine-tooth comb," Ketcham said.

"Nothing. All the screwdrivers are either short or fat, and none of them had been sharpened."

"How about a file, or an awl?"

"No awl," Terry said. "There's a file with a point, but it's pretty wide. Besides, there's no visible blood, and I don't see how it could have been wiped that clean." He shrugged. "We can run a check."

"Do that," Fred said. "Might as well take the whole box over."

"Sure, Lieutenant," Terry said.

"Let me know if you turn up anything else," Fred said. "Come on, Joan, I'll take you over to the courthouse."

SEVENTEEN

My object all sublime
 I shall achieve in time—
To let the punishment fit the crime—
 The punishment fit the crime.

—MIKADO, *The Mikado*

THEY RODE back in silence. At the station Fred ducked in to call the clerk so that she'd meet them at the courthouse door. When she did, he introduced Joan and left.

Maude Kelly welcomed her with a warm smile. She looked like somebody's grandmother. Probably was.

"Call me Maude," she said.

"I don't know anything about this," Joan said, following her down the dark stairway to the basement.

"Don't worry, honey, there's really nothing to it," Maude said over her shoulder. "Watch yourself on these steps, though. I keep telling the commissioners we need more light on them, but you know how it is, they'll put it off until someone breaks a leg. We don't want it to be you. I think it's just grand of you to volunteer like this. David was such a sweet man."

"You knew him?"

"Since he was a little boy. He loved my cookies. My, but that boy could eat. And I was so proud of him when he turned into a lawyer and then a judge." When they reached the well-lighted room at the bottom, Maude turned, and tears welled in her eyes. "Did you know him too?"

"Just a little. I met him after the tornado."

"Wasn't that a terrible thing? They almost lost their little girl in it." Maude's tears stopped as she warmed to her story. "She ran off to play in the park, and they couldn't find her. Some woman saved her, thank goodness. Threw herself down in the creek to do it."

"I know," Joan said.

"Really?" Maude stared. "It didn't make the news—David and Ellen are pretty private where the children are concerned. Unless you…" She stopped.

Joan felt suddenly shy. She nodded.

"I was walking home across the park when it hit, and there she was."

"Mercy! I've been praying for you ever since I heard that story, and here you are in my courthouse. Well, I never."

Joan didn't know what to say. She smiled, instead.

"I shouldn't be rattling on like this, when you've come to help find David's killer. The police said they'd send someone back, but right now it's just you and me down here. I don't want to waste your time."

Joan looked around at the metal shelves filled with large, gold-lettered volumes bound in black and red. An aluminum table in the middle of the room held three of the books, several pads of paper, and a mug full of pencils.

"What do I do?"

"Check the indexes in these docket entry books against this list of names. If you find any of them, we'll keep that book out. Otherwise, we'll reshelve them as we go. Do it any way you like. Detective Terry was reading one at a time, standing up, but they're too heavy for me to hold for long."

"How do I know if the case was in David's court? Isn't that what we're checking?"

"That's right." Maude flipped one of the books open and

pointed to the page. "Look here for CO1 right after the number for Alcorn County—that's the one that matches the county number on your auto license plate. CO1 is the first circuit court—that's David's. The next numbers tell you the year and month, and the letters after that tell you what kind of case it was—DR for Domestic Relations, CT for Civil Tort, SC for Small Claims, and so on. The last number is a serial number."

Whew. "I hope I can keep it straight. Are they all mixed together?"

"Oh, no, each kind of case has a separate book. Besides, we don't know what kind we're looking for. So you really don't have to know all that. Just watch for the names on the list, and then look for CO1."

"Have you found anything?"

"Not yet. Maybe we won't. Trouble is, I don't go back very far. Before I was clerk, I only knew about cases that made a big splash. And I didn't pay all that much attention to those. I don't know what made me think I could do this job, except that I'm an organized person, which is more than you can say for my predecessor."

"Where do we start?" Joan didn't see any need to get into partisan politics.

"Right here." Maude replaced the fat volumes from the table in a gap on a shelf and pulled down the next three.

The legal-length pages were bound at the top. Probably cheaper than binding those long sides, Joan thought. She flipped through a few pages, looking at the neat handwritten entries. Then she buckled down.

Half an hour later her arms were aching. Despite what she'd said, Maude Kelly slung the books around as if they weighed nothing, and checked half again as many as Joan. She's considerably tougher than she looks, Joan thought. And less likely to get sidetracked by interesting-sounding cases or other names she might recognize.

By now Joan had memorized the list of names to watch for.

These must be all the people who were onstage or backstage at the time David was killed, she thought. Nice of someone to put them in alphabetical order. Probably Maude—that wasn't Fred's scribble.

"Here's one," Maude said, and set a volume aside.

"Who?"

"Christopher Eads. His wife sued him for divorce. The clerk's notes say the marriage was dissolved."

"That's two of them."

"Pardon me?"

"Liz MacDonald, his ex-wife—she's in the cast, too, though I don't see her on this list. That's the one case we already knew about."

"Wouldn't you know it."

"He's pretty unhappy. I guess the divorce isn't recent, if the record's down here in the basement."

"No. According to the clerk's entries, he tried to open the case again, but he didn't succeed."

"I could see Chris killing someone over Liz. But killing David wouldn't help him get her back." Unless it made Liz turn her attention from David back to Chris, but I doubt it. Question is, did Chris doubt it?

Maude made sympathetic noises and went on searching. Joan found her mind wandering as she scanned the lists of cases. She was in Civil Torts when she was brought up short.

"Here's Dr. Cutts!"

"Dr. Cutts? I know him, of course, how could anyone forget a doctor with a name like that? But I'm blessed if I can remember him in court."

"It's a malpractice suit. He's not on the list, but he's in the cast."

"Set it aside, then."

Joan read the clerk's entry. "Judgment for plaintiff for $750,000." Ouch. She supposed the doctor had malpractice insurance, but that was a hefty amount. Had it increased his

premiums? Hurt his reputation? There hadn't been a long wait
in his office the day she was there. Even so, would that make
him go after the judge years later? She found it hard to believe,
but she set the volume aside.

By the end of the afternoon they'd finished the books on
the shelves and found two more names on the list. Virgil
Shoals had been sued by a customer dissatisfied with a house
he had contracted to build. But the case had been settled out
of court. He could hardly hold that against David.

And David had ordered a man named Zachariah Yoder to
use a slow-moving vehicle emblem on the back of his horse-
drawn vehicles. Maude said she had opened the Traffic In-
fractions books because she didn't think the city cops would
have cases involving the sheriff or state police in their computer. Joan didn't think this could be the Zach she knew. This
case was only three years old, and she was sure from what
Ellen Putnam had told her that Zach had been living among
the "English" considerably longer than that. She'd said as
much to Maude.

"There are scads of Amish Yoders," Maude had answered.
"They're probably related, but it could be pretty distant, even
with the same first name. But it's on the list, so we'll keep it
out."

Hardly a motive for murder anyway, Joan thought, and
rubbed her sore arm muscles. I was crazy to do this in the
afternoon before a performance. But maybe I won't have to
play tonight after all.

"I'm glad we made it through all the books," she told
Maude. "I was going to have to quit now even if we hadn't."

"Oh, that's not all of them," Maude said. "There's another
whole roomful, and it's a mess." She flicked on the light in
an adjacent room.

Joan groaned when she saw the boxes.

"Don't worry about it, honey. It had to be a long shot
anyway, doing this. David was so fair, I can't see why anyone

but a criminal would come after him for something he did in a case—much less one so long ago that it's in those boxes.''

Chatting all the while, Maude walked upstairs with Joan and saw her safely out of the building. They'd worked hard together, and Maude certainly seemed to appreciate her efforts, slow as they were.

And what did we get out of it? Joan wondered while walking home from the courthouse. Some unlikely suspects, that's all. One Amishman—probably the wrong Yoder—ordered to display the red slow-moving triangle when on the public roadway, presumably against his convictions. One doctor ordered to cough up for malpractice. One builder who had to pay when a contract went sour, but who never came before the judge. And one divorce that created a triangle in which only the judge was unscathed. Only the divorce felt murderous, and they'd known about that before the search began.

And sore arms and shoulders, she added to the list. Feeling the hot sun on them, she swung her arms as she walked and hoped she wouldn't need them for the rest of the day. But when she walked into the kitchen, the phone was ringing. In one breath, Alex told her that the police had given tonight's performance the green light and asked her to notify the players.

''Alex, I'll be there, and I'll call John Hocking if you like. But if I don't spend the next hour or so in hot water, I won't be able to play at all tonight.''

''*Hot* water?''

''I know, it sounds crazy on a day like this. Maybe I could try ice, instead. Anyhow, I can't call. Sorry.''

For once, Alex folded quickly. How can she argue with me when she's sure I've taken leave of my senses? Joan thought. I should try it more often.

She left a quick message on John's answering machine and then climbed the stairs to let the shower pound on her. The heat felt good after all. Afterwards, she shut the door on the muggy bathroom and stretched out on her bed in her lightest cotton robe to avoid chilling her arm muscles, now wonderfully loose. Half an hour later, the alarm she'd had the foresight to set woke her from a sound sleep in time to pad downstairs barefoot for a supper of yogurt and last night's fruit salad and to change into orchestra black.

Andrew rolled in when she was on her way out the back door.

"What's for supper, Mom?" he asked.

"Whatever you can scrounge up. I ate all the fruit salad—the cantaloupe is good, though."

"I could go out for pizza."

"You could. How's your cash holding out?"

"Okay. See you, Mom."

"See you."

What a joy to see him so independent after those years of being the only parent, responsible for both of them. Again, her heart went out to Ellen Putnam. It would be hard to play tonight with David and Ellen missing from the cast, but not nearly so hard as what Ellen had in front of her.

EIGHTEEN

I love him—he loved me once. But that's all gone.
Fisht! He gave me an Italian glance—thus—and
made me his. He will give her an Italian glance,
and make her his. But it shall not be, for I'll
stamp on her—stamp on her—stamp on her! Did
you ever kill anybody? No? Why not? Listen—I
killed a fly this morning! It buzzed, and I
wouldn't have it. So it died—pop! So shall she!

—MAD MARGARET, *Ruddigore*

DOWN in the dressing room and in the pit, the cast and orchestra seemed more relaxed than they'd been before the first performance. Joan didn't think it was her imagination. Was it because they had been through it once, she wondered, or because the music was the last thing on their minds tonight?

"We're sold out," her old friend Nancy Van Allen reported from the trombone section. "I tried to buy a ticket for my husband, but no luck."

"It figures," Joan said. "I'll bet everyone wants to see the scene of the crime. They're all probably sorry they missed last night."

"Hang on for disasters tonight," said John next to her, when the pit began to climb the wall.

She stared at him. Did he know something?

"Think about it," he said. "We'll have a new Mad Margaret and a new Sir Roderic."

"That's right. And they couldn't so much as walk through it today." Now it was John's turn to raise an eyebrow. "According to Fred, the police kept everyone off the stage until tonight," she explained.

They tuned and the lights dimmed, but Alex didn't give the signal to begin. Instead, she looked expectantly toward the left side of the stage. Joan understood why when a man in a dark suit stepped out from behind the curtain into a spotlight.

"Ladies and gentlemen," he said in a voice that might have carried as far as ten rows. "We are presenting our remaining performances of *Ruddigore* in memory of our colleague David Putnam." He paused, and the audience was still. "The part of Sir Roderic will be sung tonight by Peter Wylie, and the part of Mad Margaret by Catherine Turner." Now there were murmurs. The word would reach the back of the hall.

So Catherine was Ellen Putnam's understudy. Catherine, whose tongue was as sour as her pastries were sweet, especially when she was talking to Joan about Fred, on whom she had once staked a claim. Joan tried to wish her well, but her true feelings leaked through her good intentions. For the sake of the show she hoped Catherine would be good enough. That was genuine. It gave her a certain satisfaction, though, to know that Fred had heard Ellen, not Catherine, sing Mad Margaret.

The spotlight vanished and the man disappeared behind the curtain, Alex raised her arms to give the downbeat for the overture, and they were off again.

Most of the first act went well, but when Mad Margaret entered, Joan felt oddly sad to hear Catherine struggling with the part. Margaret's almost tuneless music was not easy to sing, especially at the beginning, when, with her clothes in tatters, her red hair a wild tangle, and flutes introducing her, she was a caricature of theatrical madness from Ophelia to Lucia de Lammermoor. Only someone who knew the notes well would have heard that Catherine missed some of them, Joan told herself, and Catherine's dramatic flair carried her through the worst of it.

At the tricky Allegro vivace and even in the next section, where pizzicato strings played on the beat and Margaret was supposed to sing on the offbeat, Alex was clearly following the singer, rather than attempting to set her straight. Joan concentrated on staying with Alex's baton. Its movements were as erratic as they had been when the most recent winner of the annual youth concerto competition had taken enormous liberties with his concerto's rhythm. But she had to credit Catherine with a sense of comic timing that milked all the laughs in the spoken dialogue.

"But see," Margaret said at the end of the scene, "they come—Sir Despard and his evil crew! Hide, hide—they are all mad—quite mad!"

"What makes you think that?" asked Rose Maybud.

"Hush! They sing choruses in public. That's mad enough, I think! Go—hide away, or they will seize you!"

The two women left the stage to a round of applause that was rare following anything but singing. When Catherine returned, it was to sing the second stanza of the brisk first act finale in duet with Dr. Cutts as Sir Despard. She managed it well enough and gave a mad flourish to the dance at the end, which Joan could see even while she played.

"Not bad," John said when the curtains closed for the intermission and the pit began its slow descent. "A little underrehearsed, but not bad at all."

"I suppose so." Joan felt relieved that it hadn't been worse.

"Your enthusiasm is underwhelming."

"She's not nearly the singer Ellen is."

"No, but she makes up for it." He chuckled. "Did you see her face when she was telling Rose Maybud how she'd stamp out her rival?"

"All too well," Joan said drily, and John leaned away as if she'd swung at him.

"I take it you know the lady?"

"Just a little better than I want to." She'd had no intention of saying such a thing to John, but it had slipped out of her. She hoped he would let it pass without comment, and he did.

"It should be downhill from here on," he said instead. He wiped his viola strings with his sleeve and then brushed without effect at the four thin stripes of white rosin on the black tux.

"Yes, her part in the second act is easier," Joan said.

"I was thinking of Pete. He sang the bulk of his part last night, so he won't have to go it cold tonight."

"You know him?" It was Joan's turn to ask.

"He directs our church choir, and my kids had him for music in school. He's a good Joe with a terrific voice. I don't know why he didn't go further as a singer."

Joan thought back, but after the shock of last night, she couldn't remember anything about Pete Wylie's singing except that he had come through when it mattered.

The pit hit bottom, and someone opened the doors.

"I don't remember his voice at all," she confessed. "I'll listen better tonight." She stood up. "I need to get out of here for a few minutes."

John waved her out.

"Enjoy yourself—I'm not battling that crowd."

He had a point, she thought, but she made her way to the dressing room and parked her viola in its case while she went into the rest room. She waited in line to use the toilet, wash her hands, and wipe her face and neck with a damp paper towel. For a few moments, at least, she'd feel cooler. She left her arms alone, though—they were holding up better than she'd thought possible after lifting all those monster books. Playing night after night had to be helping her endurance, but she didn't want to chill the tired muscles.

She had tossed the towel into the trash and was about to open the rest room door when Catherine slammed into it. Her fiery hair stood out in wild contrast to the sober black costume she was already wearing for Act Two. Joan just escaped being hit.

"Does anybody have a comb? I can't find mine!"

"I think I do." Joan dug into her black shoulder bag of emergency supplies. She found a clean comb sturdy enough to do the job. "Here. You can return it later—I have to get back."

"Thanks." Catherine attacked her unruly mop without so much as looking at the face of her rescuer. One comb down the drain, Joan thought. Turning her back on Catherine, she went out into the dressing room, picked up her viola, and hurried back to the pit.

John Hocking took one look at her face and grimaced.

"Is it that bad?" she asked.

"That's what I was going to ask you," he said. "What happened?"

"Nothing, really. I shouldn't let her get to me." She couldn't bring herself to tell him.

"Who?"

"Never mind." He'd probably guess, but she couldn't help that.

I ought to be bigger than that. If it had been anyone else, I wouldn't have thought twice about it.

Un-huh, her inner voice said. But it wasn't anyone else.

So what's that supposed to mean? I begrudge Catherine a pocket comb?

No. You mind one more in a long series of insults, all because of Fred.

This has nothing to do with Fred, or me. She didn't even see me.

Didn't she, though? You sure she didn't look straight through you? If she hadn't needed that comb so badly, she never would have accepted it from you. Maybe it irked her to have to.

Joan smiled at the thought, and John smiled back.

"Atta girl," he said. Now she knew she definitely couldn't tell him what she'd been thinking. Could she tell Fred? I could, but I won't, she decided, and turned her attention to checking her strings against the oboe's A before the second act.

This time the ghosts marched as they should. Hearing Pete Wylie sing "When the Night Wind Howls," Joan finally remembered how much she had indeed liked his voice the night before. Full, strong, and well-trained, it was perfect for the role. As she had then, she wondered now why he hadn't been cast as Sir Roderic in the first place. David couldn't compete with Pete's professionalism, and yet he'd won the part.

But Dr. Cutts and Catherine stole the show as the reformed Sir Despard and the scarcely tamed Margaret. Her hair slicked back under a severe bonnet, Margaret thanked him passionately: "Master, all this I owe to you! See, I am no longer wild and untidy. My hair is combed. My face is washed. My boots fit!"

The hair you owe to me, Joan thought darkly, but she laughed with the audience when Catherine, unlike Ellen, substituted Ellettsville, the one-stoplight town near Bloomington, for Gilbert's Basingstoke as a signal that Margaret needed to quiet down. Dr. Cutts didn't miss a beat when he responded in kind—he had to be in on that one. And the contrast between Margaret's newly demure deportment and occasional wild shenanigans was funnier than anything Ellen had done. Catherine has a real gift for comedy, Joan thought. Who would have guessed it?

After the performance, when she picked up her case and climbed the stairs to the stage door, she was not surprised to see Pete and Catherine surrounded by well-wishers. She was surprised, though, to see Fred standing off to one side. He spotted her, too, and came over.

"Good show tonight," he said, as if that were his only reason for being there, but she was sure he was listening to what was being said around them.

"You just dropped by?"

"Wouldn't have missed it." He gave her what Mad Margaret had demonstrated as an Italian glance. Joan couldn't help wondering whether it was for her benefit or Catherine's, and then kicked herself for not simply enjoying it.

"I heard it was sold out," she said.

"Not backstage."

Oh. "You going home?"

"I'll hang around awhile yet, maybe ask a couple of questions."

"You're no closer than you were, are you?"

Fred looked suddenly tired.

"No. Looks as if we'll have to reinterview a whole mess of people we've already talked to. Thank God I don't have to interview Catherine. She was downstairs during the second act last night."

"Catherine? Why would Catherine murder David?"

"She's over there telling people she'd kill for a chance to sing a part like that. Pete's not saying any such thing, but he had opportunity."

"Oh, Fred. Nobody would really kill over something like that."

"You wouldn't think so."

Joan went home wondering.

NINETEEN

Oh, the man who can rule a theatrical crew,
Each member a genius (and some of them two),
And manage to humour them, little and great,
    Can govern this tuppenny State!

—ERNEST, *The Grand Duke*

FRED WATCHED JOAN go until he lost sight of her in the crush at the stage door, where Catherine, flushed with success, was displaying the sparkle that had once attracted him to her. Still in costume, the cast members were congratulating each other and shaking hands with members of the audience. He left them to it.

Backstage again, he flipped open his notebook and peered at the list of names he'd had people searching the court records for: Duane Biggy, Steve Dolan, Christopher Eads, Edward Kleinholtz, Walter Rice, Virgil Shoals, Anthony Ucello, Peter Wylie, and Zachariah Yoder. By now he knew that Biggy and Ucello were college professors, Dolan a student, Eads a farmer/woodcutter/hunter who lived on the edge of economic survival, Kleinholtz an engineer at Oliver's electronics manufacturing firm, Rice an Oliver fireman and housepainter, Shoals a builder, Yoder a carpenter who worked for him, and Wylie a high school music teacher and church choir director. Dolan, Eads, Rice, and Wylie were natives of Alcorn County. All the rest had lived in the county at least as long as Fred.

Each of these men had been backstage tonight before or during the first part of the second act. Fred deleted the lighting man from the list when Ketcham pointed out that the control booth was high up in the back of the auditorium. Shoals had opened and closed the curtain and helped with sets, as had several chorus members and ghosts, but they were now enjoying themselves instead of striking the set for Act Two. Fred had asked Duane Biggy to leave it up, and so he stood alone in the cool dimness behind the picture frames, the jubilant voices by the stage door muted.

Only Dolan and Kleinholtz, as Robin and old Adam, had been onstage before Amy Putnam had seen her father's head on his chest after she entered with Biggy, Esther Ooley, and the bridesmaids. Fred had eliminated the chorus and Ooley on that basis.

Maybe I shouldn't have, he thought now. Maybe one of them got Putnam on the way in. Besides, after Ooley's little melodrama last night, I ought to have included all the others who were supposed to be downstairs. Maybe one of them sneaked up during the performance.

Don't get sidetracked, he told himself. Nobody came up here early tonight when I was watching. Start with the obvious.

The ghosts had been up in their frames for most of the time in question, but it was likely that before that they'd been moving around behind them and climbing into position at the time Putnam was attacked. He'd made a quick map tonight. From backstage, Wylie had stood at the far left, substituting for Putnam. Then Eads, Yoder, Rice, and finally Ucello, who was nearest to the stairs. On Friday Wylie had been on the other side of Eads, but tonight they'd left one of the frames back by the wall, omitting Wylie's ghost altogether, so that he could sing Sir Roderic. These were the only cast members who had not entered from stage left, where Putnam's frame had been on Friday. Ucello and Yoder, however, had crossed behind him to pick up swords from the prop box before taking their places.

The other cast members had passed behind all the ghosts and gone by the clothes rack and prop box. Any of them might have stabbed Putnam on the way in, and then spotted the dagger in the prop box and stabbed him again. The more Fred thought about it, the more likely it seemed that Joan was right. Whether or not it was premeditated, the second stabbing had been to make the police focus on an obvious weapon and let the killer carry off the one that had struck the killing blow. It had certainly had that effect. All of which got him nowhere.

"Can I help you, Lieutenant?" Duane Biggy asked at his elbow, still in his sailor suit, pigtailed wig, and makeup.

The question that was nagging at Fred insisted on coming out.

"How sure are you that no one downstairs came up early last night—say, before or during the first scene?"

"I'm sure." Biggy didn't hesitate. "I stood at the top of the stairs and watched them like a hawk until I signaled Esther and the bridesmaids to go on. No one could have got past me. After that, I can't be sure, because I was onstage, too. But it's the young girls I was most concerned about—they giggle, and the audience can't help hearing." Hearing more laughter from the stage door, Fred could believe it.

"So if one person wanted to come up—an older woman, say, or a man in a later scene—you might allow it?"

Biggy shook his pigtail emphatically.

"You can't keep discipline that way, Lieutenant. No, I make no exceptions."

"And you're sure nobody distracted you last night?"

"I don't distract easily. I've been doing this a long time. Besides, there was nothing else going on. Only Virgil Shoals and I were backstage, and he was on the far right, opening and closing the curtain. I listened to Steve and Ed sing, but I didn't budge from that stairway, believe me."

Fred was inclined to believe him. "How about before that? What happened before the curtain opened, when there was no need for silence?"

"I came over here early, but you're right, I was watching the ghosts climb into their frames. If they needed help, I was there to give it. Or Virgil and Zach could have helped—they built the things. But it went smoothly last night. The usual horsing around, that's all."

"What kind of horsing around?"

"Oh, you know, people giving David a hard time about falling asleep, that sort of thing. Zach and Tony had a little sword fight. I had to stop it before they tripped or tore a costume or something."

"Uh-huh. And then what did they do?"

"Then Tony went up here." He patted the nearest frame.

"And Zach?"

"Same thing, I guess—over there." He pointed to the next one down the row.

"You didn't actually see Zach do it?"

"No. He might have been helping someone else get settled on those armrests first." Putnam? No one would suspect Zach Yoder of anything if he climbed Putnam's steps, not even if he touched him.

"Were these frames individually designed for the height of the men in them?"

"You'll have to ask Zach. He built the supports."

"Can you remember who was joking with Putnam?"

"Not really."

"Tony?"

"Noooo." Biggy drew the word out slowly. "No, he was still over here by the stairs."

"Zach?"

"I don't know. The way the portrait gallery curves at both ends, you can't see David's frame from here."

It was true. Less obvious from the middle of the stage,

where Fred had been standing, but he should have spotted it sooner.

"Do me a favor, would you?"

"What's that?"

"Go stand behind that frame."

Biggy nodded, and walked along the wall to the far side. Fred went to the top of the stairs.

"Here?" Biggy called.

Fred could still see him and the prop box.

"Maybe. Am I where you were last night?"

"Looks about right."

"Okay. Now walk up to the frame until your toes are touching it."

Biggy took two steps and disappeared.

"Okay. Now would you climb up to the top step, please, but don't go all the way in." Still invisible. Fred started down the row of frames toward him. By the time he reached the second one, he could see Biggy looking back at him. So Biggy couldn't have seen Putnam's murder, if he was where he said he was. The other ghosts couldn't either, if they were already in their frames. Nor could Shoals, if he was waiting at stage right to open the curtain. That left Dolan and Kleinholtz, waiting at stage left to begin the first scene. They'd claimed not to have seen anything last night. They could probably alibi each other, though. Might as well get it over with.

"Thanks," he told Biggy. "I'd like to talk to Shoals, Dolan, and Kleinholtz, if they're still here."

"I'll get them. You still need the set?"

"No, go ahead. One more thing—are the frames always in the same position?"

"Sure. At least, they have been since we settled an argument about whether to put the ghosts in chronological order or the way the original stage directions read. Chronology won out—never mind how it looks onstage." Fred gathered that Biggy had lost that argument.

"How sure can you be that they're in exactly the same spot?"

"Plenty. See the tape?" Looking down where Biggy pointed, he saw that the back steps of each frame were lined up against short strips of dark tape, almost invisible on the stage floor.

"I see. Can you send Shoals back first?"

"Sure thing."

While he waited, Fred curved the ends of the portrait gallery on his sketchy map. It wasn't accurate, but it would remind him. With luck, the lines of sight would be documented in the police photos of the crime scene. If necessary, they could re-create the scene from the tapes on the floor.

"Lieutenant?" Blue-eyed, with straight blond hair falling across his forehead, the slight man in dark jeans could have been a brother to Chris Eads.

"Mr. Shoals?" The man nodded. "Thanks for coming back."

"No problem. What can I do for you?"

"I'm just sorting out a few things. I understand you built these sets."

"That's right."

"Take you long?"

"I had one of my men do most of it."

"That would be Zach Yoder?"

"That's right."

"He a pretty good worker?"

"Most days." Shoals wasn't going out on any limb for Yoder. No wonder, from what Joan had said.

"I hear you had a little dust-up about Judge Putnam's falling asleep on the supports Yoder built."

"He fixed it." Shoals was closemouthed now, defensive.

"And you're here now during performances to make sure there aren't any other problems."

"That's right."

"Good of you to take so much time."

Shoals expanded a little. "I like to give back to the community when I can."

"I understand you also take care of the curtain."

"Might as well."

"Uh-huh. So you'd see a lot of what goes on backstage during the performance."

"Not really." Shoals studied his toes.

"Oh?"

"I generally sit in that chair over there and rest my eyes."

"How do you know when it's time to pull the curtain?"

"I listen."

It made sense. "And did you hear anything out of the ordinary last night?"

"I heard Pete Wylie sing David Putnam's part, and let me tell you, I wasn't happy about it."

"You thought you were going to be blamed again."

"You got it."

Fred thanked him and asked him to tell Biggy he was ready for Dolan. He marked Shoals's chair on his map.

"Sir?" This time he heard the steps. He looked up at the tall young redhead still in costume as Robin. Six two, maybe six three.

"Dolan, thanks. I have a couple of questions." Around them Shoals and the stage crew, most in costume, were pushing the heavy frames back to the brick wall. It was over in moments. Fred waved at the nearest steps. "Take a seat."

"Yes, sir." Dolan folded his long legs and rested his arms on his knees. He sat without fidgeting, like a veteran of long waiting.

"Tell me again how it was before you went onstage in the second act last night."

"Well, sir, Ed and I were back in the corner on those two chairs—" He broke off. "Well, there *were* two chairs over there."

"I saw them. Go on."

"We were running over our lines. Especially mine. I was still a little weak."

"And then?"

"And then it was time to go on."

"Nothing happened while you were sitting out here?"

"Just the usual. You know."

"Suppose you tell me."

"There's not much to tell. Biggy was on the other side, by the stairs. He laid down an order that you had to stay downstairs if it wasn't your turn to go on. Made people mad, but he's tough. The guys were climbing into the pictures. That's about it."

"Anyone come over and talk to you?"

"No, they could see what we were doing, and they left us alone."

"You had a good view of David Putnam from where you were sitting."

"Only when we were looking. And we weren't looking, you know? I didn't see anything wrong."

"What did you see? Did anyone come over your way at all?"

"Only people picking up props." His face changed. "Oh...you mean, did I see someone pick up that dagger?"

"Did you?"

"No. But I wouldn't have noticed. There was a crowd around there anyway, talking and laughing, and two of the guys were sword fighting. Biggy came over and broke that up—they were getting kind of raucous, and he likes it quiet backstage, even between acts."

"Is that the only time he left the stairs?"

"Yeah, until we went on."

"Anyone need help with the supports?"

"The what? Oh, yeah. I don't know. I wasn't paying much attention to anyone but Ed."

"Who came up first, you or Ed?"

"We came up together when Biggy called. He cracks the whip."

"Then you sat in those chairs. Then what?"

"Then we went on together."

"Was Ed out of your sight between the time you came up and the time you went onstage?"

"No." For the first time, Steve Dolan looked nervous.

"You both stayed right there the whole time."

"That's right. What are you doing, collecting alibis?"

"That's my job." Fred smiled at him. "Don't worry, son, you're one of the few people who had someone else watching him the whole time we're concerned about, and you've just given him the same alibi."

"You mean it happened right then, while we could have seen it?"

"Maybe. Or maybe while you were onstage, with hundreds of witnesses."

"Oh."

"Or maybe even before you came up."

"Oh, no. David climbed into his frame after we came up. I saw him." He looked startled.

"See? You *were* watching."

"I guess. Is that all?"

"You see anyone else up there with him?" Dolan shook his head. "Then let's go find Ed." Fred escorted him to the stage door, where the crowd had thinned out and most of the cast had left. Ed Kleinholtz, the short fellow with the big ears, was waiting, though he'd gone downstairs long enough to change into slacks and a short-sleeved shirt. Without makeup, his baby face made him look almost as young as Dolan, although he had to be in his early thirties.

"Where do you want me?" Kleinholtz said.

"Back here is fine," Fred said, and led him to the steps of the frame nearest to where the chairs had been.

The conversation he'd had with Dolan repeated itself in substance, if not word for word.

"Is that normal, to be rehearsing lines like that on opening night?" Fred asked finally.

"I don't know what's normal—I never did any of this before. But the kid was nervous, so I figured why not?"

"Did it work?"

"Yeah." Fred waited. "He settled down, and when we went on, he was fine. He's young—worries too much anyway—and Biggy scares him."

"What about Biggy? Did he come back here?"

"No, only that once when Zach and Tony staged the sword fight. He was too busy protecting us from the chorus." He grinned up at Fred. "Good thing, too. You can't hear yourself think around those girls."

"And then you went onstage together."

"He went first. I was his steward, his 'former faithful *valley-de-sham*,' don't you know, so I had to follow a step behind him." He looked Fred in the eye. "Not far enough behind to run up there and stab David Putnam after he went on."

"I know. I was in the audience."

Kleinholtz relaxed visibly. "That's all right, then."

"Let's back up a little. From where you were sitting, did you see anyone near Putnam, once he climbed up into that frame?"

Kleinholtz was silent for a moment. Then he shook his head.

"No. That doesn't mean no one was, but I don't think so."

"Anything else I ought to know?"

"I wish I could help you. I've been wracking my brains, but nothing comes."

"You've already helped." They stood up, and Fred looked down at him. "Thanks. And tell Dolan not to worry."

"Not about you, maybe. Nothing's going to keep him from worrying about Biggy."

Me either, Fred thought as they walked to the stage door

together. If you're right, and no one approached Putnam before you went on, then the man on the spot for the next couple
of minutes is Duane Biggy. The ghosts all had their backs to
him, Shoals was beyond the curve of the set—with his eyes
closed, at that—and the chorus was still downstairs until Biggy
called them up. Who could have seen what he did?

TWENTY

Here's a how-de-do!

—YUM-YUM, *The Mikado*

JOAN PUT HER bare feet up on the sofa and leaned back to
check out the funnies between loads of laundry. Sunday, never
a day of rest for a minister's family, was little more so now
that she supported herself and attended church only sporadi-
cally. This morning she had thrown her sweaty black things
in the washer with Andrew's jeans. Some mothers might tell
him to do his own wash, but to her it seemed a fair trade. She
was sitting in the relatively cool house, and Andrew was out
working in the heat—the whir of their old rotary mower told
her that he was keeping his promise to cut the remnants of
their small lawn, though the grass had survived the tornado
better than the trees and bushes. One day he'd leave home for
good. Then he could match his own socks and she could mow
her own grass.

The whirring stopped abruptly. Andrew couldn't be finished
yet, and she didn't hear the clickety-whir of the mower's trip
back to the garage. Instead, voices, and then the back door
banged.

"Hey, Mom," Andrew called.

"I'm in here."

"You've got company."

"Who is it?" She hated to move, but she folded the paper,

tucked it between the sofa cushions, and poked around on the floor with her toes for her sandals.

"Me."

"Fred!" Forgetting the sandals, she jumped up. He strolled in from the kitchen as if he'd been doing it all his life. She felt suddenly grubby in her floppy T-shirt and worn cutoffs next to his crisp summer suit. "Why didn't you tell me you were coming over?" I might have carried that basket of wash-and-wear stuff upstairs, for one thing. At least it's clean.

"Didn't know it to tell." He hugged her as Andrew might have. "How are you?"

"Recovering."

"Oh?" He quirked that eyebrow.

"I'm not cut out for pit orchestras, especially after a day of lifting weights."

He got it. "Those books. I'm sorry. How's the leg?"

"It's all right," she said, surprised to realize that it was true. "I'm fine, really. Can I feed you?" It was a risky invitation—grocery shopping was something else she generally left for the weekend, and yesterday had been no day for it. Alone, she and Andrew would graze the refrigerator for leftovers.

"Not today. I just wanted to see you."

"Good." Both ways. "Come sit down. Tell me how it's going." She tucked her feet underneath her and patted the sofa cushion. He sat down, stretched his long legs out in front of him, and draped an arm over the back of the sofa, like a teenager working up courage to make a pass, or a husband taking her closeness for granted. She relaxed under it.

"It's not going," he said. "What I wouldn't give for some solid physical evidence. But I'm down to sorting out who had opportunity. With the stage manager guarding the stage the way he was, it almost seems as if nobody could have killed Putnam. By the time I left last night I'd about convinced myself it had to be Biggy himself.'' She heard the doubt in his voice.

"You don't believe it?"

"Not really. No apparent motive, for one thing. And it would put him in the position of having to depend on understudies.''

"I don't suppose I could sell you on a random act of violence by a stranger or a thief?''

"Nothing was stolen. And there are easier ways to commit violence than twice stabbing a man on the far side of that stage, even if you can believe that nobody would have noticed a stranger back there.''

"Okay, scratch the stranger.''

"With Biggy on the job, you just about have to scratch everyone who wasn't in the first part of the second act, before the chorus entered. I have a hard time picturing one of the ghosts climbing down and back up again without being noticed, though Eads would be a likely possibility. And no one would have noticed Yoder—they'd all think he was helping, not stabbing. They're the most likely ghosts.''

Joan couldn't imagine Zach doing such a thing. She fought back. "But suppose it happened later. I mean, once Duane was onstage, it could have been anyone.''

Fred groaned. "Amy Putnam noticed her father slumped over right away,'' he argued.

"Even so. It could have been a bridesmaid on the way in.'' Even Catherine, Joan thought. "Or someone who came upstairs as soon as Duane had his back turned.'' Dr. Cutts. He should have come up with Ellen Putnam. If they stuck together, that would eliminate both of them, but what if they didn't? A doctor would certainly know where to aim. So would a nurse, and Liz MacDonald might have been angry at David—a woman scorned, and all that. Joan sighed.

"Hmm?'' That arm reached down and patted hers gently but then retreated to the back of the sofa.

"Fred, I hate to think that any of them could have killed him."

"Somebody did, you know."

"I know."

"We'll get him, Joan. It's not your problem."

She looked up at him then. Was he putting her down? But he was staring into space, looking nothing but tired. She liked it that he had come over to relax with her. She remembered a day, years ago, when Ken had called her in midafternoon. When she'd asked what was on his mind, he'd said, "Nothing. I've been counseling people all day, and I just wanted to talk to someone normal." Would it be like that with Fred?

Whaddya mean, would it? her inner voice asked. It is already.

You know, she thought back. If...

If you were married, is that it?

Well...

Don't even think about it.

All right, I won't. He's a friend, that's all.

Uh-huh. A friend who drops in as if he lived here. A friend who kissed you the other night as if he meant it. And you liked it, you know you did.

He was showing off. He's not really interested in me. He's not interested in anyone. He's sour on marriage.

What would it be like, anyway, being married to a policeman? Interruptions at all hours of the day and night, she was sure. She knew about interruptions—she'd learned long ago not to expect dinner without phone calls. People got sick and died at the least convenient times. Political pressure? She supposed the pressure on Fred could be worse than pressure from a whole congregation and board of trustees, but that would be saying a lot. What social obligations would a cop's wife have? She had no idea.

Don't even think about it, the voice said firmly.

Fred pulled his arm away from her, clasped his hands above

his head, stretched, and yawned. Then he stood up in one smooth movement.

"Thanks, Joan. I needed that." He bent down and kissed her cheek. "I'll see you." And he left.

How about that? Joan thought. But her inner voice was silent. So was the dryer, she realized suddenly, and slipped her sandals on to go down to the basement. When she came up, Andrew was in the kitchen, drinking ice water and wiping his sweaty face with the clean dish towel she'd just hung on the handle of the refrigerator door. She hung out a fresh one without comment. Her mother would have called that "crowding the hero bench."

"Finished?"

"Yep. Next time, don't hang the sheets out when I'm going to mow, okay?"

"Sorry. Are they dry?"

"Just about. You want me to bring them in?"

"Thanks, Andrew."

Joan's mother also would have been shocked at the idea of hanging out washing on a Sunday. But death had freed her of criticism from her mother or Ken's parishioners. Annie Jordan's right, Joan thought. She always says there are advantages and disadvantages to everything. Only sometimes they're mighty hard to see.

Helping herself to a glass of cold water, Joan stared out the kitchen window at the bare yard between her house and Henry Putnam's. Most of Henry's roses were gone, and this side of his yard had been wiped clean of vegetation. What the tornado hadn't destroyed, David's digger had. Out back she knew she still had some day lilies and some irises. No flowers now, but the plants looked sturdy enough. If it rained enough to dampen the soil and cool things off a little, she would try transplanting some over to Henry's. He wouldn't be ready to dig when he first came home, but he might welcome any sign that he'd eventually have flowers again. If he came home at all, she reminded herself. And even if he didn't, it couldn't hurt. At least she'd see them from the kitchen.

She began to fold underwear on the kitchen table, leaving the socks for last. While her hands automatically flipped and turned the clothes, her mind wandered back to what Fred had said. Zach Yoder was high on his suspect list. Zach, for whom she'd been leaving her back door unlocked, so that he could help himself to a cool drink or use the toilet while she was away during the day. Zach, with whom she'd fallen into the habit of sharing a cup of coffee before getting dressed for work.

What if Fred's right? she wondered. How will I ever act normal around him in the morning?

TWENTY-ONE

Black sheep dwell in every fold
All that glitters is not gold;
Storks turn out to be but logs;
Bulls are but inflated frogs.

—BUTTERCUP, *H.M.S. Pinafore*

AS IT TURNED OUT, Zach was the least of her worries on Monday morning. Having turned off her alarm clock for Sunday, Joan had forgotten to set it for Monday. To make matters worse, Zach had begun his week's work without his usual racket. And so it was after eight when she dreamed that she was sitting in the bathroom, but that her own personal plumbing was refusing to cooperate. No matter how hard she tried, she couldn't urinate. She turned on the faucet in the sink—nothing. Maybe it's because the door's open, she thought, but she couldn't reach the door handle. She was going to have to get up and go over there. But when her feet touched the floor it was soft, much too soft to support her.

Then she was lying in bed, with the sun streaming in the window. Her mouth felt gummy. She threw back the sheet and padded into the bathroom, hoping she wasn't going to wet the bed by persuading herself that still another dream was real, but the door closed with a convincing click and the tile floor felt hard and cool against her bare feet. She ran her toes along the edges of the little hexagons and rubbed them against the grout, just to be sure.

By the time she'd showered and brushed the taste off her teeth, the breeze coming in the window was already muggy. Back in her bedroom, her traitorous alarm clock read 8:27. No time to walk to work today. Hardly time for breakfast.

She pulled on a navy blue skirt and top and slid into her sandals, glad she could wear them at work. She brushed her hair on her way downstairs and skewered it up off her neck while she walked into the kitchen.

"You're late," Andrew greeted her, his mouth full of toast. "Want some coffee?"

"Please." Joan stuck a couple of slices of bread in the toaster and opened the refrigerator for milk and orange juice. "My alarm didn't go off. I wish you'd called me."

"I thought maybe you had the day off." He passed her a steaming mug.

"No such luck. We're having a speaker today. And in the afternoon I'm going to David Putnam's funeral. I forgot about that until just now. I can't go like this—I'll have to come home in between."

"You look fine."

"For a funeral?"

"Sure. Why not?"

She looked down at herself. Maybe if her legs weren't bare... She could stick a pair of panty hose and some pumps into her handbag and change at work. She buttered the toast, feeling only a little less rushed. Andrew was saying something. She tuned in.

"Should I go?" His forehead wrinkled as it did when he was anxious.

"How do you feel about it?" she said. Andrew hadn't been to a funeral since his father's. She'd never believed in taking children. But he was hardly a child now. She didn't need to make up his mind for him, and she certainly didn't want to pressure him. Or hurry him, even today. She chewed as inconspicuously as she could and willed herself to sit quietly.

"I don't know," he said finally. "I liked him. You should have seen him over at Henry's that day."

"I liked him, too. Come if you want to, Andrew. Or maybe you could do something for his kids some other time. You know what they're up against."

"Yeah. Thanks, Mom. I will." He zipped his book bag and slung it over his shoulder. "See you." And he let the back door bang.

Joan finished her breakfast in peace. She scanned the headlines and the obituaries—part of her job, she figured—but left the rest of the paper for evening. A quick trip upstairs to brush her teeth again and grab the panty hose and shoes, and she was off. The car started, not that it had ever threatened not to. Still, with the odometer making its second pass through the numbers, she blessed it every time it did and spared it when she could.

She didn't have to unlock the doors to the center when she arrived at nine; the adult day-care staff had done that when they opened at eight-thirty. It was a good thing, because the crowd was already gathering for Dr. Cutts's talk at nine-thirty. What is it about getting older that makes people get ready so far ahead of time? Joan wondered, not for the first time. She made decaf coffee in the big urn and set out teabags by a smaller urn of hot water. This early in the day, she wouldn't offer cookies from the center's stash. She saved them for afternoon events.

I wondered how I'd act normal around Zach, she thought suddenly. But what about Dr. Cutts? Calm down. Nobody's going to do anything here today. Anyway, Fred's probably already eliminated him. I can't go around suspecting everybody in the cast.

She'd been amazed to find the doctor available on such short notice, and for a weekday morning at that. In the pediatrician's office, when her children were small, Monday morning had always found patients hanging from the rafters. Maybe Dr. Cutts didn't have that kind of practice. She had called Liz MacDonald at his office after learning that he was currently chief of staff at Oliver's small hospital, which hired no staff physicians but relied on doctors in the community.

"Oh," Liz had said blithely, "he'll be happy to do it. How about Monday?" Joan hoped he wouldn't regret it. From the comments she'd overheard, she was sure he would face some tough questioning, if not actual hostility. On the other hand, a lot of people tended to put doctors on a pedestal. They might back down when he was in the same room with them. And some folks loved him, she knew.

At least they had come. Joan had hurried to get the word out in time. She would have felt bad if he'd shown up to empty chairs, but by ten the small meeting room was comfortably filled.

Dr. Cutts arrived promptly, looking as well scrubbed as she remembered him from his office. Probably made his hospital calls already, Joan thought, and went to welcome him.

"How's that leg doing?" he asked.

She gave him points for remembering. "Much better, thank you." It was true, she scarcely noticed it most of the time now.

"Good." He gave her that pixie smile. "Morning, Mabel," he said to Mabel Dunn, who was just arriving, and he smiled and nodded at some others, both regulars and drop-ins.

Joan wondered how many of the people here today were his patients. They probably all knew him better than she did. She kept her introduction brief, mentioning his role as current spokesman for the hospital, and his willingness to answer their questions.

"I'll do my best," he said, and launched into a brief history of Oliver Hospital. Joan learned that it had been founded over a hundred years ago by local women concerned with the lack of medical care in their little town, and that it had grown from an old house whose windows children tried to peer through while operations were being performed to the small modern hospital it was today. While limited, it provided convenient local care for routine medical, obstetrical, orthopedic, and surgical cases. For most specialized care Oliver residents had to go out of town.

Only a year ago, he told them, a group working in close cooperation with the hospital had opened Hoosier Place, Oliver's first fully accredited nursing home. Bids were being taken for a new wing to be built next spring. The new wing would concentrate on elderly patients with Alzheimer's and other dementing illnesses.

"Even if all they have is Medicaid?" someone asked, not waiting for a formal question period to be announced.

"Yes," Dr. Cutts said. "Like the hospital, it's Medicare and Medicaid certified."

"And what happens if they need something Medicare and Medicaid won't pay for?"

"Or their private insurance won't pay for?" asked Mabel Dunn.

"I know you're concerned about the effects of insurance cutbacks," Dr. Cutts said. "We all are. We're doing our best to provide good patient care in spite of them."

"Like hell," Joan heard a man say quietly in a back corner, but she couldn't see who had spoken. Here we go, she thought.

"Is that what you call it when you kick people out while they're still sick, because the insurance says you can only be in the hospital a day or two after major surgery?" said a woman she didn't know.

"The hospital is negotiating those limitations with the insurance companies. Speaking for myself, though, I keep patients in the hospital until I decide they're ready to leave."

"Will you visit patients in the nursing home?" asked a man

Joan had met once or twice. "I can't get anyone to call on my wife when she comes down with an infection."

"What happens?" Dr. Cutts asked.

"The nurses call the doctor and tell him what they think is wrong, and he prescribes over the phone. He hasn't seen my wife in over a year." The doctor opened his mouth, but the man didn't let him reply. "And that's not all. He doesn't even return their calls. Last time it was two days after they told me she had an infection before she got any antibiotics for it."

"That's not right," said a woman, and others echoed her.

Dr. Cutts waited them out. "I don't know the facts in your particular case, but you may want to notify the Alcorn County Medical Association."

"Fat lot of good that will do," said the quiet voice in the back corner. But the man who had asked the question thanked the doctor and sat down.

And so it went. Dr. Cutts fielded questions about expensive hospital aspirins, indecipherable hospital bills, and more before he finally looked at his watch. Joan went forward to shake his hand and set him free.

"Thank you for your patience," she said. "We all appreciate your taking the time to come."

The applause was polite. Several people crowded forward to shake the doctor's hand—or, more likely, ask for free medical advice, but he waved a quick good-bye.

"I have patients waiting," he told them, and ducked out.

"I just love Dr. Cutts," said a woman in her eighties. "He's such a nice young man." Joan smiled.

"Nice my foot," said a heavyset bald man. Joan didn't know him, but she recognized the voice from the corner. "I wouldn't take a sick dog to that man, especially not after the lawsuit."

"What lawsuit?" someone asked.

"You must have heard," said Margaret Duffy. "Dr. Cutts sent Ada Lawson's fourteen-year-old grandson home with antacids when he had an ulcer so bad it perforated his stomach and nearly killed him. Ada's son took him to court and won."

"He didn't lose his license," Joan said, wishing she'd asked someone else to come.

"No," Alvin Hannauer said. "That was up to the licensing board, and they disagreed with the judge. I understand it's really cut into his practice, though. I know my insurance won't let me use him anymore."

"So how can he be chief of staff at the hospital?" Annie Jordan asked.

"Oh," said the man who'd made the crack about the dog, "you heard him—there's no real staff at the hospital. He probably volunteered. Makes him sound good. He needs to—you notice he had time to come over here this morning. I wish I hadn't wasted mine." And he walked out.

"I don't care what Dr. Cutts told us today," Annie said. "He's the one who made Henry Putnam leave the hospital too soon."

The complaining went on, but Joan had lost her stomach for it. The callous man they were talking about was her doctor. She excused herself from the group and shut her office door, but she couldn't shut out her own thoughts. David, Henry's nephew, had ruled against Dr. Cutts in court and, from the sound of it, had cost him earnings that no insurance would cover. Could it be that the doctor had taken his anger out on Henry? That his thirst for revenge had grown until he had murdered David?

She had been thinking of Ellen and the children and hoping for their sake that the killer would be found soon. Now, for the first time, she was fully conscious of the cloud of suspicion hanging over the heads of all the innocent people.

TWENTY-TWO

Oh, bury, bury—let the grave close o'er
The days that were—that never will be more.

—CASILDA AND LUIZ, *The Gondoliers*

BY MIDAFTERNOON the center was quiet. Joan retreated to her office again when she could no longer postpone pulling on her hose and shoes. At half past two she left the center in the capable hands of the adult day-care staff.

She was pulling into the First Baptist Church parking lot when she wondered whether anyone had offered to pick up Henry Putnam. He wouldn't be able to walk. Still, she thought, if I'd planned ahead, we could have managed it with a wheelchair. Maybe someone in the family had remembered Henry, although considering her own spacey numbness when Ken died, she doubted it. If she hadn't been so late this morning…but would she have thought of it, even then?

Let it go, Joan, she told herself.

In the crowded lot, Gil Snarr, wearing his undertaker's black, was waving cars into tight rows.

"Hello, Joan," he said.

"Hello, Gil." He had been her classmate in Margaret Duffy's sixth grade, and they'd met repeatedly since her return to Oliver. Death and decay in all around I see, the old hymn echoed inside her head.

"Will you be going to the cemetery?" He held out a purple Funeral pennant.

"Oh, I don't…" she began, but stopped. David's death was affecting her as few of the deaths of the old people she'd worked with had done. "Yes, I will." Gil affixed the pennant to her antenna and directed her elderly Honda to a spot beside a spanking new Lincoln.

"Just follow the car to your left," he told her. She nodded and went into the church.

She had just slid into a pew near the back when the organist began playing Bach's "Jesu, Joy of Man's Desiring." If the church had air conditioning, it wasn't working well enough to be noticed. Here and there people were already fanning themselves with cardboard pictures of Jesus kneeling over a discreet ad for Snarr's Funeral Home. Andrew used to call fans like those "Jesus on a stick." She hadn't seen one in years.

There was Maude Kelly down front, her face streaked with tears. That's right, Joan remembered. They closed the courthouse this afternoon.

Alvin Hannauer and Margaret Duffy sat together a few rows behind Maude, and several more of the Senior Citizens' Center's regulars were scattered throughout the crowd, as were people Joan recognized from the neighborhood and a few members of the Gilbert and Sullivan cast. She saw Esther Ooley and Catherine Turner, both dressed more sedately than usual.

Annie Jordan slipped in beside Joan, for once without her knitting. She leaned over. "Isn't that your boy, Joanie? With Henry?"

Looking where Annie had pointed, Joan saw Henry Putnam's white head above the back of a wheelchair in a side aisle down front, and Andrew's dark head bent toward him at the end of the pew. It looked as if Andrew must have brought the old man. No one else sat near them.

"Yes," she told Annie. "They're friends." And knew it was true.

How did he do it? she wondered, stifling a giggle at a sudden mental image of Henry's wheelchair on the crossbar of Andrew's bike. Andrew was nothing if not resourceful, she knew. He'd probably borrowed a car. However he had managed it, or even if he'd merely come to sit with Henry, she felt a warm glow watching her son with the old man.

"You must be mighty proud of him," Annie said, and squeezed her hand. Joan squeezed back, wishing Ken could see him.

The organ struck up "For All the Saints." The congregation rose to sing, and a double row of pallbearers—Joan recognized Mayor Deckard—followed the closed casket down the aisle and lined up in the front row on the left while the family took their places on the right. The rousing hymn set the tone for a celebratory funeral, with gratitude for the life of this good man and a minimum of sentimentality. The minister seemed to have known David well. He included personal stories that made people chuckle—at one point Joan even saw Amy and Scott Putnam laugh together.

The minister read biblical words of comfort and promise, ending with the Twenty-third Psalm. They sang "The King of Love My Shepherd Is," there was a final prayer, and it was over. The organist played more Bach while the casket was wheeled out and the family escaped by a side door. Gil Snarr and his father, Bud, stood at the end of the pews and released the congregation row by row, like wedding guests.

Following Annie down the center aisle, Joan saw Fred Lundquist standing at the rear of the church. Always the matchmaker, Annie gave Joan a little nudge in his direction and disappeared. He met her at the door.

"You going to the cemetery?" He held the door for her and they walked down the steps together.

"I said I would."

"Want a ride?"

She was tempted, but remembered her car. "Fred, I'd better not. Gil Snarr has me in line—I'd louse up the works."

His eyes crinkled.

"Did I ever tell you about the fellow who changed his mind in the middle of a funeral procession?" She shook her head. "I guess he just decided to go home. The back half of the procession followed him. I was bringing up the rear on a motorcycle, so I moved up to the head of that bunch and led them where they were supposed to be going. Sure felt funny to be leading a funeral procession without a hearse."

Later, waiting in her car for the procession to begin, Joan realized she had no idea where Fred had been a cop before coming to Oliver. She knew Oliver wasn't his home, but little more. When she'd asked him once where he was from, he'd said only "a little Swedish community in northern Illinois" and changed the subject. He hadn't sounded particularly mysterious—more as if he'd rather think about the here and now than his own past.

You'll probably never need to know, she thought. Face it, nothing's ever going to happen with Fred. He's a lonely man, and you keep running into murders. That's all. If you got serious about him, there would be more important things to ask him about his past. Catherine cracked once that Fred's wife had rocks in her head. What if Linda Lundquist played around? How do you rule out AIDS? And then there's all the emotional baggage people our age bring with them. What about Catherine herself? Has there been anyone else? He's been divorced for some time.

How do people find each other these days? Everything was so simple when Ken and I met at Oberlin. We kind of grew up together. But it's so complicated now, even for kids like Andrew and Rebecca.

Joan shivered in the heat. Her daughter Rebecca, only two years older than Andrew, was working out her life in New

York City. She'd come for a family visit just over a year ago, when she'd entered an original quilt in Oliver's annual spring quilt show. These days, in addition to holding down a day job at the bank, she was marketing her own unique designs. So far, at least, she was surviving, and loving it. Joan had learned to respect her daughter's need for distance, and they had begun to be adult friends after a period of tense separation.

Engines coming to life around her jerked her back. Joan started her car, pulled out in the wake of the Lincoln, and was startled when the procession turned, not in the familiar direction of the old cemetery near the edge of town, but out into the country, where it quickly picked up speed.

How could I not have asked where we were going? It might take hours. Why didn't Ellen bury him in town?

They'd passed a few miles of woods, corn, and soybeans when a line of dust rising from a hill off to the left told her that they had arrived, and Joan followed the Lincoln onto a gravel road leading up to a little redbrick church. She parked on the grass beside the church and walked with the others into the small cemetery beyond it, past old, tilted limestone and marble tombstones with illegible lettering. On several Joan could just make out the name Putnam. More Putnams were among the limestone angels and limestone tree stumps wound with limestone ivy, and then they came to more recent stones, mostly pink and grey granite, with sharp edges to their names and dates. The granite stones were plain shapes, but many were carved with curlicues and flowers, crosses, open Bibles, and praying hands. Here and there, a headstone rose out of a yucca or peony bush. Many more boasted plastic bouquets or sun-faded flags stuck into the ground.

There was no stone at the head of the open grave around which about fifty people had gathered, only masses of flowers from the church. The Snarrs had already poised the casket above the empty hole, and the family and pallbearers were seated in folding chairs, shaded by a tent. Joan stood in the hot sun at the back of the group of mourners and wished the maples and redbuds that edged the cemetery could move a little closer.

The service was mercifully brief. The minister's unamplified voice murmured words too soft for her to hear. When the others bowed their heads she prayed a little prayer of her own for David's family. In the silence she heard muffled sobs near her.

Maude Kelly? she wondered. But when she looked, it was Liz MacDonald who stood alone, her shoulders heaving.

Should I go to her? I hardly know her.

While Joan hesitated, Liz solved her dilemma by recognizing her.

"Oh, Joan," she wailed softly, and stumbled toward her across the uneven ground, her arms wide.

Joan hugged her.

"It's too late," Liz wailed.

"Too late?"

"I tried, but I couldn't help loving him...and now he'll never know." She broke down again.

Holding Liz while she sobbed, Joan was sure David must have suspected. What can I say to her? she thought. But no wise, comforting words came. The people were leaving now, but no one seemed to be paying much attention to two women hugging after a funeral.

Poor Liz, Joan thought. You sang Saturday night as if nothing were wrong. I didn't even wonder how you must be feeling. And I thought nothing could be harder than singing love songs with David when you knew you couldn't have him.

Finally, Liz pulled back. She fumbled in her handbag, wiped her eyes with a damp handkerchief, and blew her nose.

"Thank you, Joan. I'll be all right now."

"You're sure?"

Liz nodded.

"You've helped me so much," she said.

I never did say anything, Joan thought. Probably just as well. She watched Liz go. By now the family and most of the others had left. Her low heels sank into the lumpy ground; this little country cemetery didn't run to sidewalks. But it was a peaceful place, and a little breeze had finally kicked up. She no longer felt any great desire to return to work—the center would be closed by the time she got back anyway.

"You decide to stay all day?" Fred had come up behind her.

She smiled at him. "It crossed my mind. Did you learn anything?"

"No. But you never know."

"I think I did."

"Oh? What did you learn?" He smiled that quirky smile down at her.

Willing herself not to go weak in the knees, Joan stuck to the topic. "Did you see Liz MacDonald?"

"Was that who she was?"

"Yes. Fred, that woman had nothing to do with David's death."

"Because she was weeping? Plenty of killers feel remorse, or fake it."

"Not because she was weeping, because of *why* she was weeping. She said, 'I couldn't help loving him...and now he'll never know.' I can't believe she would have killed him. She still had hopes."

"You may be right."

"I'm sure I'm right."

TWENTY-THREE

The flowers that bloom in the spring,
  Tra la.

— NANKI-POO, *The Mikado*

THAT EVENING at supper Joan told Andrew what had happened at the cemetery. "I don't want it to be anyone I know, Andrew. At least now I'm sure it's not my doctor's nurse."

"How about the doctor?" He reached for another ear of bicolor sweet corn one of the old gardeners had brought to share at the center, and slathered butter on it.

"I don't know, and that's the truth. I just hate it, Andrew. I hate not knowing something this important about the people I need to trust."

Andrew nodded as he worked his way down the rows of kernels. It does help to have a good listener, Joan thought. No wonder Liz didn't need me to say anything. And then she remembered what Andrew had done today.

"Andrew, how could I forget? I saw you and Henry at the funeral. Did you take him?" He ducked his head and half-smiled, the way he'd always done when he was embarrassed, but she went on. "I'm so proud of you."

"Aw, Mom. Henry couldn't get there by himself."

"I know. But you thought of him, and you did something about it." Andrew was really squirming now. She didn't want to spoil it for him. "How is he doing?" She started down a sweet, bicolor row of her own, minus the butter.

"Much better. He says they're going to send him home before long. He'll have someone there to help him, and he'll get physical therapy every day. He really wants to come home."

"I can imagine. It's going to break his heart to see his garden, though." Henry had brought some of his favorite roses from his old house. And the new hybrids he'd been developing in his tiny greenhouse were sure to be dead, if they were even there—the greenhouse itself had been shattered by the tornado.

"He already knows. He saw it after the tornado, remember? Mom, couldn't we do something about that?"

"Like what?" Joan knew her ignorance about roses.

"I don't know. Plant something over there? Move some of the stuff out of our backyard, maybe?"

"We could, couldn't we?" It was, after all, what she had been thinking only yesterday. "It's pretty hard to kill an iris. Or a day lily. Or lilies of the valley, for that matter. They're not roses, but they smell wonderful for as long as they last. At least he'd have something next spring."

"We could move some right now," he said. "It'll be light for a while yet." Yesterday she'd been planning to wait for rain, but Andrew's enthusiasm was worth a lot.

They left the dishes to soak, and Joan changed into shorts, a T-shirt, and sneakers. Half an hour later she was dripping with sweat, but they had wrestled several dozen lilies and irises out of the almost rock-hard ground and dug a wheelbarrowful of compost out of the heap she'd been building casually from grass clippings, autumn leaves, and vegetable trimmings.

"I can't believe we're taking compost to Henry's," she told Andrew. "He's worked so much stuff into his ground already—digging there is going to be a snap compared to digging in ours. And these plants don't even need rich soil."

"So why are we?" He dumped another shovelful into the barrow and pulled up the bottom of his T-shirt to wipe his streaming face. Feeling a little too public to imitate him, even in her own backyard, Joan settled for a sleeve.

"Foolish pride, I guess."

But when they crossed into Henry's yard, she could see that their barrowful was a scant beginning, and sent Andrew back home to dig more compost. David's backhoe had moved Henry's topsoil away from the house, and the resulting mounds had baked as hard in places as the dirt from which they had taken the plants. Turning over several shovelfuls, though, she found some crumbly soil. It was going to be possible after all.

She peered into the gaping hole by the house. They'd have to fill it up with the hard stuff from those mounds, no easy job.

Wish I'd looked at the size of this mess before we dug the plants, she thought grimly.

"What do you think you're doing here?" a man's voice growled behind her, and she jumped.

"Oh!" She turned to see Virgil Shoals, in overalls and a painter's cap. "You startled me." Her heart was pounding.

His voice softened. "Sorry. I didn't recognize you." He took off his cap. "Out of place like that." It still felt like a challenge, though not so threatening.

"I'm about to transplant some things from our yard for Henry." She waved at them. "I hated for him to see it like this when he comes home, even though he's already seen it, of course." Her heartbeat had slowed, but she knew she was babbling. "This sure is some hole." She peered in it again.

"First time you've noticed?" He sounded as if he thought she should have been keeping tabs on Henry's house and yard. Irritation won out over startle.

"I had more than enough to be concerned with at my own house." It came out sharper than she intended.

"Uh-huh." He sounded conciliatory, not sarcastic. "Zach ever going to get done over there?"

"I hope so," she said fervently, her irritation fading. "I'll be glad to have my front door back. I guess you'll be glad to get him back."

"I guess so," he said. "I'd better go. See you Friday."

"Friday?" She drew a blank.

"At *Ruddigore*."

"Of course." I must still be rattled, after all.

"Look, why don't you just leave this mess? I can take care of it in the morning. I'm coming past here anyway."

"You don't have to do that. My son is helping me." She waved at Andrew, digging in her compost heap. I can't wait, she thought. These plants won't last that long, but it was nice of him to offer. "But thanks."

"Don't mention it. You have a good evening, now." He pulled his hat back on, walked out to the street, and climbed into a blue panel truck with Shoals Construction lettered on the side. Joan waved at him and went back to her own yard. She wasn't going to attempt this next bit without Andrew's help.

"Who was that?" he asked, continuing to dig in the compost.

"Zach's boss, Virgil Shoals."

"He getting on your case about Zach?"

"Not really. Virgil's the man who had Zach boarding up Henry's after the tornado. He offered to fill in the hole for us tomorrow morning."

"Good." Andrew wiped his face again. "I wasn't looking forward to that."

"Andrew, the plants we took over there would die by then. They're already too dry."

"Oh." He didn't say another word, but picked up his shovel.

They hauled several more loads of compost over to Henry's

and then tackled the mounds. By the time they filled the hole, evened out the ground, raked in their compost, and planted all the flowers-to-be, it was getting dark. They were both covered with dirt, and Joan's lower back was throbbing along with the ankle that hadn't bothered her for days. She sent Andrew home again, this time to stretch the hose across from their house—she had no idea where to look for Henry's, or whether it had been blown away. You've been a big help, she thought, watching Andrew.

"Turn it on so I can soak them," she called over to him.

"Thanks, Mom. You've been a big help." She looked at him—was he pulling her leg?

The expression on his face was guileless. He means it, she thought. This whole project was his idea. I'm just the assistant.

"You're welcome." Don't embarrass him again. "And so's Henry."

To ease her back, Joan sat on the steps of the little side porch near the front of Henry's house. When she saw how fast the water soaked in around the plants, she decided to saturate the ground enough to leave good-sized puddles around them. Otherwise, another day as hot as today would dry them out in no time.

The spray from the hose would eventually tire her thumb, she knew, but when she considered how her back and legs felt, it was easier to do it the simple way than to hunt up the nozzle Andrew hadn't thought to bring.

He'd disappeared around back, where she could hear him tossing pieces of glass into Henry's old metal trash can. He must be cleaning up the last scraps of the greenhouse, she thought, amazed. Was this the same boy she'd spent years trying to persuade to pick up his own room?

After a while the cicadas began, or were they tree frogs? Combined with the spray, the sound made her eyelids droop. It was joined by voices, faint at first and then gradually louder, coming toward her from the direction of the park and preceded by a wave of barking from neighborhood dogs. They usually save that for the mailman, she thought, or other dogs. Some-one must have waited for the air to cool to walk the dog.

But when they reached Henry's place, the voices seemed to be coming up his front sidewalk toward the house. Then Andrew was beside her.

"Hear that?" he said. "That's Henry's dog!"

Swinging around to look, she accidentally squirted him. He yelped, but waved off her apology and ran toward the voices.

Probably feels good, she thought. She dipped her face into the cool stream and ran water over her hands and arms. Refreshed, she was wiping her hands on the seat of her shorts when she heard her name.

"Joan, what are you doing over here?" Ellen Putnam, look-ing more comfortable now in cutoffs than in the suit she'd worn to the funeral, walked toward her with Laura, Andrew, and Henry's old dog.

"A little watering. Pull up a step." She aimed the hose back at the flower bed, and was glad when Ellen sat down beside her. "We transplanted a few things from our yard. My son heard that Henry might be coming home before long."

"It's very kind of you, though I think it will be some time. That's why we came, to check the house and see what needed doing."

"It was Andrew's idea. He and Henry are buddies." Joan looked at him, squatting a few feet away with the dog and Laura, who was already in animated conversation—with An-drew or the dog, she couldn't tell which. "I think that's why he walked the dog."

"That old mutt. He smells, and he can hardly walk, but he's been wonderful for Laura, especially since..." She stopped, her eyes filling.

"She looks good. How are you holding up?" Joan gave her time to look away.

"Better. The funeral was today."

"Yes. We were there."

"I'm sorry, I didn't see you."

"Of course not. It was a lovely service, Ellen."

"I'm glad it's over. Nothing can bring David back, but I was dreading that."

"Yes." They sat in silence for a few moments.

"We had family over at the house until just a little while ago—food, and all that—but they finally left. Most of them live nearby, so it's not as if I had to put them up. And I told them I didn't want anyone to stay with us. I had to get out. The dog's an excuse, really."

Joan nodded.

"It's getting late. I'd better tear Laura away from your son and go in there. I won't try to do anything for a while, but I need to know. We're all the family Henry has now."

"She'll be all right out here, Ellen, unless she'd rather stick close to you. I'll keep an eye on her."

"Thanks. I won't be long." Ellen spoke to Laura and Andrew and waved to Joan before letting herself in through Henry's back door.

The dog and Andrew kept Laura occupied. The soil was certainly wet around the irises, but the water was still soaking in amazingly fast. A little more won't hurt, Joan thought. And I'm not about to go back home to turn the water off. This is the child who escaped from her parents during a tornado warning. I'm not going to turn my back on her until I see her mother again.

A few minutes later, Ellen ran out the door yelling, "Joan, turn off the water! It's leaking into Henry's basement!"

Joan immediately turned the water away from the house, and Andrew ran back home to shut the faucet off.

"That tornado did more damage than we thought," Ellen said more calmly. "There's water all over the floor."

"I'm so sorry," Joan said. "It never occurred to me that I could be causing a flood."

"Why would it? This is no worse than a rainstorm, after all."

"Maybe I should have sloped the dirt away from the house. I don't remember how it used to be."

"Joan, a little dirt can't possibly make that much difference."

"You'd be surprised."

"I was." Suddenly Ellen started to laugh. "You should have seen me down there when I first realized my feet were wet!" Sitting on the step, she took off her sneakers and turned them upside down. No water poured out, but they were sodden. Then she pulled off her socks and wrung them out. This time, a thin stream wet the dust.

"Careful," Joan warned her. "There are still bits of glass in the dirt. In the grass, too."

"Right. I haven't let the children go barefoot once since the storm." Ellen stuffed the wet socks into a back pocket and forced her feet into the sneakers. "Uncle Henry's house still needs some major repairs. But right now I'd better get Laura and the pooch home and to bed before we all collapse."

Joan watched them go. Ellen could be a real friend, she thought. It's been a long time since I had a woman friend who lived nearby.

TWENTY-FOUR

Sad is that woman's lot who, year by year,
Sees, one by one, her beauties disappear.

—JANE, *Patience*

TUESDAY dawned clear and sunny, another hot one in the making. Only a few puffy clouds hinted at the distant possibility of rain. Joan was out on the almost-finished porch drinking a cup of morning coffee with Zach when Virgil's truck pulled up to Henry's house. Two young men carrying long-handled shovels hopped out of the back.

"Oh, no," Joan said. "He came back to fill in that hole David left, but we already did."

"I expect he'll notice," Zach said with a grin. He picked up a plane and began shaving long curls off the new porch railings. "Virgil's been after me to work overtime for him while I'm finishing up here. Least I can do is look busy."

Joan left their cups in the kitchen sink and collected her shoulder bag from the closet doorknob. Waving to Zach, she set off down the sidewalk. Virgil came around from behind Henry's house and met her.

"I told you you didn't have to worry about that hole," he said. "I told you I'd take care of it."

"I know you did, but it's been so hot, and I'd already dug my plants. I was afraid they'd die."

"How'd you manage it?" The smile on his face was

friendly enough, but behind it she thought she sensed the kind of male superiority that Fred never laid on her. Well, almost never. I'm not being fair, she thought. The man asked a civil question.

"Fine, thanks," she said. Unless you count the muscles that hurt with every move I make. She shrugged. "Once you're hot and dirty, what's a little more dirt?" I'm no helpless female, even if I was glad Andrew was there.

She walked on and was about to enter the park when Virgil drove up and tooted at her. Now what? she wondered.

"Need a lift?" he called out.

"No, thanks. I always walk to work."

He waved, and the truck veered off to the left. Only foot traffic could go through the park—that was part of why it appealed to her even now, with so many trees down. Just past the creek it occurred to her that she probably should have mentioned the leak in Henry's basement wall.

It's all right, she thought. Ellen will tell him, or whoever ends up doing the repairs.

She wondered suddenly whether the faulty wall could have had anything to do with what happened to Henry. She relegated it to the back of her mind until midmorning, when she saw Charlie Nikirk, a retired carpenter, arrive for a rehearsal of the center's barbershop quartet. He was early—the quartet wasn't due for half an hour yet.

"Got a minute, Charlie?" she asked him.

"Oh, sure. Time's what I've got too much of these days." There was a bitter edge to his voice. So far, at least, Charlie and retirement were a poor match. Joan thought his failing vision and gnarled joints had probably forced it on him, though he'd never said much, and she hadn't wanted to pry.

"I want to pick your brain."

"Such as it is." This time a half-smile softened his words.

"About building."

"That's different." Charlie eased himself down onto a chair, and his smile broadened. "Shoot." Joan sat down, too.

"A specific building, actually, Henry Putnam's house."

"What about it?" Charlie and Henry were buddies. Another reason he might be feeling bitter.

"Well, I was watering some flowers over there last night, and it seems I watered his basement, too. There's a crack in the wall."

"Uh-huh."

"I just wondered, could that have anything to do with why Henry got hurt?"

"Henry? Naw, a leak in the basement isn't gonna make the floor collapse. Not unless it was so bad it made the whole house collapse. Anyhow, didn't a tree fall on that house?"

"That's right. A big old silver maple."

"Well, there you go."

"How would a tree do that much damage?" She was skeptical.

"Oh, I don't know. Maybe if it hit something that was nailed in a half—" He caught himself. "In a slipshod sort of way. Or maybe if something was measured wrong. People get in a hurry. They don't slow down and do it right."

Joan thought suddenly of Tony Ucello's experiment. Was that what had happened there? Was Professor Ucello more slipshod than dishonest? Or was there all that much difference, when it came right down to it? But Charlie was talking about Henry's house.

"You mean it could be the carpenters' fault?" she asked.

"It could. There are men I wouldn't let touch my house."

"I'm lucky to have a good one."

"You building on?"

"Just a new porch. The tornado blew mine off."

"Seems like anybody who knows one end of a hammer from another is working this summer, and some who don't." Charlie's rheumy eyes twinkled, and Joan rose to the bait.

"Zach's not like that."

"Zach Yoder? Young feller works for Virgil Shoals?"

"That's the one. You know him?"

"Knew his father, and his grandfather before him. Couple of stubborn old Amishmen."

"Were they carpenters, too?"

"You could say that. They could frame you a good house, but you wouldn't want them to finish it."

"Why not?" She pictured Zach as she had left him, patiently smoothing her railing.

"You hear about how the Amish are craftsmen—how their quality work is their reward, and all that—well, I've worked with them, and I'm here to tell you that's a line of bull. They work cheap, all right, but they're primitive." She'd never heard Charlie talk so much at one time. His vehemence made her wonder whether he had lost out on jobs to Amish carpenters willing to work for less.

"David Putnam recommended Zach," she said quietly, and David would have known. He was a carpenter, too, she thought, but she didn't say so. Somehow she doubted that Charlie would consider him anything but a rank amateur.

"Maybe so. He got out, of course."

"He what?" What a thing to say about a murder victim.

"He broke away from the Amish."

Oh.

"Married a Jordan, didn't he? Ask Annie. She'll know."

Joan didn't doubt it.

The rest of the barbershop quartet arrived then, and the four of them greeted each other with cheerful insults. Watching Charlie among them, Joan was sure that he missed the company of other men as much as he missed the work itself. She could picture him swapping stories on the liars' bench in front of the hardware store before long.

Benches. Now there's a thought. I wonder whether Charlie would be up to making us some benches for the sidewalk out in front of the center. With the shade from the tree plot, it's pleasant enough to sit out there much of the year. I'd better make sure the board of directors would fund it before I ask him. Maybe he could even teach some of the other men. They make jokes about the women and their quilting bees, but I'll bet they'd love working together on a project like that. That ought to convince the board, even if they don't think benches are essential in and of themselves.

"Cat got your tongue?"

Joan jumped. It was Annie Jordan, who had sat down in Charlie's place with her knitting. Today she was clicking around a sock on four needles.

"Hello, Annie. I was thinking."

"I noticed. You didn't answer the first two times I spoke to you."

"I'm sorry. Funny thing, Charlie Nikirk just said I should ask you something. Now what was it?" Not benches.

Annie shook her head. "You're gettin' old, Joanie."

"I'm afraid so." Times like these, I get an inkling of how it must feel to have Alzheimer's. "Oh, I know. He was talking about Zach Yoder's wife. He thought she was a Jordan, and said I should ask you."

"Susie Yoder? Her mother was a Jordan. Susie's my second cousin twice removed."

Joan let it go. Genealogical terminology mystified her. "So you don't know her very well?"

"I know her. You've probably seen her yourself. She works right down the street from here, at Esther's."

"Esther Ooley's?" Much farther from the plain Amish people than Esther's bridal shop would be hard to imagine. But then, it was Zach who had grown up among them, not his wife.

"Sure. She does alterations and fancy embroidery, too, when it's called for. And sometimes Esther lets her dress the window."

When she passed Bridal Delights at lunchtime, Joan wondered which of them had dressed it today. Instead of the usual jumble of formal wear and lingerie, the window was dominated by a full-length ruby-red nightgown, cut to the waist from above and slit almost as far up from below, and displayed against a white satin drapery. The matching negligee lay crumpled elegantly on the white satin floor, as if it had been discarded in a moment of passion. On an impulse, she went in.

"May I help you?" Esther came toward the front of the small shop, which had several fragile-looking chairs covered in white velvet, and only a few dresses on display. No wedding gowns. It was plain that Esther would keep yours secret from the world until the moment you walked down the aisle.

"Oh, I'm just looking."

"Something for yourself?" Esther raised her carefully penciled eyebrows. The light in the shop was kinder to her face than the light in the theater had been, but she was still no ingenue.

Joan's eye fell on a tray of embroidered handkerchiefs.

"Actually, I was thinking of a small gift for an old friend. These handkerchiefs are lovely."

"They are, aren't they?" Esther smiled warmly and held one out to her. "Feel this fine Irish linen. They're all handmade, of course, and we'd be happy to add a monogram."

This would be just right for Margaret Duffy, Joan thought, stroking it. I'd love to give her something, after all she's done for me. A handkerchief shouldn't be so big as to embarrass her.

She took her time over the choice. Here in the shop, Esther displayed the patience and gracious manner that had been sadly missing during rehearsals. By the time Joan had decided on the subtle white-on-white design she liked best, she could only gulp and take out her charge card when Esther told her the price.

"That includes the monogram, of course?" she asked, as if she always paid twenty dollars for a handkerchief.

"Certainly, Mrs. Spencer," Esther said, glancing down at the card. "And we'll be happy to gift wrap it for you at no extra charge." She swiped the card through a slot and handed it back. "When would you like to pick it up?"

"I'm in no hurry. But I'll want to see the monogram before you wrap it."

"Of course. Let me show you how it will look. Susie," she called into the back room. "Bring us a sample, please."

Susie had clearly been close enough to hear what was needed. She came through the velvet curtains with a single white handkerchief, so beautifully embroidered that Joan would have thought the letters had come from the same hand that had worked the flowers and edging.

"I chose this style of lettering," Susie said. "But if you'd prefer something different…"

"No, that's just right," Joan said, and smiled at the fresh-faced beauty that put Esther's careful cosmetics in the shade. Zach had picked a winner. "Aren't you Zach Yoder's wife?"

Susie looked startled.

"Yes, I am," she said. "You know Zach?"

"I'm sorry. I should have introduced myself. I'm Joan Spencer. Zach's been putting the porch back on my house." Already Susie was nodding and smiling. "And I'm in the pit orchestra for *Ruddigore*."

"Oh, forevermore," Esther said. "I thought your face looked familiar. Wasn't that a terrible thing?"

Joan had no trouble following her. "Yes, it was. It was David Putnam who sent Zach to me," she told Susie. "I'm so grateful to them both."

"The judge was a good man," Susie said.

"Even though he wouldn't let Zach drive without the slow-moving vehicle emblem?" Joan asked. She'd been wondering about that.

Susie laughed. "That wasn't Zach. That was his grandfather. Even his dad gave in on that issue, though he's pretty strict. I guess he and Zach's brothers had to drive the old man around a lot after that. He would ride in their buggies, but he wouldn't put that devil's triangle, as he called it, on his own."

"I don't know much about Amish ways. What's it like, marrying into an Amish family?"

"Oh, I'm not in the family—Zach's out of it. It's hard on him, but he'd already made the break before I came along. He can't go home again. We take the children to visit my parents, and they love Zach, but it's not the same. I know he misses everyone. He still sees his brothers once in a while when they come to town, and he subscribes to the *Budget*, the Amish newspaper, just to hear about his family and old friends."

"You never told me all that!" Esther said.

"You never asked." Susie said it simply, with no defensive bristling. Nor did she play it for laughs. Joan liked her for it. It was time to leave them.

"I'd better get back to work," she said.

"We'll have the handkerchief for you in a day or two," Esther said. "And I'd be happy to give you a demonstration of our line of skin care products. They'll take ten years off your face."

If they took ten years off your face, Joan thought, it's amazing you still have a voice at your age. But she didn't say it. On her own turf, Esther was likable enough.

TWENTY-FIVE

You booby dense—
You oaf immense,
With no pretence
To common sense!
A stupid muff
Who's made of stuff
Not worth a puff
Of candle-snuff!

—CHORUS, *The Grand Duke*

BY THE END OF THE DAY, Joan had forgotten all about Virgil, and she was surprised to see his panel truck in front of her house when she was half a block from home, and when she came closer, to see him on her new porch chewing Zach out. She couldn't hear his words, but he waved a clipboard in Zach's face and punched at it with his forefinger. Zach just stood there, not arguing back. By the time she got within earshot, though, Virgil had stopped his harangue, and Zach was packing up his tools.

I don't want to know about this. Joan climbed Zach's steps, feeling them solid under her feet, and slid her hand along the satiny railing. He's been doing a beautiful job. David was right about him.

Still silent, but with a face like thunder, Zach tipped his cap when he passed her on the steps. She watched him go down the walk to his pickup.

"See you tomorrow, Zach," she called after him, hoping it was true. Zach didn't answer, but she took his raised hand to mean yes. If Virgil drives you away, she thought, I'll have something to say to Virgil.

"I'm sorry you had to hear that," Virgil said from the porch. He was smiling an apologetic sort of smile at her. It stopped short of his eyes.

"I didn't, actually." And with luck, I won't. "Isn't he doing a lovely job on the railings?" She stroked the one around the porch.

"Oh, sure." Virgil didn't even look. "Zach loves wood. That's why I keep him on." He fiddled with the clipboard, but made no move to leave.

He's going to tell me, she thought. She held onto the railing to stand up for Zach.

"I appreciate the care he takes," she said. "He's conscientious with every little step."

"Don't misunderstand me, I use Zach a lot—he was chief carpenter on your neighbor's house." Virgil pointed to Henry's. "Trouble is, he has no sense of urgency. He should have been done with your job last week. There are houses down and damaged all over town, and I'm bidding on the new nursing home. I've got work lined up for him like you wouldn't believe. But do you think I can get him to do it? He takes his sweet time, and nothing I can say or do will persuade him to work any faster." The words were pouring out of him now, and his knuckles had tightened on the clipboard. "He doesn't care how backed up I am. He works when he wants to and not a minute longer, no matter what I offer to pay. In fact, I can't pay too much, or he'll cut his hours. The man doesn't have a shred of ambition. You'd think with a family, he'd want to get ahead."

With Susie and their children to go home to, Joan thought

it was no wonder Zach didn't want to work any more than he had to for Virgil, who bad-mouthed him to his face and behind his back, too, though maybe Zach didn't know that part. She wondered about Virgil, who was sounding a little like Charlie Nikirk.

"So you're working long hours these days," she said.

"You better believe it."

"And your wife doesn't mind?"

"No time for a wife."

She let it hang in the silence, but he didn't seem to notice. "No family at all?" she asked finally.

"Just my mom." His face warmed to a real smile, and his startlingly blue eyes suddenly reminded her of Fred's, the way they squinched up at the corners. "Mom's a peach. She's getting on in years, but she's always there for me."

"Does she live here in Oliver?"

"No, I built her a little place down near Lake Monroe when she gave up the store."

"What kind of store?"

"Oh, you know—groceries, beer, bait, firewood."

"Your mother ran it?"

"Not alone. After Dad died, she couldn't understand why the profits went down. Mom had no head for business." He grinned a lopsided grin and shrugged one shoulder. "She always said she never wanted to shortchange anyone. Dad was a natural. He knew just how many logs to tie in a bundle with kindling for the city folks, and exactly how much he could get them to pay for it. He'd buy a rick of firewood for forty bucks and end up selling it for at least ten times that."

Unsure what he expected her to say to that, Joan thought she'd better stick to his mom. Lake Monroe was only a little more than half an hour to the south. With his workload, though, he might consider that an impossible distance.

"Do you see your mom often?" she asked.

He shrugged again. "I don't get down there as much as I'd

like. She's doing okay, though. We talk on the phone almost every week.''

"That's wonderful," she said, and meant it. Her daughter was so far away. Since her good visit last year Rebecca hadn't called even once a month. And she still hadn't given Joan her phone number.

"Well, you know how it is," he said. "She won't be around forever." Now those blue eyes focused on something in the distance, as if he were embarrassed to have revealed a weakness.

"Yes, I do know," she said quietly. He looked at her then, but she didn't feel like telling him about her own mother's death.

Eventually he said he'd have to let her go, although she was at home, and he was the one who left. Joan made friendly noises and watched him down the front walk before going into the house. It felt strange to be using the front door again, even if only temporarily—the porch would need painting when Zach was finished.

"Andrew?" she called, heading for the kitchen. "Anybody home?" No answer. She checked the refrigerator. Good. He hadn't been home to raid the leftover beef stew. Grateful for food that improved with age, she dumped it into a pot with a little water, gave it a quick stir, and turned the burner on low before going upstairs to change into jeans and a T-shirt.

When she came back down, Andrew was lifting the lid and sniffing.

"I didn't hear you come in," she said.

"I just got here. Smells great. When do we eat?"

"In a minute. Set the table, would you?" She made a green salad while he did, and soon they were sitting down together. She hadn't realized how tired she was, or how tense, but suddenly Andrew was looking at her expectantly. A dim echo registered—he'd been talking to her, and she hadn't heard a word.

"What did you say?" she asked him.

"You must be beat, Mom. That was twice."

"Sorry. Try me again."

"I've been thinking about that business with Professor Ucello's experiment."

"Uh-huh." She ladled stew onto her plate. "What about it?"

"I feel kind of caught in the middle."

"You?"

"Sure. Because of Steve. You know. You were here."

"I'm sure I was, but I'm too tired to remember."

"You will. Steve and I signed up as subjects in Ucello's experiments. He pays us out of his NSF grant."

"That's good." But the rest of it came back to her, even as she said it.

"Right. But Steve could see from the results Ucello published that he misrepresented at least some of last year's data—the data he collected from Steve. He left out the stuff that didn't fit his model."

"I remember now."

"Steve's not going to blow the whistle on him, because he needs the money. So do I, but I don't want to get it dishonestly."

"Uh-huh." Let him tell me, she thought.

"So I have this ethical dilemma, see? I don't know that he's going to mess with any of *my* data. I could wait and see. Or I could turn him in because I do know what he's already done. I can't prove it if Steve won't talk, but I know."

"Uh-huh."

"It's not as if it's hurting anyone—that's what Steve says, anyway. So is it right to hurt Steve by telling? He didn't do it; he's just an innocent bystander, but he depends on the money."

"Uh-huh."

"Only I keep thinking that Ucello's making his results look

more important than they are, and that's going to give him an unfair advantage compared with other people who want NSF grants.''

Andrew was getting there on his own. ''Trouble is, I can't think of any way to be fair to those people that won't hurt Steve.''

''Has Steve talked to Ucello?''

''Talked to him? Like threatened him? He wouldn't do that.''

''No,'' she said. ''But he could give Ucello a chance to fix it himself. He'd end up with egg on his face, but it wouldn't be as bad as if someone else turned him in, as you put it.'' That had been the essence of the honor code at Oberlin when she was a student. Mostly, of course, it had meant a great freedom compared to her public high school. Professors weren't allowed to proctor exams or even be in the room during them, and Joan could blow her nose during a test without worrying about being suspected of using a cheat sheet. To her relief, she'd finished four years of college without ever having to apply the code beyond writing and signing the pledge at the end of her blue books: ''I have neither given nor received aid on this examination.'' But she knew that it had conferred an obligation on her beyond her own personal honesty, and she'd often wondered whether she could have made herself turn in a fellow student to the student-run honor court, or even ask a cheating student to confess.

That was not far from the position Andrew was in right now, only without the support of the formal honor code. Even with it, she had dreaded such a confrontation. How much harder would it be for Andrew and Steve?

''I see what you mean,'' Andrew said. ''I don't know if Steve could do that, or if I could. I could talk to Steve, though. You think Professor Ucello might keep his grant if he did that?''

''I don't know,'' she said. That was the hard part, and there was no way to make it easy for him. Honesty at all costs could be painful, even if you excepted social fibs. Her dad had lived by that awkward honesty, as had Ken, and she had loved them both for it. Now here was Andrew, working his way through it. Look at the men in my life, she thought suddenly. No wonder I'm falling for a cop.

"Thanks, Mom," Andrew said. He took another bite of stew and chewed slowly. "Is this how you feel when you tell Fred Lundquist something that might get someone convicted of murder?"

"Yeah."

"How do you make yourself do it?"

"It's easier with murder, Andrew."

"Yeah, they couldn't say no one got hurt, could they?"

"No. But you don't want to make a mistake about it, either."

"If I knew anything that would help catch the person who killed David Putnam, you bet I'd tell. That little girl is so sad. She doesn't understand."

"Neither do I. He was a good man, Andrew. And from all I've seen, he was almost always a nice one. Good or otherwise, some people can be so annoying you can understand the urge to kill them. But no one has talked like that about David."

"Henry said he was full of beans when he was a little boy. But you're right. He made a point of saying that David's pranks were never malicious. He liked to make people laugh. That's what Henry said, anyway. I wish I'd known him better."

"Me, too." They fell silent, and she wondered what Andrew would end up doing about his ethical dilemma. It occurred to her that she ought to tell him what she'd already done. "Andrew, about Professor Ucello."

"Yeah?"

"I don't think it will come out in public unless it turns out he had something to do with David's murder, but I did tell Fred he fudged the data.''

"Why?'' Andrew didn't sound upset.

"I don't know. He was onstage at the right time, and Fred needs all the information he can get about those people. If you like, I can tell him your concern about Steve.''

"Yeah, I guess.''

He's already decided he's not going to keep the secret forever, she thought.

"I'll talk to Steve,'' he said. "And I think I'll have to talk to Ucello if he won't.''

TWENTY-SIX

*It isn't pleasant to have a fellow constantly
jumping down your throat—especially when he
always disagrees with you. It's just the sort of
thing I can't digest.*

—MERCURY, *Thespis*

THIS IS NO everyday offense, and this is no everyday victim.
We're talking about the cold-blooded murder of a judge, for
God's sake! You've wasted almost a week, and you don't have
so much as a suspect in custody. I don't want excuses, I want
results!'' Mayor Deckard's words carried clearly through the
walls of Captain Altschuler's office. Fred could picture the
cords standing out on the mayor's neck, and knew that he was
pounding Altschuler's desk during the last sentence. Warren
Altschuler, who never made excuses, would be coming to a
slow boil.

A man with common sense would find a good reason to
leave the building before the meeting broke up, Fred thought,
but he stayed put. When the mayor finally left, Altschuler was
going to need to yell at someone, too.

And I'm it, he thought gloomily. I caught this one fair and
square, and I blew it. I was so sure. I never considered the
possibility that the thing sticking out of his back wasn't the
murder weapon. I established where it came from and thought

I had a handle on what was going on. Instead, I let the real weapon get away with the man who used it.

Or woman, he reminded himself. It could be a member of the chorus. It could be almost anyone. The mayor's right. I've wasted most of a week, and we still don't have a solid lead. Everything peters out for lack of evidence, if it even makes sense in the first place.

Not for lack of trying, he knew. They had interviewed and reinterviewed all the witnesses and suspects, but learned little that hadn't been apparent almost from the beginning. The best he'd been able to do was eliminate a few possibles. Not good enough.

The mayor's voice had subsided and Fred was digging into the reports on his desk when he heard the knock. He steeled himself.

"Come in."

Altschuler left the door open. Great, Fred thought. Not only am I going to get a reaming out, but it's going to be public. Well, why not? What I just heard was public, too, whether you know it or not.

But Altschuler dropped his stocky body onto a straight chair and put his feet up on Fred's desk, a favorite posture of his. Fred leaned back against the wall with his hands behind his head, catching his toes under his desk as insurance against the day his old oak swivel chair would give up altogether. It creaked in protest.

"Politicians!" Altschuler said, and grimaced, as if he weren't already homely enough.

Fred came as close as he could in his precarious position to nodding.

"Deckard's been raking me over the coals about the Putnam thing. He seems to think we can pull a suspect out of a hat, just to make him look good. I wish."

Fred could scarcely believe his ears. After that session, Altschuler was going to be nice about it? He let the old swivel chair crash forward and leaned toward Altschuler before he could lose his nerve. "Warren, it's my fault."

"Oh?" Altschuler left his feet on the desk. It was like a yawn.

"I didn't search anyone the night of the murder."

"Search them for what?"

"That's what I thought," Fred said. "We had the knife in the body. But you know how that turned out. If I'd searched them all right then and there, we would have found the other weapon."

"Maybe. And maybe not. He could have hidden it anywhere and come back for it later."

"Maybe. Either way, we didn't find it because we didn't look."

"Nonsense," Altschuler said. He put his own feet down and stood up. "You wouldn't have known what you were looking for. The citizens would have objected, and you know you'd never get a warrant for a fishing expedition like that." Fred did know. Though maybe with a judge as the victim, another judge might have bent the rules. "I would have done the same in your shoes. Deckard has no idea what we're up against, and I'm not about to give him anything to whip us with. You keep on digging."

Fred had never appreciated his chief of detectives more. "Thanks, Warren," he said.

At the door, Altschuler turned back. "You be sure to tell me anything you come up with. First. I don't want to hear it from Deckard."

"Yessir."

Fred closed the door and paced back and forth in front of his desk. There was nothing to tell. He was beginning to think there never would be. But the mayor was right. This was the kind of case that wouldn't be forgotten, no matter what excitement took its place on the six o'clock news. Killing a judge was like killing a cop. And everyone had liked this particular judge.

Almost everyone, he reminded himself. Somebody disliked him enough to go to great pains to kill him in a way that precluded sudden passion or a momentary impulse. Or did it? If Chris Eads and Liz MacDonald had another fight just before the second act, did Chris grab the first sharp object that came to hand and eliminate his rival for her affection? Just because we didn't find the actual weapon doesn't mean he didn't. And just because Kleinholtz and Dolan didn't see anyone near Putnam after he was in his frame and before they started the scene doesn't mean no one did. Eads was in the next frame, or maybe he was only on the steps, about to go up. He could have waited for their backs to be turned, made his move, and run up his own steps before the curtain opened.

Oh, sure. And what did he do with the weapon while he was onstage? Some of the others had boots, but Eads was wearing low shoes and tight pants—no hiding place there. He could have left it in his own frame, though. On the floor, likely as not. It wouldn't show from a distance, and no one else looked at those frames until we searched after the murder. By then he'd have had plenty of time to move it.

It was just possible, he decided, but only because Eads had been so close to Putnam. The next ghost was Pete Wylie, whose only apparent motive was the opportunity to take over Putnam's role, and Fred couldn't make himself take that seriously as a reason to kill.

Besides, he thought, if it would be hard for Eads to zip over there without being noticed by Dolan and Kleinholtz, it would be that much harder for Wylie. Zach Yoder's another story. He had such a good excuse for being on another ghost's frame that they'd never have noticed him. But he had even less motive than Wylie.

Not even the court case had checked out, flimsy as it would have been as motive for a murder. Chuck Terry had reported

Zach's laughter when he heard that the police were checking on his grandfather's problems with the slow-moving vehicle emblem. Chuck said he sounded "really tickled," and Fred trusted Chuck's antennae.

Fred was so close to the door that another knock made him jump. He reached for the handle and opened it to find Ketcham looking as startled as he felt.

"You going out?" Ketcham backed away. "I can come back later."

"Come on in, Johnny." Fred walked back to the swivel chair. "I'm not going anywhere, in more ways than one. I've been trying to think. I'd give a lot to have that weapon."

"Yeah, well, we just got the report back from Doc Henshaw. No blood on those tools we sent over."

"You knew that."

Ketcham nodded, sat down, and took off his wire rims. "We've got the dagger," he said.

"Oh, sure."

"The killer had to get to it." He blew on the lenses and polished them with his handkerchief.

"They all passed it. One time or another."

"But some more than others. There was that sword fight. Maybe it was a cover. Either one of them could have bent down and picked up the dagger."

Ucello and Yoder. Hmmm.

"What do you have on Ucello?"

"Nothing much." Ketcham hooked the glasses over his ears. "He's a research type—psychology professor. Active in party politics. Some people think he'll run for office—council, maybe—in the next election. Some people would like to see him run against the mayor. They say he's keeping his hair cut shorter than he used to, and he's quit wearing an earring in one ear. He grew that beard for the part, but they expect him to shave it off next week. Seems Mrs. Ucello doesn't approve of whiskers, whether the voters would or not. I know her family wouldn't.''

"Her family?"

"The Coxes. Old Oliver family with money. They never expected him to amount to a hill of beans, but she fell for him in a big way when she was at Radcliffe and he was a graduate student at Harvard."

"How do you know all this?" Fred marveled at the wealth of hometown information Johnny Ketcham always brought to an investigation.

Ketcham shrugged. "Barbara was in my sister's class. Imagine, a family that dismisses a Harvard Ph.D. just because he's teaching here. They look down their noses at him and Oliver College both—that's why they sent their daughters to Radcliffe. And then Barbara came home with a man whose parents never even went to college. Hell, she might as well have married a cop." He didn't say "after all," but Fred wondered. He didn't ask.

"I heard an odd bit about him from Joan," he said, instead. "I'm wondering how it fits in."

Looking over his wire rims, Ketcham raised his eyebrows.

"Seems Ucello took a shortcut in a research paper he's just published, and Steve Dolan, who plays Robin Oakapple in *Ruddigore,* caught him out in what looks like a deliberate distortion of his results."

"Did he challenge him?" Ketcham asked.

"I don't think so. Dolan's one of his experimental subjects, and they're both dependent on grant money to fund the research. Joan says Dolan doesn't want to jeopardize that, so he's not telling. But her son is a subject in the same study, and she was there when Dolan read the paper and spotted it."

"I can hear the Coxes now if Barbara's husband gets involved in an academic scandal." Ketcham shook his head, but Fred thought his eyes sparkled.

"All very interesting," Fred said. "And if someone stabbed

Dolan in the back, we'd have to check into it. But I don't see any real connection to Putnam."

"Me either. Still, it's a crooked side of him I hadn't heard about—if it's deliberate. He needs all the publications he can get. But maybe he just goofed, Harvard Ph.D. or no Harvard Ph.D."

"Maybe. Keep your ears open there, though, would you, Johnny? I'm going back to Yoder and Eads."

FRED FOUND Chris Eads at home, splitting firewood. Long rows of beautifully stacked split wood stretched beside his small green trailer. In town, it would have been slum housing, but here, next to the state forest, it blended into the woods behind it. Eads stood between a large pile of freshly cut fireplace-length logs and a smaller heap of split ones. Sweat emphasized the well-defined muscles of his bare back. Blond as he was, he already had a good tan.

"Hot day for that kind of work," Fred said.

"If I wait for good weather, I'm already behind." Thwack. Eads tossed the split logs aside and stood another length on end. "Besides, I got better things to do in hunting season." Thwack.

"What kind of wood is that?" Fred wrinkled his nose. Eads laughed.

"This old piss oak?" Thwack. "Burns great, but most folks don't like the smell." He reached back for a red log. "You'd probably rather have sassafras." Thwack. He tossed one of the fragrant pieces to Fred, whose nose announced sweet kindergarten paste.

"I'll say. Why would anybody use the other stuff?"

"Sassafras is fine for starting your fire, but it burns too fast. You want to keep warm all day, you need a hardwood like this oak. It's not so bad when it dries out." Eads leaned on his ax and wiped his streaming forehead with a bandanna. "I could make you a good price on a couple of ricks."

"Nothing to burn it in. I'm not here about wood." Eads nodded and waited. "I'd like to run over Friday night one more time."

"I already told you. It was just the same as always. Nothing different until David keeled over."

"I know. But I'd appreciate it if you'd tell me one more time about what was the same."

Eads gave a last thwack and then started through the litany Fred had heard many times by now. He wasn't likely to announce himself as the murderer, but if he had done it, there was always the chance he might slip up somewhere, get some detail wrong this time. Even if he hadn't, he might add something so obvious no one had thought to mention it. Fred wasn't holding his breath, but it was all he had left to try.

He heard again about Biggy's firm discipline, about the swordfight between Ucello and Yoder, and about Putnam's last few words to Eads.

"After that, I just don't know much."

"Anyone come over to help you get settled in that frame?"

"Nope. Didn't need help."

Fred nudged him with another couple of questions, but Eads didn't add anything he hadn't heard before, much less anything inconsistent with his and everyone else's stories. He thanked him and headed for the car, waiting until Eads picked up the ax again before turning back. "I forgot to ask you about that fight you had with Liz MacDonald the night before Putnam was stabbed."

Eads swung and missed, burying his ax in the dirt. His tan face paled. "You leave her out of this! She don't have nothin' to do with it!"

"You know that for a fact?"

"I know Liz. She's a nurse, for God's sake!" As if that cleared her of suspicion.

"But you're not."

"What's that supposed to mean?" His voice rose.

"You were jealous of her and Putnam. You once threatened to kill him if he didn't stay away from her."

"We were married then." Low, through clenched teeth.

"And you wish you still were. She throw you over for him?" Fred asked conversationally, but watched him carefully—Eads was, after all, still holding the ax. He raised it high, only to swing on another log. Thwack.

"No. I did it to myself." Thwack. "I cheated on her, and she never gave me another chance." All the anger had drained out of his voice, and he looked at Fred with sorrowful eyes. "It like to killed me, though, watching her moon over him."

Driving back into town, Fred thought how different his own situation was. When Linda left him, she left town. He didn't have to watch her feel her way into relationships with other men. He supposed the divorce had gone as smoothly as such things ever did. At least there were no kids, and no alimony, not in Indiana. Just a hole in his life, a numbness, until Catherine's sparkle charmed him, before the jealous, backbiting ways he'd eventually backed away from surfaced. No wonder he was pussyfooting around Joan. With her warm smile, not that the rest of her was a punishment to look at, she made him feel safe, as if she cared for him the way he was. So far, though, for all he teased her and enjoyed her company, being with Joan was like being with a good friend. Maybe she didn't think of him as a man. No, he knew better. But maybe he ought to leave it at that. He never wanted to find himself in Chris Eads's shoes.

The man didn't seem murderous so much as miserable. And Fred still couldn't picture him stabbing someone in the back. Barring new evidence, he moved Eads far down on his list.

He pulled up in front of Joan's house now, knowing she wouldn't be home, but hoping to catch Yoder. He found him near the back, working on the posts that supported the long wraparound handrail. But Yoder, like Eads, added nothing to his earlier story. Fred leaned on the railing.

"Tell me about the sword fight. Who started it?"

"I don't know." Yoder kept his eyes on the post. "Nobody, really. We were both picking up our swords—I think we needed to do something like that. We were all kind of jittery."

"Someone must have been extra jittery. And after the fight? Where did Ucello go?"

"I saw him climb into his frame before I climbed into mine." Yoder looked up, his eyes intense. "He didn't do it, Lieutenant. He couldn't have."

"Were you watching him after you climbed into yours?"

"No, but he was at the far end from David. Don't you see, it's just not possible." Yoder's voice was earnest, and he tapped the railing with "just not possible."

"But he can't say the same for you."

"Well, no. I don't guess he can. I don't know who was watching me."

"We have a witness who says you were helping one of the others with his supports," Fred lied without blinking.

"Someone said that?" Yoder raised his eyebrows. "He must have meant during rehearsal."

"I don't think so."

"Then he's wrong. I forgot my tools here on Friday. But we didn't need them. Nobody had a problem."

Fred looked at him. "Tell me something, Mr. Yoder. Is it true that an Amishman never lifts his hand against another man?"

"People bait them a lot to find that out." Not a direct answer.

"And how do you respond?"

"That's a different question, Lieutenant."

"Sorry?"

"I grew up Amish, it's true, but I left. People don't bait me like that anymore." But you're doing it, his eyes accused.

"Ah. And if they did?"

"I would still find it hard."

"Hard to take, or hard to fight back?"

"Both."

TWENTY-SEVEN

A very great deal may be done in a day!

—LUDWIG, *The Grand Duke*

LIFE WENT ON. It wasn't that people stopped talking about the murder, but they hadn't found anything new to say about it for days. It began to fade into the background.

Thursday morning, Esther called the senior center with the message that Joan could pick up her purchase anytime.

Annie Jordan was the volunteer answering the phone, knitting between calls, while Joan sat across the desk from her and caught up on correspondence. No good fairy had yet donated a computer to the center, but she managed what they needed with an electric typewriter and an inexpensive desktop copier.

"I'll tell her," Annie said in a businesslike voice, and then at a level that could be heard clear across the activity room, "Joanie, your order's ready at Bridal Delights. You and Fred finally getting serious?" Warmth rushed to Joan's face, and she could feel all the eyes on her.

"Thank you, Annie," she said. "But it's not for me."

"Esther said it was monogrammed."

"That's right." She kept her face straight. "I finally found the perfect source of gifts for the board of directors." One of the men in the bridge group guffawed, the others chuckled, and she was off the hook.

She meant to pick up the handkerchief on her lunch hour, but when one of the noontime workers didn't arrive, the center was left shorthanded, and Joan ended up ladling apple dumplings for the senior nutrition project—what Annie called "eats for old folks." By afternoon, having made her own very tasty, if borderline nutritious lunch out of a glass of milk and an apple dumpling, she was charging through typing the last of the letters at a speed she couldn't maintain.

"Rats!" she said, and crumpled another letter with too many typos. "You'd think I could at least goof on the first line, instead of practically at the bottom of the page."

"Don't be so picky," Annie said. In between knitting and answering the phone, she was addressing the envelopes in a beautiful clear hand. "You'll never notice it on a galloping mule."

Joan threw the crumpled page into the wastebasket, rolled another sheet of letterhead into the old machine, and started hitting the keys harder than she needed to.

"Why don't you have a computer?" Charlie Nikirk stood in the open doorway of her tiny office.

"No money, I guess," she said.

"Time's money—for people with jobs, anyway."

"I don't think that means me, Charlie. They don't pay me by the hour."

"That's not what it means," he said. "If you didn't have to spend all this time retyping, you'd be doing something else worth a lot more."

"Tell it to the board. No, that's not fair. I haven't even asked the board for one."

"There you are. If you don't ask, the answer's no."

"I suppose. Trouble is, right now I don't have time. These letters need to go out this week, and it's already Thursday."

"What did I tell you? Time's money." He wandered off to the pool table, and Joan sat thinking.

Maybe that's why Professor Ucello ignored the data point

that didn't fit his theory. He was in a hurry to publish and thought he didn't have time to go back and find out what it meant. That wouldn't make what he did right, but it sure would make it easier to understand.

By the end of the day Joan had come close to the quota she'd set herself.

"I couldn't have done it without you," she told Annie. "Being able to ignore the phone made it possible, not to mention the envelopes."

Annie shrugged it off. "I think a lot of you, Joanie. I was glad to help."

"Well, you certainly did. I'm going to scoot out a little early, take these letters to the post office. Then I have to talk to a painter about my porch before supper. That'll have to be quick—I play *Ruddigore* again tonight." She'd been surprised when she first heard they planned a Thursday night performance, but Alex said they'd have out-of-towners to fill the seats, and now, with all the publicity from the murder, she was sure they would.

"Don't forget to stop at Esther's." Annie grinned at her.

"Oh, you! I really did order a nice gift from her, Annie. After today, I'd get you one, too, if she weren't so darned expensive."

"Uh-uh. Don't bring me anything from that place. I'd be embarrassed to go out in public in it, even if it didn't show."

Joan dropped the letters in the post office first and decided it would be no trouble to stop at Esther's before the painter arrived. If she was late, he could look at the porch without her—it was outside, after all.

The window display hadn't been changed. This time she heard a bell tinkle faintly somewhere in the back when she opened the door. Esther Ooley came toward her, hands out.

"Joan! So good to see you again." As if they were old friends. "Come see what Susie has done for you." She led Joan to the counter and brought out a flat white box with

Bridal Delights embossed on the lid. Opening the box, she unfolded the tissue and waited. It was like a curtain call.

"It's lovely," Joan said sincerely, glad to be able to applaud. "I'm sure Margaret will be pleased. Please tell Susie for me that I think she did a beautiful job."

Esther stroked the linen and folded the tissue back over it. "You did want it gift wrapped, didn't you?"

"Yes, please." While she watched Esther measure and cut the elegant paper, Joan wondered how much Fred had asked her. "I suppose you had to talk to the police after David Putnam was killed."

Esther's fingers stopped. "Wasn't it awful? Awful about the murder, of course, but awful for the rest of us, too. I was exhausted by the time I got home that night."

"Oh? That's right, June is your busy month." As if the rest of us weren't busy, Joan kept herself from saying out loud.

"Well, yes, and then the police kept coming back. Johnny Ketcham is an old friend. He knew better than to wonder about me. But that Lieutenant Lundquist just didn't let up. He wanted to know where we all were before the second act, and I had to tell him I was too nervous on opening night to pay attention to much of anybody else, except Duane Biggy, of course—we played the first scene together. The lieutenant came back later and asked me about the chorus, but honestly, I don't see how any of them could have done it. They all went in ahead of Duane and me, and he didn't let any of them come upstairs until the last possible minute. You heard how he was."

"Did you go up early?"

"No, of course not!" Her hands fluttered. "The lieutenant asked me that, too. How could he suspect me?"

"He has to suspect everyone."

"I suppose. Even if I had gone up, I don't know what I could have seen. There was always such a confusion while they were running back and forth between the props and those picture frames. And then so many of the ghosts look alike, I could mix them up. Do you think Duane cast blond men on purpose, for the family resemblance?''

"I doubt it. I think he was lucky to get that many good singers in a town this size.'' Joan looked at her watch.

"Oh, dear, I'm keeping you.'' Esther went back to wrapping. "I don't know why anyone would want to kill David. He was such a lovely man.''

"He was a judge. They do make enemies.''

"I guess.'' Esther curled narrow strips of white ribbon. "The only case I ever heard about was settled out of court.''

"Really?'' There had been one like that on her list, Joan remembered.

"My neighbors took Virgil Shoals to court when their new foundation turned out to be defective. They were fit to be tied.'' That was the one. "They said he didn't reinforce it with enough rebar, and they even did tests on the concrete and proved it wasn't up to specs. He blamed it on Sands Building Supplies, his subcontractor. They said it was his fault anyway. They settled for some huge payment, but they had to promise not to talk about it to anyone. They'd already talked to me, though, and I didn't promise. About the only thing I don't know is how much he paid them. They sold that house for pennies on the dollar and still had enough to build a new one twice as nice, I know that much.'' She tied the curly strips into a cascade that dwarfed the handkerchief box and tucked it into a plastic Bridal Delights bag with handles. "There you go. I hope she likes it.''

"Thank you,'' Joan said, and accepted the bag. "I know she will.''

Walking home, she mulled over what she had just heard. Had David known the outcome of that case? Even if he had, that wasn't a reason for Virgil to kill him—he chose Virgil to build the new addition on his house. He must have had some faith in him.

I don't, she thought. I'll bet he used the same crummy subcontractor for Henry's leaky basement. But that doesn't make him a killer.

Walter Rice was chatting with Zach when she got home. Two young blond ghosts, Joan thought, looking at them. Esther's right about that.

Walter handed her a written estimate that seemed reasonable. She accepted it at once—Zach had recommended him, and that was good enough for her.

"How much more time will you need?" she asked Zach.

"I'm about done. I'll just drop off my bill tomorrow. There's a couple places still need sanding, but Walt could do that. I'd like to do it myself, stretch this out another half-day. I've really enjoyed working for you. But Virgil's been pressuring me. He's got a ton of jobs lined up. He's a hard man to work for, but he'll keep me in groceries the rest of the year."

"Better you than me," Walt said, punching Zach lightly on the arm. Zach laughed and punched him back. Like a couple of kids, Joan thought.

"When can you start?"

"First thing in the morning, if you want. I'm just coming off another job."

"Good. I'll see you tomorrow. Bring your paint chips, and I'll choose a color." Knowing they all had to be fed, dressed, and ready to perform in less than two hours, Joan was glad to have it settled so quickly, and a little surprised when they went back to the conversation her arrival had interrupted.

"Anyhow, the cops came back and talked to me again," Walt said. He perched on her new railing while Zach put his tools away. "But when you didn't see a thing, you can't tell them much. And I didn't. I don't know who would kill Judge Putnam."

"Me either," Zach said.

"Now if someone knocked off old Virgil, I'd think it was

you, for sure." Walt laughed so hard at his own joke that he lost his balance on the railing, flailing at the air before falling forward onto the porch, instead of much farther backward onto the ground. Sprawling on the new boards, he sent Zach's toolbox skittering past Joan's feet and off the edge of the porch.

"Why'd you have to do that?" Zach yelled at Walt, and jumped after it. The tools had scattered.

"Sorry, old buddy," Walt said, scrambling to his feet. "I'll help."

"Get outta here," Zach said, and gave him a shove that looked less friendly than the light-hearted punches they'd been exchanging, but Walt ignored him and started picking up tools. Tight-lipped, Zach turned his back on him.

Joan went to help. Fortunately, most of the tools had landed on the front steps rather than disappearing into the grass. Sure that he would prefer to put his own things away, she passed them to Zach, who had already picked up his box. Like the box, most of his tools looked old. Many had handles of woods she couldn't name, and some looked hand carved. Had he done that himself?

"Look what this one did!" Walt called, and pulled a redhandled awl out of the grass, where it had stuck like a lawn dart. He handed it to Joan, who gave it to Zach, but not before seeing how different it looked from most of his tools. Newer and more commercial. An expression she couldn't name flickered across Zach's face, and then he turned his back to her and dropped it quickly into the box. A few minutes later she spotted a second awl at the bottom of the steps, a shorter one with a dark wooden handle, which clearly belonged with the others. She thought Zach stowed that one away even faster. By now, he and Walt were hurrying. Maybe they'd finally realized how tight the time was getting.

"That's it," Zach said to Joan. "See you tonight." He stashed the tools in his truck. Walt tipped his painter's cap to her and climbed into his own truck, and they were gone.

Joan walked slowly up Zach's steps and into her house. Why did he have two awls? And where did that red one come from? The police hadn't found an awl in David's toolbox, she remembered that. She hadn't seen David's tools, though. Were they a matched set? With red handles? Ellen would probably know, but she didn't want to alarm Ellen. The police would know. They had sent all David's tools to be tested for blood— or maybe not all, at that.

She hadn't seen any blood. This is silly, she thought. This isn't evidence. Why shouldn't Zach have two awls? They were right out in the open. If he were a murderer, wouldn't he hide the weapon, not just throw it in with his own tools?

What better place to hide it? her inner voice argued. He wouldn't know that anyone was even looking for it. The police haven't released that information. For all the killer knows, they still think the dagger killed David. He'd feel perfectly safe.

But not Zach! Zach wouldn't kill a fly. Well, yes, he would. But not a person! And even if he would, what possible reason would Zach have to kill David?

In the back of her mind she heard Andrew saying, "That little girl is so sad." All right, she had to call. She picked up the phone and dialed Fred's home number. No answer. After eight rings, she called the police station and asked for him.

"I'm sorry, ma'am, but he's not here. Could someone else help you?"

"No." She really didn't want to explain her feelings about Zach to the others.

"I can take a message."

"That's all right. It wasn't important."

Yes, it was. But there's no hurry. David's dead, and Zach's not running away. And I'd better move, or I'll be late.

TWENTY-EIGHT

Keep no one in unnecessary suspense.

—ROSE, READING ETIQUETTE BOOK,
Ruddigore

ANDREW hadn't come home yet, and so Joan ate a quick supper of cheese, crackers, and fruit and left him a note. He could fend for himself. After her years of single motherhood, his adult abilities were a continuing joy to her. Then she brushed her teeth, pulled on her orchestra black, brushed her hair into a twist up off her neck, and was ready to go. John would bring the viola music. All she had to do was arrive with her instrument.

The car coughed and sputtered when she first started it, but then quickly settled down. She'd made friends with a mechanic whose mother attended the adult day care at the Senior Citizens' Center. Between them, they'd been nursing the old car along, but she knew it wouldn't last forever.

She patted it on the dashboard. Just hang it there till we get Andrew through school. Scholarship or no scholarship, this is no time to have to buy a car.

She put the thought out of her mind, or as far back as she could push it. She managed. Except in emergencies, her frugal nature stuck to a budget without much trouble. Her health was good, and as Ken's widow she'd been able to continue his health insurance plan. Insurance would cover the tornado damage to her house, too. New strings for the viola had set her back sixty-five dollars this spring, though, even with Mr. Isaac's friendly discount. And her bow badly needed rehairing. Maybe after *Ruddigore* and before the fall season, she thought. If I could buy Margaret a handkerchief from Esther's, I can treat myself to a little horsehair.

Not that anyone but me will ever hear the difference, she thought as she rosined what was left of the hairs on her bow in the women's dressing room. It looks bad, but it can wait.

"You're looking awfully serious tonight." It was her old school friend Nancy Van Allen, who was putting her trombone together. "Something the matter?"

"Oh, no. I was just thinking about money."

"That'll do it to you. Though I can't complain. We're doing all right these days. I remember when I used to have to watch what I bought at the grocery store, and new clothes were out of the question. Good thing we were young and healthy."

"I'm okay." One out of two's not bad.

"Well, of course you are. It's the young people who have a rough time." Nancy turned her back and blew warm air into her horn.

You have no idea, Joan thought. True, she did worry how her own two would make it, especially because she could give them so little help. But many of the older people she knew were struggling, too, and her sample—those who came to the center—didn't include the ones who couldn't afford even the basic necessities. Sooner or later, though, if they had enough illness, a lot of people went through their savings long before they died. It scared her to think about it.

Joan carried her viola and bow to the pit, squeezed past the winds and cellos, and joined John Hocking, who set the music on their stand.

"You all right?" he asked.

"I'm fine." Two of them asking me that. I must look awful.

"That's good." His cheerful face beamed at her, and she felt her spirits lift again.

"Thanks, John."

"For what?"

"Being there."

"Any time, kid." He opened the music to the ghosts' chorus, "He yields!" and ran through the arpeggios in fast sixteenths. The notes were really only doubled eighths, which made them possible, but they did demand a person's full attention, and it was easy to get tangled in them unless they were familiar. Joining in, Joan was relieved to find her fingers remembering from the previous Saturday.

From the beginning, the performance went well. Joan thought it might be the best so far, although she missed Ellen's elegant singing. Esther's Rose Maybud was amazingly convincing and her tones were pure. Catherine's rhythm was steadier in the mad scene and she wowed the audience with her comic turns. Pete Wylie sang as if he'd been Sir Roderic all along. Even the diction of the chorus seemed to have improved. Had they been rehearsing? It didn't seem likely.

The audience responded wonderfully. Their hearty laughter at all the right places seemed to give new energy to all the performers. Down in the pit, Joan was free to laugh as the people in character onstage could not. Good thing, she thought, and chuckled at Steve Dolan's line, "So this is what it's like to embark upon a career of unlicensed pleasure!" when Liz MacDonald challenged him to a duel instead of meekly letting him carry her off. Tonight it would be hard not to laugh, even as many times as I've heard it.

When Pete came down from his picture frame and asked, "What is the matter? Have you carried her off?" and Steve answered, "I have—she is there—look at her—she terrifies me!" the audience roared again. It suddenly occurred to Joan that Gilbert and Sullivan's domineering women—Dame Hannah and Mad Margaret in *Ruddigore,* Katisha in *Mikado,* and the sisters, cousins, and aunts in *H.M.S. Pinafore*—had more than a little in common with Alex Campbell, who at the moment was watching benignly enough from her conductor's stool. The faint smile that crossed her lips from time to time seldom reached her eyes.

And then it was over. Somehow Joan wasn't as tired as she had been before, even though she hadn't practiced since last Saturday. The rest must have restored her.

"That went well," John said.

"I thought so, too. It was a great audience!"

The pit rumbled down, and she headed for the dressing room, but the chorus had beaten her to it. Joan didn't feel like pushing her way in. She could wait to get to her viola case. Leaning against the wall in the downstairs hall, she exchanged greetings with a few chorus members on their way out.

She congratulated Liz MacDonald. "That was really good tonight."

"Do you think so? I was having fun. On Saturday I could hardly stand it, but tonight I could hear the jokes again."

Liz is going to be all right, Joan thought. She saw Zach leaving the men's dressing room, close to the exit, and felt relieved not to have to speak to him.

I can't believe Zach would do it, she thought. But she couldn't ignore what she had seen. She no longer trusted him, it was that simple. She felt betrayed by him, not safe, as she always had before. That's not fair, she thought. I'm not giving him a chance. But her feelings wouldn't listen.

And now she saw Virgil coming down the hall toward the men's dressing room. He wasn't in costume—just jeans and a T-shirt—nothing to change out of, but the toilets were there, too. She knew suddenly that she had to talk to him. She waited outside the men's room door, trying to look natural, and waylaid him when he came out.

"Well, hello there," he said. "You going home?"

"When I can get to my instrument case. It's still pretty crowded in the women's dressing room."

"I'd offer to help, but not in there." He grinned at her.

"No." She smiled back. Now that she had him, she didn't know what to ask. "Virgil, you've known Zach for a while, haven't you?"

He pounced on it. "What's he done?"

"Done?"

"I meant to come over and check your porch for you. Just because he's slow doesn't mean he's always careful." His voice was so mournful and his eyes so sad that she had to believe him.

"It looks fine. Walter Rice is coming over tomorrow morning to start painting."

"Well, then, I'd better look at it first thing. Once it's covered up, you'll never be able to tell what's under there."

"Is that what happened over at Henry's?" His eyebrows rose. "Did Zach do something to that beam that made it fall on him? Is that what you were telling David about?"

"What I was...?"

"I overheard you two down here that night. I was mad at David for talking like that about Zach behind his back. I had no idea." He didn't deny it, and she rushed on. "But now...yesterday when he was packing up his things I saw something that's worrying me."

"What's that?"

She hesitated. She probably shouldn't talk about it except to Fred. "I'm sorry. I shouldn't even have mentioned it until I talk to the police tomorrow. I don't suppose they came back tonight."

"No. They finally left us alone."

"No wonder everyone sounded so good tonight. That has to have been a relief."

"I think you're right."

"Thanks, Virgil. And I'll take you up on tomorrow, if you

really mean it. The porch seems fine, but it won't hurt. I appreciate your taking the trouble.''

"Sure thing."

Joan found her case, made it out to the car, and drove home on automatic pilot.

Andrew looked up when she opened the back door and parked the viola on the floor beside it. He waved a slice of pizza in her direction.

"Try some, Mom, it's terrific."

"Whose is it?" She didn't see a box. He'd apparently warmed it on a cookie sheet. The oven was still putting out heat, the last thing they needed tonight.

"Mine."

"Thanks." She reached for a piece. "That's not what I mean."

"Yes, it is. I made it."

"From scratch?" She lowered the slice without tasting it.

"How about that? It's easy. I figured if pizza started life as poor man's food, I shouldn't have to fork over ten bucks. So I found a recipe and tried it. You had yeast and flour and mozzarella and tomato sauce. I put a few spices in the sauce and some vegetables on top, and I was in business. Turned out okay."

Amazing. Biting into the pizza in her hand, Joan was pleasantly surprised. Chewy crust, flavorful sauce, and plenty of cheese, mushrooms, green peppers, and broccoli florets. He was right, it was terrific pizza. Though why she should be surprised, she didn't know. Andrew hadn't had a cooking failure yet. Omelets, popovers, and now pizza. She wondered why he didn't do it more often, but it was good to know he could manage on his own.

Andrew had stopped chewing. She realized that he was waiting for her verdict.

"It's more than okay, Andrew. It's delicious."

He smiled and helped himself to another piece.

"Thanks. How was *Ruddigore*?"

"Better than last week. But I'm more tired than I thought." She had just about enough energy to chew. They sat in companionable silence for a little while. Then Andrew snapped his fingers.

"I forgot. Rebecca called. I told her where you were, so she said she'd call back later tonight."

"What's on her mind?"

"I don't know. She sounded all right."

"Good. I'd better get ready for bed. I have to go to work tomorrow morning. That's the trouble with a Thursday night performance. Of course, the rehearsals lasted even later, and they were on weeknights, too."

She dragged upstairs and changed into her coolest gown.

Why am I so tired? I felt fine at the end of the performance. But she knew. At the end of the performance she hadn't been thinking about anything else. Seeing Zach and then talking with Virgil had brought her worries down on her shoulders again.

The phone rang. After the usual preliminaries, she found herself telling Rebecca all about the murder. Almost all. Andrew, who had picked up the extension in the kitchen, added bits he knew. But she hesitated to tell Andrew about the awls before she told Fred.

"So what's wrong, Mom?" Rebecca didn't miss much. "Are you holding something back?"

"You always know, don't you? Yes, I am. And I'm going to keep it that way until tomorrow."

Now they both pounced on her.

"Look, you two. I saw something today that suggests who killed David. But there's nothing we can do about it tonight. I'll tell the police in the morning. Then I can tell you." And she wouldn't budge.

"Don't get in trouble, Mom," Rebecca said. "You don't owe the police anything. You take care of yourself first."

"I *am* taking care of myself. Telling Fred is the best thing to do about this."

"Well, if it's Fred." Rebecca had developed an amazing soft spot for him during her visit to Oliver. "He'll know what to do. I wouldn't trust those other bozos."

"I won't."

"Make her call him, Andrew."

"I'll call him, Rebecca," Joan said. "Don't fuss." Is this how they felt when I mother-henned them? Now the shoe's on the other foot, and it pinches.

"I'll call you back tomorrow night," Rebecca said.

"You do that. I'll be back late. We still have two more performances."

"That's okay. I'm a night owl."

"Good night, Rebecca. I love you."

"I love you, too. Be careful."

TWENTY-NINE

Life's perhaps the only riddle
That we shrink from giving up!

—QUINTETTE, *The Gondoliers*

IT FELT STRANGE on Friday morning not to hear hammering. Andrew would love the peace and quiet. Early-morning painting wouldn't disturb his summer sleeping habits as Zach's power saw had done. Today, though, Andrew had already left for the day—the signs of his breakfasting were unmistakable. Joan put his dishes to soak with her own and retied the bread wrapper he had folded over casually. The bread was still moist enough. Just as well he got up early. Ordinarily, she'd have left before he did and missed it. He hadn't mentioned any special plans for this morning, but he seldom did these days. The good part was that she no longer felt the need to hear them. It might be lonely when he left the nest completely, but she expected to have no trouble letting him go.

And maybe if I start doing it now, he won't have to carry breaking away to extremes, like Rebecca. Even last night she didn't leave her phone number. You'd think she'd trust me better by now. It's okay. If she needs that much distance, I won't take it from her. It's just funny that she has no hesitation in telling me how to live.

In the sunshine of morning, she smiled at the memory of Rebecca's long-distance hovering. Rebecca hadn't been wrong, though, about talking to Fred. Joan made another attempt. Again, his home number didn't answer, but he wasn't at the station. She didn't leave a message. She could try again from the center.

Neither Zach nor Walt had come by yet, which rather surprised her. She'd shared so many cups of breakfast coffee with Zach that she'd expected to see him early today. It didn't matter, really, when he showed up. He was only going to drop off his bill. She was just as glad not to have to face him. And Walt hadn't exactly specified a time. She wrote him a note asking him to bring his paint chips to her office and taped it to the front door.

No sign of Virgil, either. Well, he knew she wouldn't be home. Maybe he'd give her his verdict on Zach's work tonight, after the performance. Or maybe he forgot. It was a nice offer, but the porch looked and felt solid to her. She'd be surprised if he found any problems.

She ran upstairs one last time. Loving the feel of her bare feet on the floor during these hot days, she generally delayed putting on shoes as long as possible. Now she strapped on the sandals she'd been wearing the day of the tornado, slung her bag over her shoulder, and went out to face Friday.

Wispy white clouds in the brilliant blue sky offered contrast to the eye without threatening rain. The air felt dryer than it had for at least a week, and even though the sun was already beating down on her, she was comfortable in her cotton dress and sandals. She'd probably be dripping before she got to work, but it would be worth it to walk on a day this beautiful.

"Morning," she called to half a dozen neighbors reading their papers on their front porches before the heat would make them retreat into air conditioning. Not that they all had air conditioning to retreat into. Joan's wasn't the only house in the neighborhood that still relied on shade and open windows, but it was in the minority. The smaller the house, the more likely it was to have boxes protruding from windows. She thought there would soon be more. Now that the tornado had destroyed some of the biggest trees in the neighborhood, some people were going to have a hard time making it through July and August.

And crossing the park these days was more like walking through a farm field than a park. Looking into it now, Joan mourned the lost trees. Contributions were already being solicited for replacements to be planted in the fall. It would be twenty years before they'd produce much shade.

She started across the street, but jumped back onto the sidewalk when a panel truck came speeding toward her, its horn blaring. It pulled up beside her in a squeal of brakes, and she saw Shoals Construction on the side and Virgil himself in the driver's seat. What had gotten into him?

He leaned over and opened the passenger door.

"Get in," he said.

"What?" She stood there, not about to wreck her morning walk to ride with this cowboy.

"Lieutenant Lundquist sent me. It's your son. There's no time to talk. I'll tell you on the way."

"Andrew?" She ran to the truck. "What's the matter?" She climbed up, and Virgil pulled away from the curb almost before she could shut the door. She fastened the seat belt and shoulder harness. At the rate he was accelerating, she was going to need it.

"He's hurt," Virgil said. She opened her mouth, but nothing came out. "Out at the old quarry. He was swimming out there. Hit his head in a dive."

"Where is he? Where are you taking me? This isn't the way to the hospital."

"I'm taking you to the quarry. He didn't come up from that dive. I left before they found him."

"Dear God." Please, God, not Andrew. Let it be a mistake. Somebody else. Some other mother's son. She didn't want to wish it on anyone else, but she couldn't help it. "Are they sure it's Andrew?"

Virgil nodded somberly. "He was swimming with a buddy who saw what happened and ran for help."

"Why didn't someone call me?"

"You were already gone when they tried. Lundquist wouldn't leave the search. I told him I knew the route you took to work." He took a corner too fast, and she grabbed hold of the handgrip above the door.

She tried to think, but her mind wasn't working. Looking out the window, she thought she saw Zach Yoder driving by in the opposite direction. You're a little late, Zach, she thought. And then, oh, God, don't let *us* be too late. And oh, God, how could we not be?

"How far is it?" They were at the edge of town now. Virgil picked up speed again. He rounded a curve and flew down a hill. She hung on, physically and emotionally.

"Not far. Only a few miles."

"I used to think the quarries were all south of here."

"No, they're scattered all around. This whole area is full of stone of one kind or another. I get all the gravel for my concrete business from a gravel quarry north of town. There's lots of good limestone right under Oliver. Makes construction expensive. We're always having to blast out basements. We drill samples so we'll know what we're getting into, but the stone is unpredictable. Just when you think you're not going to have a problem, you run into a shelf of limestone right next to where you drilled."

If he was trying to distract her, it wasn't working. Who cares about basements? she wanted to yell at him. My son…if I still have a son… Tears filled her eyes. Her throat ached. How far did his friend have to run for help? He must have been under water a long time. Even if he lives, he'll be brain damaged. Unless maybe the water is cold enough. Quarries are so deep, it might be. But in this weather? Oh, Andrew, how could you? I *told* you never to swim in a quarry. You *knew* it was dangerous.

Stop it, Joan. This is doing you no good. She sat up straight. Virgil was still talking. She wanted to throttle him, but she needed him.

"Indiana limestone's wonderful building material, though," Virgil said. "Most folks think it's too expensive. In the long run, they'd save, but they don't think of the long run." He meant well, she knew.

"I saw limestone angels and tree stumps in the cemetery." She was squeezing the handgrip so hard her fingers were starting to go numb.

"Yeah. Old-time carvers trained the younger ones."

"Was your father one of them?" Dear God, now I'm asking polite questions. Virgil, never mind me. Just drive!

They careened around another curve.

"No, he always kept a store. So did his father. Grandpa had an old-fashioned general store, down in the Amish country. They'd act as if they were the only people who ever did a lick of work. Some of those old guys drove a hard bargain, but he never let them get the best of him."

No wonder Virgil felt that way about the Amish, if he heard that kind of thing from his grandfather.

"Look, we're almost there." He pointed to enormous chunks of dark gray limestone tilted at crazy angles along the side of the road. "This is the old part of the quarry. After a woman drowned in her car a few years back, they hauled those damaged quarry blocks over here so no one else would slide into the pit. In winter this road's really bad. There've been lots of accidents along here."

Joan could believe it, especially if people drove the way Virgil did. She held her breath more than once, but the last thing she wanted was for him to slow down. Her heart beat faster when he did exactly that and turned through wrought-iron gates into the quarry. They jounced and jolted along a deeply rutted, tree-lined gravel road. Straining to peer through the trees and underbrush, Joan kept expecting the flashing lights of police cruisers and an ambulance around every bend in the road.

At last she could see through the trees to sun reflecting off water. The place was deserted.

"They're gone!"

"They were here when I left," Virgil said. "Parked over there." He swung down out of the truck and pointed toward the edge of the pit in front of them, where stones jutting out over the water made an almost irresistible diving platform. "You can see the tire tracks where they left the road."

She got out and looked where he was pointing, but all she saw were trees and weeds and rocks and water. Then a truck roared up behind them, and she whirled to see Zach's pickup spew dried mud and gravel in their direction as it spun to a stop. What was Zach doing here? And why was he running toward her?

"Zach?"

"Joan! I've got to talk to you."

"Get back!" Virgil called to him. In Joan's ear he said softly, "I didn't want to tell you."

"Tell me what?"

"Your boy didn't dive in. He was pushed."

"Pushed! But who...?" Who would push Andrew into the pit, and why?

"You're looking at him, right there." Then louder, "Don't come any closer." This to Zach, who was already backing off. "That's right, leave her alone." For the first time Joan saw the shotgun he was aiming at Zach. "Nice and easy. You just keep going."

Zach climbed into his pickup.

"You're letting him go?" How could he?

"He won't get far. The police are watching for him." Virgil

kept pointing the gun while Zach drove off and lowered it only after the curving road took the pickup out of sight.

Joan's head was whirling, but one thing was clear. She had to find Andrew.

"Virgil, take me back to town!" she said. "Take me to the hospital!"

THIRTY

*Though but fifty-five, I am an old campaigner in
the battle-fields of Love; and, believe me, it is
better to be as you are, heart-free and happy, than
as I am—eternally racked with doubting agonies!*

—PHANTIS, *Utopia, Limited*

WHEN FRED woke up on Friday morning he could hardly drag
himself in to work. He stopped at Dan's Donuts on his way,
putting it off a few minutes more. Dan pumped him for information, but only half-heartedly, as if he no longer expected
Fred to know anything.

Just as well, Fred thought, since I don't. He sat at one of
Dan's tables to munch a sour-cream doughnut and drink coffee.

"So, Lieutenant," Dan said, as he filled Fred's cup for the
third time, "I hear you went out to visit my old buddy Chris
Eads."

"Where'd you hear that?"

"Oh, word gets around. You know how it is. A little bird
told me."

"We're talking to everyone." *Why am I even bothering to
answer?*

"Just routine, is that it?"

"That's it." *You're not going to get my goat. See me
smile?*

"Can I interest you in another doughnut?"

"Nope. I'd better go. Unless your little bird has told you something you think I ought to know."

"Not a chirp."

"That's the trouble with those birds. See you, Dan." He licked the last bit of glaze off his lips and walked glumly over to the station.

Today he didn't feel like running up the worn limestone steps. When the police dispatcher greeted him cheerfully, he almost bit her head off.

"Morning, Lieutenant. Your lady friend find you?"

"You want to translate that?" He glowered down at her.

"I didn't mean anything by it. We logged a couple of calls for you from a woman who didn't want to leave a message. One before I left yesterday evening, and one just a few minutes ago. I figured it was personal."

He headed down the hall without answering. He was in no mood to have civilians twit him about his personal life. As for the calls, he'd find out soon enough. Right now he was so down on himself, he didn't want to have to deal with any woman, not even Joan. Her very cheerfulness would be more than he could bear.

He was walking into his office when the phone rang. He sat down and took a deep breath before reaching for it.

"Lundquist," he growled. But it was a young man.

"Mr. Lundquist, this is Andrew Spencer."

"Hello, Andrew." He relaxed. "What can I do for you?"

"It's not me, it's my mom." Andrew's voice croaked, making him sound much younger than he was.

"What about her?"

"Zach Yoder just called and woke me up—I went back to bed after breakfast—and said he thinks she's been kidnapped or something."

"She's *what?*" Fred leaned into the phone.

"Zach saw her in Virgil Shoals's truck. Virgil was speeding, he said, and Mom looked really scared."

Fred leaned back. Probably a false alarm.

"You sure he wasn't just giving her a ride to work? Maybe she was worried she'd be late."

"No, Zach was calling from a place out on Quarry Road. He told me to call the police."

"Why didn't he call himself?" He was afraid he knew the answer already.

"He took out after them." Oh, great. "But he gave me a description of the truck." Fred grabbed a pencil and paper.

"Shoot."

"It's a blue Ford panel truck with Shoals Construction in white letters on both sides. He didn't get the license number. Please, can't we go make sure she's all right?"

"You sit tight, son. I'll see what I can find out and call you back."

"Okay." Andrew's voice sounded very small.

First check the obvious. Fred found the Oliver Senior Citizens' Center in the phone book.

"Mrs. Spencer, please."

"She hasn't come in yet this morning," said a pleasant older woman's voice. "Can someone else help you?"

"This is Lieutenant Lundquist, Oliver Police Department. When do you expect her?"

"Lieutenant, we don't know." Now the voice sounded concerned. "This isn't like her. She's never this late. We were about to call her house, in case she's sick."

"Don't bother. I'll call her."

"Thank you. Thank you very much. We don't want anything to happen to our Joanie." Aha. This was the woman with the topknot and the knitting who liked to tease Joan.

"No, ma'am. Are you all right over there?"

"Oh, yes. The day-care people opened the building, and the

rest of us can take care of things for one day. You tell her we'll be just fine."

"I'll do that."

Now he was worried. Annie—that was her name—was right. It wasn't like Joan. Did that mean Yoder had it right? He tried to remember the odd thing Joan had said about Yoder and Virgil Shoals. Putnam had bad-mouthed Yoder to Shoals, that was it. She knew them both, and as far as Fred knew, she had no reason not to trust Shoals. He wouldn't have to carry her off at gunpoint—just convince her she was urgently needed somewhere, or maybe threaten harm to Andrew if she didn't do what he said. That would get her. But why would he abduct her? It didn't make sense. Both men were on the spot when Putnam was killed, but that hardly suggested a reason to carry Joan off. Or make up a story like that.

He called her number.

"Hello." Andrew's voice was steadier.

"Fred Lundquist, Andrew. You mom didn't show up for work, so I'm going after her. If she comes home, you call the station again and ask someone to page me right away."

"Okay. But there's one more thing. I just remembered something she said last night."

"Yes?"

"Rebecca called, and Mom told her she saw something yesterday that made her think she knew who killed David Putnam. She was going to call you."

Damn! Fred thought.

"She tried. What else did she say?"

"We couldn't get it out of her. She wouldn't talk about it until she could tell you." So, maybe this abduction that looked more and more like the real thing tied in with the Putnam case.

"Thanks, son. Try not to worry."

Automatically, he filled Ketcham and Terry in.

"This could be the break we need," Ketcham said. But

looking at Fred's face, he subsided into silence and moved fast. They took a squad car for speed and turned on the lights and siren. Terry followed in another unit with Jill Root.

Flying out Quarry Road with Ketcham at the wheel, Fred had all too much time to imagine Joan in the hands of a killer. She'd be terrified at best, injured or dead at worst.

If I hadn't dawdled at the doughnut shop this morning, she would have reached me. Then she could have told this creep the police already knew whatever he was afraid she would tell us.

Fred scanned both sides of the road without success for the blue panel truck, but the closer they came to the quarry, the surer he was that it would be there. The abandoned quarry hole, filled with water that hid enormous, unusable quarry blocks, wrecked automobiles, refrigerators, and other large items that rural residents didn't want to pay a landfill fee to dump, was such a logical place to dispose of a body that he'd been half-expecting something like this ever since he first saw it. The junk and stones on the bottom would make dragging to find a corpse useless. And there were natural injuries every year or so. People insisted on diving into what looked like a beautiful rural pond, no matter how often you warned them they'd probably break their necks—or heads—on the invisible hazards below the water. A body that floated to the surface on its own would be ruled accidental death if it didn't have an obvious bullet hole or two in it, unless something made the coroner suspicious enough to order an autopsy and the autopsy proved that death occurred before it hit the water.

Something like cops looking for a body before it's even dead, he thought bitterly. And then hoped he was right about the before part. What was going on out there? Were they already too late?

Traffic was light. About a mile from the quarry, Fred spotted a pickup parked at a schoolbus turnaround across the road and a man standing beside it, waving both hands at them. He recognized Zach Yoder.

"There's Yoder!"

Ketcham pulled over, and their backup followed suit. When they jumped out, Yoder ran across the road. Terry and Root ran up to join them.

"I got your message," Fred said. "Where is she?"

"At the quarry." Yoder pointed a shaky finger down the road. "I followed them there. Virgil's got a shotgun. I saw her, but he wouldn't let me talk to her."

"Was she all right?"

"I think so. She looked scared."

"Was he threatening her?"

"I don't know. He wasn't touching her. I couldn't hear what he was saying to her. He was aiming at me, so I did what he said." He shrugged.

"How long ago was that?"

"Not long—I just got here."

"Did he say he was holding her hostage? Or what he wanted?"

"All he said was to get out."

"You think he's drunk or on drugs?" Terry asked.

"Not that I could tell."

"You have any idea why he's got her out there?" Ketcham asked.

Yoder just shook his head. "Virgil's got a temper, but I've never seen him do anything like this. He's come by while I was working at her house, but nothing ever happened. It doesn't make sense."

Not unless Joan would have told me she suspected him, if I hadn't been pigging out on doughnuts.

"You want me to go back with you?" Yoder was asking.

"No," four cops said at once.

"Call it in," Fred told Terry and Root. "And don't let

anyone spook him. Thank you, Mr. Yoder. We'll handle it from here.'' They left Yoder standing in their dust.

He heard Root's voice on the radio: "We have an abduction with a weapon involved at the old Beasley Quarry, on Quarry Road north of Oliver. Lieutenant Lundquist and Sergeant Ketcham enroute with Detective Terry and Officer Root. Request a signal one hundred. The lieutenant's handling this code two.''

The dispatcher relayed it. The signal killed all chatter and routine inquiries on the police radio frequency until the emergency was over, while alerting every police agency in the area to it, and the code warned them to use red lights only. No sirens.

If he kills her, I'll tear him limb from limb, Fred thought. No, if he kills her, I'll never forgive myself. I don't belong here. I know that. But nobody better stop me. He looked over at Ketcham's calm face, the sunshine glinting off his glasses as the road curved to the east again. You wouldn't even think of getting in my way, would you, Johnny?

THIRTY-ONE

Life is one closely complicated tangle:
Death is the only true unraveller!

—DON ALHAMBRA, *The Gondoliers*

THE SOUND OF Zach's pickup had faded into the distance. Virgil stood on the lichen-covered stone jutting out over the green water and peered down as if he expected to see Andrew's footprints under the trees reflected in it. Sunshine played on the water, which splashed musically over a narrow dam between the large quarry hole and a smaller hole that looked just as deep.

"I guess they got him out, all right," Virgil said. "I'll bet he got caught under one of those old quarry blocks down there. A quarry's a dangerous place to swim. And dive. You have to be crazy to dive here, or young, or both. I used to do it back home, when I still thought I had to prove myself to my buddies."

I can't believe this. What do I care what you thought?

"I want to go to Andrew now!" Joan hated the quiver in her voice.

Virgil made no move to leave, but kept staring down at the water. She was suddenly frantic. Andrew could be dying! Why was Virgil dragging his feet like this? She wished she'd asked him to take her home the moment she heard Andrew was in trouble, so she could have driven herself here instead of jumping into his truck and putting herself in the position of having to beg.

I could have found it. Andrew told me the old quarry hole was out this way. That's why I knew he might do such a dumbfool thing as dive into it.

"Come *on*, Virgil. Take me back or I'll drive it myself." She ran back to the truck and was halfway across the storage divider to the driver's seat before she saw that he'd taken the keys with him. She scrambled back to the passenger door and down out of the truck. Not that she expected him to hand his keys over to her—putting them in the ignition and driving her back would be plenty good enough.

Virgil jumped down off the stone. She heaved a sigh of relief and was starting to get back in when out of the corner of her eye she saw him stoop down and pick up a good-sized rock. But when she turned toward him, he turned away, so that his body hid his right hand from her. The shotgun crooked under his left arm was pointed safely down at the ground. What on earth was he up to?

"Joan, you'd better come see this," he said, as if he hadn't heard her. He leaned over the rock-strewn rim and waved with the gun for her to do the same, like the witch telling Gretel to check the oven.

"It was you!" Her hand flew to her mouth, but the words were already out.

You brought me out here to get rid of me. You got rid of Zach so you could brain me with that rock and throw me in to drown. You're not going to shoot me, or you would have done it by now. You want it to look like an accident. It'll be Zach's word against yours, and the way you've bad-mouthed him I don't know why the police would believe him. They'll believe you, instead. Why wouldn't they? I did. When I think of how I taught the children they should never go with anyone who told them Mommy needed them, not unless he used our secret family word...Andrew couldn't give the word underwater, but I could have checked some other way. All I had to do was call the police, but I climbed into your truck without asking a soul whether you were telling me the truth. I'll bet Zach didn't push Andrew. Maybe he's not even hurt. I'm the one in danger. Rebecca would kill me if she knew, except that you're going to beat her to it.

While her mind raced, her feet were putting the truck between her and the shotgun, just in case she was wrong about that, too. Crouched behind the truck, she gauged the distance to the stacked quarry blocks on her left and ran for them, dodging trees and shrubs on the way.

The ground was uneven, made more so by smaller stones and fragments that had been dumped in piles here and there. Old grass caught her ankles and greenbriar scratched her bare arms and face. Her bad ankle, which had been doing fine in town, jabbed her with new sharpness the first time her foot turned on an unexpected hummock, and kept jolting her with every step. She heard Virgil calling her, but she didn't slow down to look back.

At last she slipped into the maze of stones taller than she was. Overhead, the next layer blocked out the sun, except for bright cracks between the stones. She could stand upright in this man-made cave with slanting holes and rows of wide grooves drilled in its walls. Even as she twisted and turned her way through it, Virgil's voice seemed to be coming closer, calling her name. Reaching the other side, she peered out from between two huge blocks, but the truck was invisible. She saw only the dam that separated the two quarry holes. From this angle, it looked just wide enough and flat enough to walk across. The trees on the bank would hide her until she reached the open stretch in the middle, and the water spilling over it would cover any noise she might make. Once on the other side, she could disappear into the woods.

She tested her painful ankle gingerly, hoping it was the same old injury, and that she wasn't doing some new kind of damage by walking on it. It didn't matter. She had to. She wished for sneakers and considered taking off her sandals. The dam looked slippery—the stone was covered with algae—but the rough stones might cut her bare feet, and if nothing else, the straps gave a little support to that ankle. No time to hesitate—Virgil was gaining on her. She kept the sandals.

Abandoning the comparative safety of the quarry blocks took all the courage she could muster. She had to, that was all there was to it. She made her feet pound the few yards to the bank as if her ankle weren't killing her. Now she couldn't hear Virgil at all over the waterfall's music. Either he was in the maze and the stones muffled the sound of his voice, or he'd quit calling and might actually be much closer. Her heart was thudding loudly in her ears.

I have to.

When she put her good foot out onto the dam the surprisingly frigid water took her breath away. The stone that appeared so near the water's surface actually lay just below it. For the first time she realized that water was flowing over the whole dam, not just at the obvious waterfall at the center. Cautiously, she stood on that foot and brought her sore one forward. Maybe the cold would numb the ankle. She inched forward on the slick surface. Could she keep her balance when she couldn't trust that ankle? Ahead of her, rippled by light wind, the water in both quarry holes reflected the stand of pines on the far side. She looked down at the water at her feet, greenish blue on the right, above the dam, greenish gray on the left, below it. She couldn't see the bottom, or the hazards lurking there. Maybe it would be safer to crawl across.

She risked glancing back. No sign of Virgil. Good. And then she spotted the cave. Half-hidden by shrubs and the roots of a sycamore, it opened into the bank she had just left, a couple of feet above the level of the water in the lower quarry hole. It looked big enough to hide her.

I'd better do it. I'm never going to make it across the dam before Virgil catches up with me.

Virgil, in sturdy boots, would be able to march across the dam without blinking. She knew she'd been fooling herself to think she could outrun him an inch at a time. Even so, it was all she could do to make herself turn back toward him. She managed the slippery turn and the few steps back to the bank. Still no Virgil. With a feeling of déjà vu, she slid down off the edge of the muddy bank, hanging onto bushes as she went, crawled over the exposed roots of the sycamore, swung her feet around them and into the cave, and lay panting on the cave floor.

The floor of the cave was a limestone shelf several feet below the water level of the higher quarry hole. The red mud of its walls and ceiling must have eroded to form the cave at some earlier time, before the dam was built. The dam had lowered the water in the second hole and exposed the entrance.

She couldn't stand up, but it didn't matter. She'd be invisible from the bank and could crawl in far enough to be invisible even from the dam. It would buy her time to think.

If he doesn't hear me breathing.

At first she herself could hear little else, and fought to control it. Gradually her respiration slowed, the pounding in her ears subsided, and she heard the water again, and the birds. Somewhere in the trees outside, two cardinals were threatening to duke it out. Still no sign of Virgil.

Doubt washed over her.

Maybe he's *not* after me. Maybe he really did see something in the water back there. Maybe he had a perfectly good reason for picking up that rock, and it was just a coincidence that he hid it from me. I blew it up in my own head into a threat that was never there in the first place. Now I'm stuck in a hole in the ground. And I need a toilet.

You do not, she told herself. You can lie here for hours. And if worse comes to worse, you can just let go and wash in the quarry hole later on, when... But she didn't know when. When someone came? When she decided it was safe to leave? Virgil couldn't see her, but she couldn't see Virgil, either. For all she knew, he was sitting comfortably on the bank above her, waiting for her to emerge. Her arms were already threatening to ache from leaning on the limestone. She pulled her knees up under her and maneuvered herself into an almost comfortable cross-legged sitting position.

She could last. But why had she been so sure it was Virgil? And what had she meant by that, anyway? The words had popped out of her mouth and she had acted on them without thinking what they implied beyond her own immediate predicament. She tried to think now.

She'd talked to Virgil down by the dressing rooms, asked him about Zach. She hadn't mentioned the awls, she knew she hadn't. But she had mentioned David. And Henry. How could any of that have set him off like this?

Suddenly she heard Virgil's voice quite close. He was still calling her name, but he was also muttering something just too soft for her to catch. Torn between curiosity and fear, she inched forward until she was crouching just inside the mouth of the cave, ready to move again if she had to.

"Joan!" he called again. And then, sotto voce, "Bitch! Where'd you go?"

If you only knew.

She was holding her breath. She heard a splash, and risked looking. Right, left, ahead, no Virgil. A second splash gave him away. Looking straight up, she saw the heels of boots covered by blue jeans. He was standing on the dam, with his back toward her. And he was still holding the rock, huge from this angle.

"Bitch!" he shouted suddenly, and his voice cracked as it rose. "You'll never tell them! Never! I killed Putnam and I'm gonna get you, too!"

Joan stretched out her arm. Not quite long enough. Leaning

far out of the cave, she hung onto the sycamore roots with her right hand and stretched her left up through the bushes. She thought again, I have to, reached around a denim-clad leg, and yanked.

As slick as the dam was, that was all it took. He flew backward, his arms outstretched, and the shotgun and rock made their own separate arcs to splash in the water. Drenched and gasping, Joan clambered back out of the cave and onto the bank, ready to run again. She risked pausing to check on Virgil.

He lay very still, half on and half off a stone ledge that extended into the water of the lower quarry hole. From the peculiar angle of his left leg, she was sure he wouldn't be running anywhere for a long time. She thought he might even be dead. Then he opened his eyes.

"Bitch," he muttered, and tried to get up, only to grunt with obvious pain. He leaned back on his elbows and glared at her. Relieved, she nonetheless felt responsible.

"Virgil, you're hurt. Throw me your keys, and I'll go for help."

"The hell you will." His eyes blazed.

"Have it your way." His injuries didn't appear to be life threatening. There was nothing else to do but wait. They'd come eventually, she was sure. Even if they didn't believe Zach, they'd have to check his story.

She sat down at last. Now maybe she could figure where she'd gone wrong.

THIRTY-TWO

Let us grasp the situation,
  Solve the complicated plot—
Quiet, calm deliberation
  Disentangles every knot.

—MARCO, GIUSEPPE, TESSA, GIANETTA,
                                    The Gondoliers

THAT WAS HOW they found her, sitting on the bank dangling her feet in the water above the dam. In the absence of sirens and with the waterfall so close, Joan's first inkling that help had arrived came when she heard the concerned voice of a young woman.

"Are you all right, ma'am?"

Joan swiveled her head to see a young blonde officer in uniform blues standing over her.

"Yes. But he's not." She pointed down at Virgil, who was mumbling something she couldn't understand.

"Is he armed?" the officer asked softly.

"Not anymore."

"Over here!" the young woman called out, and started down the rough slope around the end of the lower quarry hole.

Arriving in a nice-looking tan suit, Detective Terry watched her, too. He smiled down at Joan, who patted the grass behind her for the sandals she had set out to dry.

"Time was, I would've torn holes in my new suit to beat her down there. But it looks like he'll keep."

"That's kind of what I thought." She accepted the warm brown hand he offered and stood up, her sandals dangling from her left hand. "Don't let me get mud on you—I must be a mess." Then she remembered—how could she have forgotten, even for a moment? "Tell me about my son. Is he all right?"

Terry looked blank.

"He's fine. He's worried about you." It was Fred, coming around the quarry blocks. "Terry, ask the dispatcher to lift the signal and call her son." Mud and all, Joan ran into his arms. She hardly felt her ankle, or the stubble digging into her still-bare feet. He hugged her hard. "If he'd hurt you..." he said into her ear, and kissed it.

"Oh, Fred, I was so scared."

"Me, too." He was holding her away from him now, checking her over. "Thank God you're okay. Andrew called me," he said, and the crinkles around his eyes reassured her more than mere words could have. "Zach Yoder told him he thought he saw you being abducted."

"Zach showed up here, but Virgil turned a shotgun on him. Virgil told me Zach pushed Andrew into the quarry, and you sent him to find me."

"Ah." The crinkles again.

"Oh, Fred, I believed him!" she said. "I came with him, but when no one was here, and he wouldn't take me back, I got scared. Then, when he picked up a big rock, I knew something was wrong. I got away, and, well, he's still down there." She pointed to where Ketcham was picking his way down to the quarry hole, and Fred nodded.

"So you weren't calling me about Shoals?" He was still holding her hand, as if he was afraid to let her go.

"How did you...?"

"The desk said a woman had been calling for me, and Andrew said you had something you wouldn't tell anyone but me.''

"Oh. But that was about Zach. At least, that's what I thought then.'' She told him about finding the extra awl in Zach's tools. "Zach knew I saw it. I figured he thought I wouldn't know why it was important. But maybe he's the one who didn't know.''

"He didn't...?''

"Virgil put it there, not Zach. Virgil was backstage, and he was involved with building those picture frames, too. He could go anywhere without being noticed. Remember, I first thought the killer might have dropped the weapon into David's tool-box? Only there wasn't any awl in David's tools. I think that's because Virgil took it *out* of David's tools to kill him and dropped it into Zach's tools, then, or some other time. It wasn't enough to hide the thing, he had to set Zach up. He was chewing Zach out when they were on my front porch the other day—it could have been then.''

"Where is it now?''

"Unless I'm all wrong again, it's still in Zach's tools. And I'll bet a cookie it matches David's.'' That would be easy to establish since the police had David's toolbox. "Zach and Walt and I all handled it, but maybe Virgil left his prints on it, too. Maybe there's even blood on it. I couldn't say anything last night, of course.''

Fred nodded. Two more OPD cars pulled up, and men hopped out. He waved them toward the quarry hole and turned back to Joan.

"You thought Yoder had killed Putnam, and you were going to tell me.''

"Yes.'' It had made such good sense at the time. Now she felt foolish, but safe, with her hand in Fred's.

"Why would that make Shoals go after you?''

"I think he thought I knew more than I did, or maybe that I would give too much away without actually knowing what

I was doing. He's had his eye on me for some time, and when I asked him about Zach, I must have said too much. While I was hiding, when he thought I couldn't hear him, he said he was going to kill me the way he did David.''

"Whaaat? Are you sure?"

"I'll never forget it. He said, 'You'll never tell them! I killed Putnam and I'm gonna get you, too!' Fred, he was *bragging* about it."

"He was, was he?" Fred looked happier than she'd seen him since the murder. "He had opportunity, all right, and access to the weapon. But why? He was Putnam's builder."

"I've almost figured that part out, but I need to ask Zach something. Could we do that?"

"Sure. Soon as I go settle this guy's hash." His face turned grim.

"You're going to arrest him?"

"You bet, thanks to you. Then we'll evacuate him to the hospital and post an officer to keep an eye on him."

While Fred went off, Joan sat on the dry grass and buckled on her damp sandals. She had soaked her feet clean, but the sun was rapidly hardening the red clay on her clothes. She'd ask Fred to take her home first. Much as she wanted to talk to Zach, she wanted even more to see Andrew. If he was half as worried about her as she had been about him, he shouldn't have to wonder another minute. Clean clothes would be a bonus.

Several more cars arrived, including two with Alcorn County Sheriff's Department on the side, and one from the Indiana State Police, all with lights flashing.

In a few minutes Fred was back.

"Let's go. They don't need me. They'll have to wait for a basket to haul him up. He's still shooting off his mouth about Putnam, and cussing you out something awful. I'm afraid he's not too comfortable." The set of his jaw and the malicious twinkle in his eye suggested that his true feelings would have been expressed in words he either didn't consider professional or didn't want her to hear. Was it because he knew Virgil was the murderer he'd been seeking? Or—and it gave her a silly little flutter to think it—was it because Virgil had put her in danger?

Fred handed her into the police car with the kind of solicitude she thought cops reserved for little old ladies. But the kiss he gave her while he fastened her seat belt was anything but solicitous.

"I was sure we'd lost you," he murmured in her ear. "I don't think I could have stood it." And he kissed her again before closing her door and coming around to the driver's seat. He turned on his siren to clear a path through the crowd of police and civilian vehicles that continued to arrive. At last she was on her way home. Fred patted her hand except during the worst curves.

"So," he said while negotiating the road that had terrified her when Virgil was at the wheel, even while she still trusted him, "why do you think Shoals wanted to set Yoder up?"

"So you wouldn't believe him," she answered promptly, and knew it was true.

"Yoder hasn't told us anything."

"He wouldn't. Zach depends on Virgil for his family's livelihood. You should see what he puts up with from that man. Maybe it's his pacifist upbringing. But just in case he ever did, Virgil tried to make sure you wouldn't trust him. It worked with me, didn't it?"

"There he is." Fred pulled over to the side of the road at a wide place. Sure enough, Zach's pickup was parked just ahead of them. When they stopped, Zach jumped out and ran over to them.

"You got her!" he said, leaning through the passenger window to shake Fred's hand. And then, to Joan, "Are you okay?"

"I'm fine. Zach, thank you so much for sending help. And for coming yourself."

"I had to. When I saw that awl in my toolbox, I knew Virgil put it there, and I thought I could guess why. Then I saw him taking you out to the quarry, and I could guess why he was doing that, too. I wanted to stay, but..."

"I know." She patted his hand, resting on the window opening. "You did all you could."

"You did exactly the right thing, waiting for us here," Fred told him. "He's under arrest."

"And you can help now," Joan said. "Will you?"

"Well, sure." He looked puzzled.

"Tell us what happened when you were building Henry's house," she said. Fred's eyebrows rose, but he kept quiet, and she went on. "On the drive out to the quarry Virgil let it slip about his concrete business, so I know that part." Zach nodded. "But you know the rest. And you know why it matters."

"Yeah." Zach scuffed his toe in the dust before meeting her eyes. "For a long time I convinced myself that it didn't. Virgil's always in a hurry, always taking shortcuts, always going for the cheapest way to throw up a building. He's not the only one, by a long shot. But he goes over the line. It was bound to catch up with him someday."

"Uh-huh." Like Ucello and his data fudging. "What did he do?"

"You know his concrete is below standard. And he never uses enough rebar. But he usually gets away with it. Nobody inspects that below-ground stuff. By the time the inspectors come around, he's buried it. Later on, if the wall cracks, he blames it on settling, and on his subcontractor, Sands Building Supplies. Only there isn't any subcontractor. It's just Virgil, with another name. Sands, Shoals, it's the same thing. He keeps different books and all, of course."

Kind of risky to choose a name like that, Joan thought. But

maybe not. I didn't think of Shoals when Esther mentioned Sands.

"So we know why there was a crack in Henry's foundation," she said. "But that doesn't explain the beam that fell on him. I'm sure Virgil would say you measured wrong."

"I told him it wouldn't work. It wasn't big enough in the first place, and it was only bearing half an inch. But he wouldn't pay for a bigger beam, and he wouldn't wait for a longer one."

"He wasn't worried about the inspectors?"

"They never size the beams—they're often not even sized on the blueprint. Bigger beams cost so much more, it's really tempting to a guy like Virgil to undersize them. But an undersized beam can crack. And if it arrives short, like that one, you know you're in trouble. I tried to tell him, but I couldn't make him do anything about it."

"What could he have done?"

"He could have sent for a longer one, but that takes time, and time is money. Or we could have changed the framing, so it would bear on more cripples—" He looked at the blank expressions on their faces. "Each end of a beam that size ought to rest on two or three two-by-fours, or cripples, so it would bear on at least three inches. More is better. But that one ended up barely hanging over part of one cripple. Almost anything could knock it loose when you install it that shallow, any little change in the foundation, or maybe that tree that hit the house. But old Virgil was in a hurry. He left it. Then he even wanted me to hurry and skimp on nailing the floor joists above it." Zach shook his head. "That would have made it that much more dangerous."

"Did you agree?"

"No. That's where I drew the line. He pulled me off the job, sent me across town. I don't know what happened after that."

"I'm surprised a man like David used him," Joan said.

"Virgil never cut corners on the judge's house. Might have overcharged him, but he didn't skimp."

"So Putnam didn't know," Fred said. He'd been following well, Joan thought. And jumping to the connection, or seeming lack of one.

"He knew some of it after the tornado," she said. "He took a backhoe over to Henry's and dug out the foundation, right where the big crack was. Virgil must have blamed that on Sands. I heard them talking about it at a *Ruddigore* rehearsal, only I thought they were talking about Zach and the picture frames. He'd blamed Zach when they weren't right, and it sounded as if David was agreeing with him. David told him that someone else's sloppy work could wreck his good name. I thought he was awfully heavy-handed, and that he shouldn't have stood up for Zach to his face and then bad-mouthed him behind his back. I was disappointed in David. He'd seemed like such an honorable man. I should have known he wouldn't change all of a sudden."

"When did they have that conversation?"

"The night David fell asleep on the supports, the night before he was killed. Oh!"

"Uh-huh," Fred said.

Now the pieces were falling into place, and they made sense. Joan blurted it all out.

"Bad enough that David found the leak. Virgil talked him out of that. But he had to shut him up before he measured the beam. He would have, you know, once he was suspicious, and Virgil couldn't have blamed that on any subcontractor. For starters, with David on the hospital board, Virgil would have lost any chance at the new nursing home contract. He buffaloed Zach—sorry, Zach—but there was no way he could buffalo David. David no longer trusted him, I know. After he was dead, Ellen told me he'd had cold feet about their new addition. Besides, he loved that old man. You should have seen him when he was calling the ambulance for Henry from my house. He stomped around hollering, 'It shouldn't have happened!' If he'd suspected the truth—that Virgil risked Henry's life to make an extra dollar—Virgil ought to have been more afraid of David than of anyone David might have told. Maybe he was, and he panicked." She finally ran down.

"Maybe." Fred leaned over to Zach. "You wouldn't happen to have your toolbox with you, would you?"

"Sure. Why?"

"Mind showing it to me?"

Joan waited in the police car while he and Zach went over to Zach's truck. Exhausted, she leaned back against the seat and quit fighting the weight of her eyelids.

The siren wailing brought her back to full consciousness, and she sat up straight in time to see the ambulance barreling past them on the way to the quarry. Not far behind it her old Honda, screeching to a halt. And Andrew, his hair wild, jumping out and dashing across the road. She got out on shaky legs to meet his warm hug. Her ankle twinged only a little. It was going to be all right, she was sure.

"Andrew!"

"Mom! The police called me. They said you were safe, but I had to come see for myself. Why are you still out here?"

"We've been asking Zach some questions about Virgil Shoals."

"He was right, then? Shoals was kidnapping you?"

"I guess so. Except that he didn't want ransom. He wanted me dead."

"You should have told us last night what you were thinking, instead of saving it for Fred." He ran his fingers through his hair—again, she was sure. It was the voice of sweet reason. He was right, of course, except that it wouldn't have helped.

"Last night I had it all wrong. I thought Zach killed David, but it was really Virgil. Good thing I didn't tell you last night.

If I had, you wouldn't have believed Zach this morning, and I'd still be out there.''

"So Lundquist saved you?''

"Not exactly. But I was awfully glad to see him.''

THIRTY-THREE

And I am right,
*   And you are right,*
And all is right as right can be!

HORUS, *The Mikado*

HOME had never looked so good as it did that day. For that matter, the house hadn't looked so good for a long time. It was past noon when Joan, Andrew, and Fred arrived for a celebratory lunch. Walt was already halfway through the undercoat on the new porch.

"Sorry I didn't get over to your office to show you the paint chips," he said. "I figured I could prime it first and catch you later. And I wondered, while I'm painting the porch, you want me to put a fresh coat on the front door?"

"Why not?" Joan said, feeling reckless. "I think red, don't you?"

"Sure thing. I'll bring those chips this afternoon." Walt didn't bat an eye, not even at the red mud she was wearing.

Andrew and Fred took over the kitchen while Joan went up to shower and change. Mighty nice to have men you can trust, she thought while she let the water pound her and then wrapped her ankle in the wide Ace bandage she still had from after the tornado. But she didn't expect to find pink roses on the kitchen table when she came down. Someone had arranged them in her best crystal vase and set the table with her wedding china.

"Where did these come from?" She bent and inhaled their sweetness.

Andrew looked up from whatever he was concocting today. "One of the neighbors saw the police car and came over. She asked if there was trouble, and if she could do anything."

"I told her yes," Fred said. "Then I traded her gossip for roses. You're going to be a hero, you know that." He pulled out a chair, seated her, and poured her a cup of steaming coffee that smelled almost as good as the roses.

Andrew took a tossed salad out of the refrigerator. Then he carried a platter piled high with buttered toast, crisp bacon, and scrambled eggs with little peppers to the table.

"Fred's been telling me all about it," he said.

Oh, it's Fred now. Well, why not?

"You didn't say you disarmed him and broke his leg."

"I didn't even tell Fred that." Joan dug in, suddenly ravenous. "Andrew, this is wonderful." He beamed.

"Didn't need to," Fred said. "Virgil gave me a real earful. He seems to think you're a dangerous woman."

"And a smart one," Andrew said. "Even if you did think I'd be dumb enough to dive into a quarry. You ought to know me better than that, Mom."

"I do, I do." It was true. "Years of worrying about you and Rebecca took over. I'm sorry."

"That's all right. How did you figure all that out about Virgil?"

"I almost didn't. But Esther Ooley had just told me about the case Virgil settled out of court and how he didn't do his own concrete work. Then, while he was driving me out to the quarry—he told me you were drowning out there, Andrew, and I believed him!—he talked to me about quarries to keep me calm. He said he had to get the gravel for his concrete business from a different quarry. I didn't put those two things together until we didn't find anyone there and he wouldn't take me back to the hospital. Then he sent Zach away and picked up a big rock. I finally caught on, and I ran. While I was sitting there after I knew I was safe, I started remembering all kinds of things. Like that conversation he had with David. It was kind of like the honor system, Andrew. David was giving Virgil a chance to clear his name. Like the dukes under the witch's curse, he died because he was too good. And Virgil almost got away with it.''

"I believed him, too," Fred said, and patted her hand again. "Funny, how you believe what you expect to hear. Like old Mrs. Snarr. She wanted us to arrest Shoals after her roof blew off in the storm. I couldn't do that, of course. But I didn't blame him for a minute. I told her it was tornado damage, even though none of our spotters said the twister touched down where she lives. Mrs. Snarr always blows things out of proportion. This time she just might be right." He took a bite of eggs and saluted the cook.

"I don't get it," Andrew said. "The guy got stabbed with a dagger, right? But a little while ago you said something about an awl in Zach's toolbox. What does that have to do with it?"

Fred quickly explained that there had been two weapons, and that the autopsy had made it clear that Putnam had been dead of a wound made by something like an awl before he was stabbed again with the dagger, after he was already dead. "Only question was why. At first I thought there were two attackers, but your mom's idea made more sense, except for one little problem."

"What's that?"

"She suggested that the second stabbing was to hide the first one, so we'd let the killer—Shoals, as it turns out—take off with the awl that really did the job. Trouble was, I couldn't see how there'd be time for one person to do both without being spotted."

"I still can't," Joan said.

"Wait till you hear this. While you were upstairs just now I checked one bit of the story Shoals gave us before we suspected him. He said he sat over on stage right and knew when to open the curtain by the sound of the music. He left out the fact that he relayed a signal from Biggy, the stage manager, to your conductor, so she'd know when to start. So Shoals controlled that time we've been so worried about. It was easy for him to pick up the awl from Putnam's toolbox and the dagger from the prop box. He killed Putnam and planted the dagger in his back between when he got the signal and when he passed it on."

"And no one saw him?" Andrew asked.

"No one was looking. Once Biggy gave the signal, he was watching the stairs and the chorus, not the stage. He couldn't see Putnam from there even if he'd been looking. When I asked just now, both Biggy and the conductor confirmed that the music started late that night."

"That's right!" Joan remembered now. "After you and I talked I just made it into the pit, and then we waited forever, it seemed."

"Both the stage manager and the conductor figured it was the other one. No one thought of Shoals, and no one mentioned it to us. If Shoals had just taken that awl home with him instead of palming it off on Yoder, he'd have been home free."

"Never mess with Mom," Andrew said, grinning.

"Oh, I don't know," Fred said, with a slow smile that reached his eyes and melted Joan. He reached for her hand. "I have every intention of messing with your mom for a long, long time."

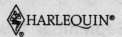 

In September 1998
watch for

BURIED IN STONE

by ERIC WRIGHT

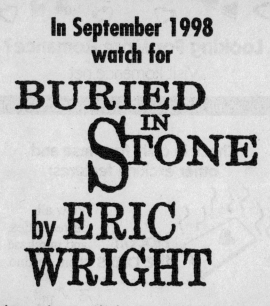

Retired Toronto detective Mel Pickett is intrigued by the body discovered near his cabin in the woods. The corpse is that of a local lothario, and Larch River folks are busy guessing who might be the culprit: a jealous husband or a jilted lover.

Someone is arrested, but Mel, with instincts honed by years as a big-city cop, suspects there's more to the case than meets the eye. His probe reveals secrets buried in stone...and a clever, nearly perfect crime and a devious killer.

Available at your favorite retail outlet only from

MYSTERY **WORLDWIDE LIBRARY**®
™